BAD IDEA

BROOKLYN KINGS 1

FELICE STEVENS

Bad Idea

Copyright © 2025 by Felice Stevens

Published by Good Man Press

Cover Art by Reese Dante
https://reesedante.com
Photographer: Wander Aguiar
Model: Kaz
Edited by Keren Reed
Copyediting and Proofreading by Flat Earth Editing
https://facebook.com/FlatEarthEditing
Additional Proofreading by Lyrical Lines
https://www.lyricallines.net/

Digital ISBN: 979-8-88949-100-2
Paperback ISBN: 979-8-88949-101-9
Special Edition Paperback: 979-8-88949-080-7

DEDICATION

To my family

ACKNOWLEDGMENTS

Thanks as always to my editor, Keren Reed. To Hope and Jess from Flat Earth Editing, you are the best. To Dianne, from Lyrical Lines, I couldn't do it without you. And to Reese for everything.

To the readers, you make it all worthwhile.

And finally. To the Jets and Giants...really, guys? Come on....

CHAPTER ONE

"All right, Monday. Let's try not to suck."

But Hayden Porter didn't hold out much hope. His boss had been away for five days on a spur-of-the-moment trip to Vegas, leaving him scrambling to rearrange meetings. Hayden didn't complain. Not that it would matter if he did. Boris was off feeling up showgirls, secure in the knowledge that Hayden was in control.

Truth was, Hayden loved his job. Checking off that last item on a to-do list was almost as satisfying as sex. More so lately, as it had been a while since he'd had a chance to get laid. His personal pleasure came in second to pleasing his boss. He had a reputation to uphold.

It was hard being the best, but someone had to be number one. And Hayden Porter—personal assistant to top CEOs in the country—was that person. There were none better. It wasn't bragging. It was a well-known fact.

Hayden understood his bosses' needs before they did, had a list for everything, and never lost his cool. He was always the first in the office and the last to leave. His mind was an encyclopedia of the-best-of lists for everything anyone who was anyone would need.

A losing day on the stock market? Hayden was there with forecasts of the next day's winners. A broken date? He'd have the best friends ready with a table at the hottest club. A mishap with lunch on that five-thousand-dollar custom suit? The best dry cleaner in the city was on speed dial.

Hayden always had it covered.

Except today.

Hayden had presumed their usual Monday morning meeting would run a bit longer because of Boris's trip. He had reports printed out—Boris hated computers—and his schedule for the upcoming week, plus a summary of the little fires he'd put out on his own with Boris away.

But Boris Kunoff—seventy-five years old, slightly shaky on his feet and possessor of one of the largest fortunes in the Northeast—had just introduced Hayden to his new wife, former Miss Something from Somewhere, Cindy Sue. They'd known each other for one whole month. The last-minute trip to Vegas? He and Cindy Sue had eloped.

Cindy Sue was twenty-four. Her age, and also, from the looks of it, her waistline in inches. She perched on Boris's lap, where the major assets she brought into the relationship rested on his cheek. But Hayden had little time for snarky, sarcastic thoughts as he listened to Boris speak and his world came crashing down. His leg bounced, the only indication that his normally tight-as-a-drum nerves were on the brink of snapping.

"So you see, Hayden, now that Cindy Sue is my wife, there will be some changes. Her degree is in marketing, and she's going to take over as my personal assistant." Boris patted her butt, and Hayden didn't miss the flicker of annoyance in her eyes, but her blindingly white smile never faltered. For a bank account of 2.3 billion dollars, Hayden would bet Cindy Sue would let a lot of things slide.

"I don't understand, sir. I've been with you for close to six years, and it's been a seamless arrangement."

"Exactly, Hay. May I call you Hay?" Cindy Sue fluttered her lashes at him.

She didn't wait for his answer, which would've been a resounding no. *No one calls me that.* He gritted his teeth and listened politely.

"Sometimes we get too comfy in our position and think nothing will ever change." Hayden didn't miss the subtle dig. "Now that Boris and I are married, I plan to be very involved in the business, and we came to the decision that I will be taking over your position. But don't worry."

Whenever anyone told him not to worry, he immediately began to have palpitations. His leg bounced faster.

"We'll give you the *best* references. I know how you kept this place running and Boris on track. But as they say in the pageant world, it's time to pass the crown."

A crown, Hayden envisaged, that would look perfect embedded in her head, but it would take too much strength to get it through the teased waves. "I-I'm just surprised, as you can imagine. I would think, that even if you did replace me"—he swallowed hard as those words he'd never thought he'd utter stuck in his throat—"you'd want me around to bring you up to speed."

Cindy Sue massaged Boris's neck, her long red nails bright against his pale, age-spotted skin. "I think I'll manage."

Meanwhile Boris, whom he'd served faithfully every day, even on weekends if needed, to the detriment of a personal life, merely sat there silent, a grinning fool. Unable to look at them any longer, Hayden drew together his torn self-esteem and rose to his feet, back stiff, eyes to the opposite wall.

"I'll be going, then. Good-bye."

He pivoted on his heel and strode out of the office. At his desk, he started removing his personal items—a coffee mug, various colored sticky tabs, pens. It all barely filled his daily work bag. Six years' worth of nothing.

The receptionist scurried over to him, goggle-eyed behind her black-framed glasses. "What's happening, Hayden? What're you doing?"

"What does it look like?" Hayden removed a bottle of extra-strength aspirin, a box of antacids, and an empty prescription bottle for migraine medication. "I'm packing." He tossed them into his bag.

"Why? What's going on?"

He huffed out a sigh and hefted the bag to his shoulder. "I've been fired. Boris got himself a wife, and she'll be taking my position." His lips pressed together until they hurt. "Keeping it all in the family."

She blinked rapidly. "You're kidding. You? They fired you?"

He winced. "No need to repeat it, please." He glanced around at the job he'd given everything to, and without another word to her or other curious colleagues, head held high, he walked out.

His act of keeping it all together crumbled once he returned home. He sank onto the couch and began to shake. Hysterical laughter bubbled up inside. He'd never been home during the week—he'd worked most holidays, didn't take vacation, and never got sick. Work was his life, his everything.

"Oh, God." His leg jiggled and his breath grew short. "What the hell am I going to do?" First thing was to check his bank account. Boris had paid him well, and as he wasn't frivolous with his money, spending little aside from mortgage payments, utilities, and food, a hefty balance greeted his eyes.

But for how long? The city was for the strong, not weak. Hayden kicked off his loafers, ditched his jacket and tie, and unbuttoned the collar of his shirt. At least twice a week for the last year he'd received calls from headhunters, and he was counting on his reputation for an excellent work ethic to find him a position that if not comparable, was at least similar to that of personal executive assistant to the head of a billion-dollar company.

First call was to Janice Butler at Platinum Executives, who'd originally placed him with Boris. His call was put through immediately.

"I know you're not calling me in the middle of the workday to wish me a happy birthday." Her raspy smoker's voice was strangely comforting. "What's going on?"

"Happy birthday. I've been let go." Hayden relayed the scene in Boris's office and listened to her huffs of annoyance.

"What a fucking moron. Another fool being led by his dick and a pair of silicone boobs."

Despite his panic, Hayden's lips twitched. He could always count on Janice for her bluntness. That and her street smarts were what had enabled her to build a business matching the highest quality personal assistants with top executives from the city. She was fast-talking, brutally honest, and people, especially men, liked to call her aggressive, which Hayden knew was simply a code word for labeling a smart woman who won't take their bullshit, as a bitch. Right now, Janice was whom he needed in his corner.

"Forget about Boris and his appendage, please. I need a new position." Hayden gazed around the condo he loved. High in the sky, twenty stories up, and only four hundred and fifty square feet, Hayden loved every inch of the space. His sanctuary. A place where he could be himself. "I only closed on my apartment three months ago. I can't afford to be out of work."

"I hear ya. Look, I'm not going to lie to you and say I've got the perfect job."

His heart sank.

"But," she continued. "I do have a roster. Give me a few, and I'll send you over to whom I think is the best match. You're a prize. Don't worry."

"I always worry," he said with a wry thinning of his lips. "It's my constant companion."

"Look, Hayden. I'm going to say something you might not like. You've been on autopilot for years. Use this time to recharge. Maybe go to a spa."

"That's a waste of money I can't afford right now. Who knows when I'll find another job?"

"Didn't you get severance? Don't tell me Boris is a cheap SOB who stiffed you on that?" Her outrage on his behalf, despite his fear, made him smile.

"Yeah, but not enough for me to breathe easily. You know how expensive it is to live in the city. Three months' salary doesn't go as far as you might think once the bills are paid." He worried his bottom lip. "And that's if everything goes smoothly and I don't get sick." He groaned. "God. It's all so damn depressing. I never thought it would happen to me. I gave the man everything I had and then some."

"Exactly. You gave him every piece of yourself, and you're worn out. If you don't want to blow a big chunk of change, at least promise me you'll go out tonight. One drink won't break the bank, and think of it as your last hurrah until you find a new job. Hook up. Relieve the stress for a couple of hours. When was the last time you had a boyfriend, or even a date?"

Hayden lay on his couch and stared at the ceiling, a sudden longing to be fucked senseless sending a thrill through him. "I don't have boyfriends, or date. You know that. Who has the time?"

"You do now," she pointed out.

He winced. "Ouch. Thanks for the reminder."

But dammit, now that Janice mentioned it, all he could think of was hot lips on his and a pair of strong hands on his shoulders. A wet mouth on his. He closed his eyes...could almost taste it. It would be nice to drown his sorrows with a big dick. All his nervous energy had to go somewhere, and Hayden had never had trouble finding men willing to take the edge off for him. After a day spent doing everything for other people, sex was one of the few things he could control for himself.

"The last time I saw you, Hayden, I wasn't happy. You were pale and jumpy."

"I'm fair-skinned and always jumpy. It's part of my charm. I'm nervous so my boss doesn't have to be."

Janice wasn't fooled.

"That's bullshit and you know it. Okay, so maybe you're not into a boyfriend. But some random guy who'll make you forget for the evening can do amazing things for your self-confidence."

"And you know this from personal experience." He grinned. Janice had never married and loved to tell stories of her wild partying life when she was younger, and Hayden had to admit he envied her. Sex had become another item to tick off his list of things to do. Shower, eat, get off. Made sense, considering he'd started out having sex as if it were a business transaction. It had taken him years to learn to enjoy sex for pleasure.

"Hell, yeah. Just because I'm in my sixties doesn't mean I don't want sex. Older doesn't mean dead, you know. I still got it. And get it." She cackled.

"Okay, okay. Enough. I get the point. We could meet up for a drink. I haven't seen you in ages," he offered.

She laughed. "I'm not angling for an invitation, and I'm not your type." He could feel her smirk through the phone. "I've got dinner reservations at Per Se tonight. All I'm saying is, try it. There's something to be said about good old-fashioned anonymous sex with someone you won't ever see again. As long as you're safe."

Shocking tears burned his eyes.

Don't go there.

Hayden huffed out a sigh. "Yes, Mother." For Hayden, anonymous sex had been the catalyst for all his troubles, but her advice made sense. Forgetting his problems for one night couldn't hurt.

"I've got to go, but I'll have something for you later this afternoon. Talk to you then."

"Bye."

He set the phone aside. Maybe she was right. The past week he'd been going double time, especially after Boris had left unexpectedly. He'd gotten to the office at seven in the morning and hadn't left until nine, nine thirty at night. By the time he walked into his apartment, he was too tired to do anything but shower and sleep. He yawned, and even with all the turmoil swirling around him, his lids grew heavy. He hadn't taken a nap during the day since he was five. His eyes fluttered shut.

He awoke with a start, to darkness. "What the hell?" The phone screen showed it was eight thirty in the evening. "I slept over nine hours?" He sat up and rubbed his face. "Damn. I can't remember the last time I had uninterrupted sleep for that long." Stretching, he winced from his cramped limbs. The couch might be comfortable, but not for his six-foot-two frame to sleep on.

And now, of course he was wide awake and hungry. With nothing in the apartment, he could order in and spend the night looking for jobs online. He scrolled through his email and found one from Janice.

I have several prospects for you, but I'm going to keep them for tomorrow. Like I said, I want you to forget about it for the night. Call me in the morning.

Amused and annoyed, Hayden grunted and tossed the phone aside. His stomach growled. Loudly. He could say he went to a club and picked up a guy but dismissed that automatically. Janice was a bloodhound and would somehow discover he'd lied to her, and that would break the trust between them.

Besides, what could it hurt? Instead of showing up at his usual hour of eleven, finding someone and getting off in a hurry, maybe he could take his time and enjoy the ride.

So to speak.

Gazing at his clothes, he wrinkled his nose at their sorry state. Scrunched up and messy wasn't how he presented himself, either in the office or when out on the prowl. He ordered sushi from a place two doors down from his building, knowing they delivered in less than fifteen minutes. Food, like sex, didn't mean much to him—it was a means to an end, and he ate, anticipating the night ahead. Now that he'd decided on his course for the evening, it was all he could think about. Anticipation flooded his veins. Damn, he was half-hard already.

He took a shower, and feeling more human, surveyed himself in the mirror:

Slim-fitting jeans that emphasized his ass. A green, sleeveless shirt that showcased his tats and biceps while also enhancing the glow of emerald eyes. His blond hair was the proper mix of messy and well-kept, and he fluffed the top with his fingers one more time before taking the clippers and trimming his stubble. One final look, then he grabbed a condom and a travel pack of lube and shoved them into his crossbody bag.

The night was warm and breezy, and Hayden decided to stay within a three-block radius of his apartment instead of wasting time and money on a car to sit in traffic for a club downtown. He stopped on 77th Street in front of The Vibe, a brand-new club he'd walked past and had been meaning to check out. Now he had all the time in the world.

The guy at the door, a six-foot-four hulk dressed in black, gave him a lingering once-over that told Hayden if he struck out in the club, he'd hit a home run outside.

The space was packed, and Hayden waited a moment for his eyes to adjust. Colored lights played over the small dance floor, and he wriggled his way through the crowd to the bar, where he ordered a Tito's and soda and stood surveying the crowd. The scent of sweaty bodies, cologne, and a faint whiff of weed surrounded him, a heady cocktail he greedily inhaled. So many choices. For the night, he allowed the problems in his life to sit by the wayside. No more worrying about Boris and the schedule of medications he needed to take. Instead of Kunoff Shipping being the main focus of his life, he concentrated on Hayden Porter. He'd think about his bank account tomorrow. His first drink finished, he decided to be reckless and ordered a second. Coupled with the wine he'd already had with his sushi, he felt loose and ready for someone to touch him. He deserved one night to go wild.

"Hey, watch what you're doing," an annoyed voice exploded to his right. "You spilled your fucking drink all over me. What the hell is wrong with you?"

"I-I'm sorry," another guy replied. "I didn't mean to. It was an accident."

Always one for a little drama, Hayden finished his drink and watched the scene unfold. The angry guy was in his late twenties, tall and skinny, covered in tattoos, and wearing a mesh shirt. A blond poof of hair was swept high on top and shaved close on the sides. Small eyes narrowed with disdain, and his lips pressed thin with an arrogant twist. In contrast, the man he'd lambasted was older, around Hayden's age, and dressed in a suit and tie. Dark hair framed a sweet, gentle face. Big eyes gazed up, wide and slightly frightened. Not the type he normally saw at a wild club like this.

"I don't give a shit if it was an accident. I'm wet now, and I smell like beer. Goddamn idiot."

Hayden moved closer. He didn't normally get involved, but seeing someone bullied wasn't fun, and he waited to make sure it didn't escalate.

The man on the receiving end looked as if he were about to burst into tears. "I'm sorry." He pulled out his wallet and handed the man a twenty-dollar bill. "Here. For dry cleaning."

The nasty prick took it, and without even a thank-you, stalked away and disappeared into the crowd. Mr. Out-of-Place sat hunched over the bar, and Hayden slipped into the vacated spot.

"That was nice of you."

The man shrugged and kept his head down. "I just wanted him to stop yelling at me." He pushed away the empty glass in front of him. "It wasn't my fault. It's so crowded, and when I picked up my drink, it spilled on his shirt." He raised his gaze to meet Hayden's. "He was rude for no reason. It wasn't nice."

Were those actual tears glistening in those clear blue eyes? A soft heart and deep conversation were the furthest thing from Hayden's mind at a club. Especially tonight. All he wanted was to forget losing his job and the tightrope he now had to maneuver. What could possibly be the reason for putting a hand on the man's shoulder and smiling at him? Must be the alcohol swimming in his blood that made Hayden aware of the sprinkling of freckles across the bridge of the man's nose, his soft full lips, and the dimples in the crease of his cheek.

"I'm Hayden. How about I buy you another?"

CHAPTER TWO

Armand Winters gazed into the gorgeous face of the man who sat next to him. "I'm sorry, what?" He must've heard wrong. Guys who looked like Hayden—sexy, messy blond hair, big green eyes, drool-worthy tattoos—didn't talk to men like him. Someone who always managed to wear what he'd last eaten on his shirt or tie. A man always late or early but never on time. One unable to make a decision because he was afraid to say no and upset people.

Not the best look for the owner of a football team. Even a reluctant one.

Hayden leaned in and whispered, "I'd like to buy you a drink."

"You don't have to." A shiver rolled through Armand, and nervous, he licked his lips.

"I know. I want to."

Their mouths were temptingly close, and Armand wondered if Hayden could hear the thunder of his heartbeat. "Uh, sure. A Stella. On draft."

A sensual grin curved those full lips, and Hayden motioned to the bartender. "Stella on draft for my friend."

Hayden held out the beer. "Here you are." Armand reached for it, and Hayden pulled the glass away at the last minute. "Ah-ah-ah. Not so fast. I need something before I give it to you."

Armand's brows knitted. "What?"

Again, Hayden commanded his personal space, bringing them almost nose to nose, and Armand's breath caught. Oh God, he wanted to kiss him so badly. "Your name."

In the heated air between them, Armand could almost feel his smile.

"Uh, it's Armi." A nickname only his closest friend called him. One he'd never felt cool enough to use with anyone else, but sitting there with Hayden made him feel daring enough to try.

"Here you go." Hayden offered the beer, their fingers touching, and Armi's hand shook. He'd never been so turned-on in his whole life. "Easy does it, Armi," Hayden murmured, curving his hand over Armi's to steady him. "We have all night."

Another full-body shiver rocked him. What did Hayden mean, all night? Did he want to…? All sorts of thoughts ran round and round in his head. Armi gulped the beer, hoping it would cool the raging fire burning through him. He'd never done this kind of thing before—a pickup at a club could be dangerous. He'd heard the stories, seen what could happen on the evening news. But Armi was tired of living an ordinary life.

What did all the dating advice say? *Ask them about themselves.*

"Uh, so do you live around here?" He held on to the glass to keep his fingers from trembling.

"Why? You want to come home with me?" A wicked smile flashed across Hayden's face.

Startled by the intense sizzle of heat those words brought, Armi stuttered. "Wh-what? N-no. I didn't mean that. I was just making conversation. I—"

Hayden laid two fingers across his lips. "Shh. I know. I'm joking." His eyes sparkled. "I guess we'll just have to find out," Hayden teased. "Why so nervous?"

Armi's shoulders sagged. "I'm terrible at all this."

Hayden shocked him by cupping his cheek. "Terrible at what?"

Everything. He was the one who could never get anything right. Armi wasn't smooth or quick-thinking. Not suave or sophisticated. Everything he should be in his new position. The one he wasn't qualified for. At least that was what his father had told him, every week, every day.

"Hey, where'd you go?" Hayden nudged their noses together.

"I'm sorry."

"You're sweet. I bet you taste delicious too." Armi forgot to breathe when Hayden's mouth covered his.

Armi's eyes slid shut, the music faded away, and he opened to the push of Hayden's tongue against the seam of his lips. He sucked its velvety softness, the pleasure melting in his mouth like chocolate warmed by the sun. He moaned. One hand fisted Hayden's shirt, pulling him close...closer, while the other tangled in the hair curling at his nape. God, he was ready. He wanted to sit in Hayden's lap and rock into him. His empty body ached to be filled.

"Two blocks," Hayden whispered. "Let's go."

He'd never done anything so wild. So free. Hayden licked into his ear, and Armi's heart hammered so fast, he grew dizzy. And then dizzier still when Hayden cupped the bulge in his pants and hummed his approval.

"*Mmm*, can't wait for this. In my mouth. You want that, don't you, baby?"

Armi hissed at Hayden's fondling of his swollen dick. He wanted...he *wanted* so damn bad. His gut told him Hayden wouldn't hurt him.

Holding hands, they hurried out of the club and through the streets until they came to a high-rise on 80th Street. Hayden's apartment was dark, but Armi had little opportunity to view his surroundings as he was pulled into the small bedroom. True to his word, Hayden unzipped Armi's slacks, yanked them with his briefs past his hips, and rubbed his cheek along the rock-hard length of Armi's rigid cock.

"Fuck yeah, you're so ready." Hayden licked the precome leaking from the slit. "So fucking hot and wet. Want you in my mouth. Now."

Hayden followed his words with action, and Armi's groans filled the quiet room as Hayden's mouth slid over the head of his cock and sucked him. Hard. "Oh God, oh please, please," Armi begged, shameless in his need. His legs started to give out, and he braced a hand on the wall to hold himself up as he continued to watch Hayden take his dick in between those gorgeous full lips.

Hayden's tongue performed delicious magic as it swirled and flickered. He bobbed up and down, and Armi lost touch with reality. His hips snapped back and forth, thrusting deeper into Hayden's warm, wet mouth.

Hayden dug his fingers into the muscles of Armi's thighs, his throaty moans vibrating along Armi's throbbing cock. Saliva coated his rock-hard shaft, and Hayden pulled off and gazed up at him with swollen lips and hazy, lust-filled eyes.

"You like that, don't you?" He sucked his fingers and pressed them along Armi's taint. "How about this?" They slid higher, to the cleft between his cheeks. "And this?"

A feral, hungry need burst through him, and he clawed at Hayden's shoulders. "Don't stop," he begged. "More, please."

"Don't worry, baby. I'm gonna give it all to you." Hayden teased along his crease and circled his rim. Armi was lust-drunk, and hearing Hayden call him baby, feeling the scratch and tickle of his fingers slipping and sliding around his hole, catapulted him to the stars.

"*Ahh*, please, please. Harder. More."

Again Hayden took him into his mouth, his lips and teeth playing along its length.

"I can't...don't stop...too good," Armi panted, his last bit of control lost. An electric shock raced up his legs, his balls tightened, and an explosion burst through the base of his spine. His cock jerked endlessly, and Hayden swallowed every drop, those sweet lips and tongue licking and sucking him dry.

"I was right," Hayden said. "You taste amazing."

Armi's face burned, and he watched as Hayden wriggled out of his jeans and briefs. His dick stuck out, red, thick, and so beautiful. Fascinated, he watched Hayden pump it, the sticky-wet crown moving fast and furious through his fist. He crouched beside Hayden, excitement spiraling, the smell of Hayden making him reckless.

"Harder, come on," Armi urged. "Do it. On my face. In my mouth. Come on." When the hell had he gotten this daring? Maybe it was his father telling him he was a failure. That he didn't have what it took to be in charge. His gay, fumbling son.

He'd never had sex like this—his mind and body voracious with want and need and a craving to be fucked until he couldn't walk. It was primitive, raw and freeing.

Through surprisingly dark, thick lashes, Hayden's green eyes blazed and he bit his lip. "Fuck, yeah."

Armi put his hand on Hayden's and his lips to that hot, hard shaft. One tantalizing lick led to another. Armi rubbed the wet, sticky cock all over his face, then sucked and flickered his tongue, playing with the slit. Hayden's eyes rolled back.

"Oh, shit." He grew stiffer, come shooting from his dick, coating Armi's cheeks and lips, and dripping down his chin.

Armi licked up as much as he could and wiped the sheet across his face to catch the last drops. Hayden lay against the bed, eyes closed, breathing steadily. It took Armi a minute to realize he'd fallen asleep. God, he was so wild and beautiful—thick blond hair laying in damp waves, body glistening with sweat, setting off all that ink. Armi's mouth watered, and he pressed his face to Hayden's chest, smelling the sharp, salty aroma of Hayden's come.

What had gotten into him?

Awkward now that the sex was over, he yanked up his briefs and pants, and with a sigh of regret, Armi left, making sure the lock clicked behind him. He lifted his head to the sky for a moment.

It took less than twenty minutes to walk to his town house on 71st Street. He showered, changed, and lay in bed, wondering if he'd always be alone.

"Good morning, Mr. Winters," the receptionist in the lobby of the skyscraper where the Brooklyn Kings were located greeted him.

"Hello, Audrey." He smiled. "Please call me Armand."

The security guard waved him through. "Morning. How are you, Mr. Winters?"

"It's Armand. And I'm fine, Jerry, how're you doing?" He held his coffee in one hand and stuck the ID card into his pocket. He noticed a grease stain on the lapel of his suit and mentally slapped himself. One day he'd manage to come to the office and not look like he'd just rolled out of bed. But after his shocking hookup with Hayden, he'd barely managed any sleep. His body buzzing with desire, he'd replayed every intense, exhilarating second, and it wasn't until almost three a.m. that he'd finally closed his eyes. He'd awoken late and shoved a buttered bagel into his mouth as fast as he could. Obviously, some had landed on his clothes.

"Good, good, sir. Have a nice day."

The elevator whizzed him up to the fortieth floor, and Armi walked into the corporate headquarters of the Brooklyn Kings, still in disbelief that he was now the owner of a professional football team. Him, the most unathletic person in the family. The gay son, who was more interested in flowers than football.

There had to be some irony in this situation. After all, his father had always said it would be over his dead body that Armi would inherit the team. And now here they were, almost three months after a small-plane crash had killed Randolph Winters, his girlfriend, Anna, and Peter, his father's personal assistant, and Armi was owner and president of the Brooklyn Kings.

He'd rather be mulching his rosebushes.

"Good morning, Mr. Winters." Josh, the front-desk receptionist, smiled brightly at him. "How are you this morning?"

"Please, Josh, call me Armand. And I'm well. How're you?"

"Oh, uh. I'm fine, thanks."

His father hadn't liked the first-name familiarity with the staff Armi insisted upon, but Armi was determined to change the culture.

"Great."

He noted the sign behind him, with the Brooklyn Kings name and logo—a football sailing between the two spires of the Brooklyn Bridge. And underneath it, in big gold letters: Randolph Winters, Owner and CEO.

It was something he'd meant to change but hadn't yet gotten around to. After the shock of his father's death, Armi had allowed Russell Anders, the Kings' general manager and his father's best friend, along with the rest of the "inner circle," to run the team, but at his mother's urging, he'd decided only a week earlier to take the reins and step into the role.

Jacob Whitmore rushed over to him. He was the Kings' chief legal counsel and chief thorn in Armi's side. "I hoped you'd be here earlier. I wanted to review those contracts."

Speaking to Whitmore always left Armi feeling inadequate and useless.

"I still have time before the meeting, don't I?" He checked his watch to see the time and promptly spilled coffee down the front of his shirt.

"Shit," he yelled and jumped, hoping to avoid the hot liquid, but the damage was done. A wet, brown stain spread across his white shirt, silk tie, and the top of his pants. Great. Tears stung his eyes at his incompetency. Maybe his father was right and he lacked the ability to be a leader.

Russell appeared at his side. "I'll get you some paper towels."

"It's not going to help," Armi called out, but Russell had already sprinted to the men's room and returned with a bunch in his hand. The man might be in his early sixties, but he was fast on his feet—Russell had been an All-Pro running back in college and had spent two years in the NFL prior to a knee injury, which had forced him to retire—and could probably beat Armi in a race without even trying.

Armi knew it was fruitless, but he dabbed at his shirt anyway. "Thanks."

"Don't worry. Happens to all of us." Russell's reassurance was tempered by Whitmore rolling his eyes.

Armi managed a weak smile. "Well, uh, I'd better get ready for the meeting. Jacob, did you email me the contracts?"

Whitmore raised his brows. "Last night. I expected a response, but I guess you were busy with something else?"

His face flamed. "I'll read them and let you know." Yeah, he'd been busy. Busy having a gorgeous stranger suck his dick, then paint him with come. Armi hurried away to his office.

Russell followed. "Don't worry. It'll be okay. I'll help you."

Armi sat behind his desk and listened as Russell talked about salary caps and trade deadlines. As a CPA, Armi understood numbers. They went through the documents Whitmore had sent, and Armi asked questions, took notes, and was able to understand the complicated world of salaries, signing bonuses, and incentives. Russell explained how their scouts spread out over the dozens of top college teams, looking for standouts they could pick up in the college draft. The nuts and bolts of putting together a winning team that could make the playoffs and win the Super Bowl all made his head spin, but he struggled to understand.

"Wouldn't it make more sense to look for excellent players who maybe don't get all the attention? We could pay them less and give someone else a chance who maybe didn't have the opportunity to make it to a big school." An underdog himself, Armi wanted to give everyone equal footing.

Russell's smile was indulgent. "That's very noble, Armand, but fans aren't going to pay season-ticket prices for nobodies. They want to see the players they've been following in college football—kids who've helped win the Bowl games and hold college records. We need the stadiums filled and advertisers buying space. The NCAA almost rivals the NFL in the money it brings in for advertising, and rabid football fans know their stuff. They don't want to see some no-name player. They want Heisman Trophy winners. Rushers who break records. Defensive ends with big moves who hold sacking records. We have to be competitive with our offers to the top college players."

While it made sense, he didn't have to like it. "Understood. However, I'd still like to see a little more effort made with lesser division schools." Nervous sweat rolled down his back. Taking a stand made him sick to his stomach, but he forced himself. "That's my decision as owner."

Russell frowned but nodded. "All right. We'd better get to the meeting. You can tell everyone your thoughts there." His hand on the door, Russell hesitated. "You're sure you really want to do this? Take over ownership of the Kings?"

He knew the organization expected him to sell the team, take his hundreds of millions of dollars, and wipe his hands clean. At the party his mother had thrown for him at his family's East Hampton home when he'd passed his CPA exam, Armi had overheard his father talking to Whitmore, Russell, and Troy Geiger, the Kings' CFO. He'd gone inside to change his pants after dropping a piece of cake on his lap, and the four men had been in his father's study, having a drink.

"To think he's my only child, a limp-wristed klutz with no head for business. All he knows is grubbing in the dirt. I still remember the first Kings game I took him to. Cried like a baby because the players were knocking each other over and he thought they were being mean."

After hearing that exchange and the laughter from all the men, Armi knew, no matter how hard he tried, he'd never be the son his father wanted. It was one thing to feel a parent's disdain, but to hear it put so bluntly to strangers was burned indelibly in his mind.

As for grubbing in the dirt...Armi's first love had always been plants and flowers. As a young boy living on their Long Island estate, he'd helped the family gardener with the vegetable flats and the profusion of prize-winning rosebushes. Here in the city, he'd turned the backyard of his town house into a rose garden and spent all his time learning grafting to create new varieties and how to keep his bushes healthy. He loved his flowers. They were his world. Their beauty brought his heart joy when he had little else to give him happiness.

In response to Russell's question, Armi raised his chin in defiance. "Yes. I'm taking over ownership of the Kings. Why? You don't think I can do it?" Russell had been the one person he'd thought he could count on to help guide him. If Russell turned on him too, Armi might have to walk away.

"That's not what I'm saying at all. I believe with work you can. But you need help. Not only from me. I've selected some candidates for personal assistants who can help smooth out the everyday busy work and let you concentrate on the important stuff."

"I appreciate it, but I've also been thinking about an assistant. My friend Trevor runs an excellent agency and—"

"No need for that. I'll take care of everything for you." Russell put a hand on his back and steered him toward the conference room. His touch startled Armi, and confused, he pulled away. Russell gazed at him steadily as they stood before the closed door. "You can trust me, Armand. I hope you know I have your best interests at heart. I always have."

Was Russell telling him something? In all the years they'd known each other, Armi had never picked up any hint that Russell might be attracted to men, but there was a glint in his eye Armi couldn't deny spoke of something different.

An odd sensation curled in his gut, one he chose to listen to.

Be careful.

It hadn't failed him when he'd decided to go home with Hayden, and he'd had the most pleasurable experience of his life.

"Thanks, but I'll hire my own assistant."

CHAPTER THREE

Hayden drew in a deep breath and rang the bell of the town house on East 65th Street. Two interviews down. Two job offers for what would amount to being nothing more than a glorified office housekeeper. Hopefully this one would pan out. The past week of job hunting was wearing on his nerves.

Was it really so hard to find a super CEO who was overworked and needed a superb personal assistant dedicated to his job? Apparently so.

A woman in her midfifties, hair drawn back in a tight bun and dressed in a black-and-white uniform, answered.

"May I help you?"

"Hayden Porter to see Charles Morgan."

Without a smile, she pulled the door open. "Please come in and follow me."

The townhome was elegant and decorated befitting someone who managed a multibillion-dollar hedge fund. Hayden spotted several museum-quality paintings on the wall, and the furniture looked like it came from Sotheby's auction house.

He was brought to a family room, where a fireplace dominated the twenty-foot space. Shining wooden floors stretched out before him. Various cabinets held antiques behind glass doors. There was more money in artwork in this one room than he'd probably earn in a lifetime. Hayden stayed in the center of the room, and under his feet was a thick, gloriously patterned Turkish carpet. "Mr. Morgan will be with you shortly."

Having worked with these types for years, it should have surprised Hayden that Morgan wasn't holding their interview in the library or his office, but he'd grown used to the idiosyncrasies of the very rich. After only a few minutes, the door opened and Charles Morgan appeared in a bathrobe and silk pajama pants. The housekeeper hovered by the open door.

"Hayden Porter? I'm Charles Morgan. How are you?"

"I'm well, sir. How are you?" He took Morgan's outstretched hand and received a firm, warm handshake.

"Sit, please. Come to the couch. I'll have Claire bring us something to drink. Scotch?"

"No, thank you."

"I insist. I don't drink alone."

"Whatever you're having is fine." He had no intention of touching alcohol on an interview. Waiting for Morgan to continue, Hayden forced himself to keep still. While outwardly he presented a calm presence, inside he was a jangling mess of nerves.

Morgan turned his head. "Claire? Two on the rocks, then close the door behind you."

"Of course, sir." She fixed their drinks, placed them on coasters before them, and withdrew. The door clicked shut.

"So. I've heard good things about you, and Janice only deals with the best. As do I."

Morgan was a good-looking man, his face smooth and pampered with facials and Botox, and his brows, like his chest, were waxed to perfection. Steady brown eyes never left Hayden's face, and a slight smile kicked up the corner of his lips.

Hayden got an interested vibe from Morgan, but they were in a boss-employee situation, and that was a line Hayden never crossed. He knew many assistants who gave truly personal service to their employer—from spreadsheets to bedsheets—but luckily, Hayden had never been put in that position.

"I pride myself on my unique ability to anticipate what you might need at any moment. I always try to be one step ahead."

"I need that. I'm busy from six in the morning to around seven at night. Overseas markets compose a vast majority of my business, so when the day starts here, it's already half over for that part of the world, and you would need to coordinate the two sides." He sipped his drink. "Is that something you think you can handle?"

"Not an issue. My last position was at a worldwide shipping company, so I'm well versed in handling international work." He kept a careful watch on Morgan's eyes and saw the approval. His pulse quickened. This could be it. The work sounded like something he could immerse himself in.

"I know. You worked for Kunoff. I'm looking for someone who shares my passion for perfection in everything." His gaze lingered on Hayden. "You have that same drive, I feel."

"I do. I'm very driven in everything I do."

Morgan's lips tugged up. "I'm glad to hear that." He finished his drink, while Hayden hadn't touched his. "How do you feel about working late hours? Or early mornings? Do you have a wife or girlfriend making demands on your time?" There went that enigmatic smile again. "A needy doodle-dog?"

"No. Nothing. I'm there for you."

"Whenever I need you?"

Like a cobra, Morgan struck quickly, and Hayden found himself under a very hard body, being kissed until he swooned, not from passion but from lack of air. Then Morgan reached to cup his groin and Hayden froze. A man like Morgan could do whatever he wanted to whomever and get away with it. Money gave him that power. Hayden had to stop it.

Now.

"Don't. Please. I don't want to."

"Oh, come on. You know the score. You do for me, and I'll do for you. You're giving all the fuck-me vibes."

"No, I-I—"

"Two hundred fifty thousand a year, plus benefits," Morgan murmured. "I'm very generous."

More than double what Boris had paid him. All his money problems would be solved, and he'd just have to grin and bear it. It would be so easy to say yes.

"No." He pushed Morgan off. It must've been the first time a man like him had heard that word in years.

Breathing heavily, Morgan regarded him. "I'm not giving options. If you want the job, take off your clothes." With a sneer he reached for Hayden again.

"I said no." It might hurt personally, but he had no choice. "That's not up for discussion."

Still, Morgan shrugged off his robe, revealing a fit, muscled body Hayden knew was achieved with an everyday personal trainer. "Yeah? Well, I say yes. Who're they going to believe, you, or me?"

Hayden's gaze was steady. "Oh, you, no doubt." A vicious smile curved his lips. "But where there's smoke, there's fire, right? And my accusation will always be out there in the press because I will drop it into the very willing ears of reporters who are my friends. People will always wonder if it's true or not. You won't be able to get away with this shit."

Morgan scrambled off the couch. "Get out."

Hayden couldn't leave fast enough.

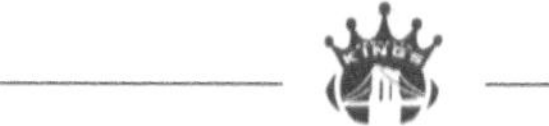

At seven thirty the following morning, Hayden flung himself into the chair in front of Janice's desk and huffed. "I thought you loved me."

She glanced up at him from her computer screen. "I do. Why?"

"One interview was with someone who wanted me to be nothing more than a glorified housekeeper. First"—he ticked off a list on his fingers—"get his coffee and have his breakfast waiting on his desk. Second, bring his laundry to the cleaners and pick up from the tailors, whenever necessary. Third, make not only his personal appointments—something that's part of my job, of course—but his wife's, his children's, and even the dog's vet appointments." At Janice's snicker, he glared. "And take the dog for three walks a day. And the second appointment was no better. More of the same, but they had *three* little dogs. I am not a shit cleaner."

"Just a shit-stirrer?" She cackled, then became serious. "Look, I didn't know that's what they wanted. They're running Fortune 500 companies and put out requests for personal assistants." Her finely arched brows drew together. "What about Charles Morgan? He's a smart financier. Manages a multibillion-dollar hedge fund. He couldn't possibly think you're simply a step-and-fetch-it gofer."

A shudder ran through Hayden. "He was the worst of all. My interview was at his house. It started in the family room. He wanted it to end in his bedroom."

Her expression revealed a combination of shock, annoyance, and amusement. "I'm sure you handled that appropriately."

His lips twitched upward. "I threatened to tell the press."

Janice's coffee spewed over her desk. "You *what*?" she squawked. "Oh, dear God, to have been a fly on the wall."

He frowned. "It's not funny. He kissed me. Someone else could be assaulted if they're not quick enough to come up with a story."

"Do you want to file a police report?"

Hayden sighed. "I debated, but it's a 'he said, he said.' Those cases are hard enough to prove. Billions of dollars make him the winner in most situations. I'll end up being hurt more."

All business now, Janice nodded briskly. "I'll take care of it. Not only will I blacklist him from my agency, but I'll put out the word to all the others not to accept him as a client. Are you all right?"

"Yeah. It might've gone further, but I held my own."

"Good. That dirty prick," she cursed, then studied him, and Hayden wondered what was going on behind her intense gaze. "I got an email yesterday from the son of a friend of mine who runs another agency. He has someone who's looking for a personal assistant."

"Okay. Why do I sense there are issues?"

"It's a different situation than you're used to."

Hayden folded his arms and cocked a brow. "Go on."

"Well...call him a reluctant CEO. Are you into sports?"

He snickered. "In or out of bed?"

"Bad boy." She cackled. "Football, Hayden. Football. The Kings, to be exact. The owner and CEO, Randolph Winters, died in a plane crash in New Jersey three months ago."

He nodded. "I remember hearing about it. He was with his pregnant girlfriend and his assistant."

"That's the one. He has a son, Armand, who's taking over, and from the talk I'm hearing, he's unqualified."

"So? What does it matter? Sounds like a richy rich who plans on playing at being an owner. Nothing new."

A grin spread across her face. "That's where you come in, my darling. Being unprepared, he hasn't a clue what to do. The scuttlebutt is, he's in way, *way* over his head, totally unprepared, and kind of a bumbler. More interested in his rose garden than acquiring talent. He needs someone to keep him in line and tell him where to go and how to get there. That one won't give you any trouble—no repeats of Charles Morgan."

He sighed, feeling older than his thirty-seven years. "Does this Armand need an assistant or a babysitter?"

"Maybe a little of both. But think about it—you could help yourself. Armand Winters is bound to lean on you, as his second, so to speak. He might not have much going for him in the management department, but he's got one thing you want."

"And what's that?"

Her eyes gleamed. "Hundreds of millions of lovely dollars."

But Hayden wasn't impressed. "I'm used to that. Boris was a billionaire. Didn't help me one bit."

Janice, of course, had an answer for him. She had answers for everything, which was why she was the top recruiter for top assistants. "Armand Winters isn't seventy-five years old." She paused. "Or straight."

Shock rippled through him. "Are you serious? After I just told you that Morgan wanted me under his desk as well as in front of it, you're suggesting I sleep with Winters?"

"No, of course not, but would it kill you to keep your options open? You're good-looking, bright, ambitious. Morgan is a bastard who's used to getting his way. Armand Winters seems to be a sweet person, and he's single." She leaned in closer. "It couldn't hurt to turn on that sexy smile and bat those pretty green eyes."

"You are something else." He shook his head. "I don't fuck where I work. If I get the interview and the job, it's strictly business. I'll do what I can to help him, but only as it relates to the Kings."

She narrowed her eyes and gave a brisk nod. "Okay. Whatever works for you. From what I hear, Armand Winters is only doing this to prove his father wrong."

Despite his annoyance, Hayden was curious. "Wrong about what?"

"That because Armand is gay, he can't run the team. Trevor—that's my friend's son who also runs an HR agency and is looking for a PA for Armand—said that for as long as he's known Armand—they went to prep school and college together—Armand has lived under the shadow of his father's less than kind behavior. Randolph Winters constantly made disparaging remarks about Armand's qualifications to run an NFL sports team, calling him weak, foolish." She met his eyes. "Limp-wristed."

Having heard some of those whispers throughout his life, Hayden winced. But where Armand Winters seemed to have buckled under the name-calling, it had only made Hayden stronger, though ultimately more foolish.

"Son of a bitch. Sounds like Armand didn't lose much when his father died." Hayden had been one of the lucky ones—his parents stood steadfast by his side, taking on anyone who treated him differently. God knew he'd put them through the wringer, but they still loved him despite his mistakes and stupid choices.

Surprisingly sympathetic, Janice pursed her lips. "It's a sad story. They had a very tense relationship. Early on, Armand insisted on trying to prove his father wrong, even though Trevor believes he has no desire to really run the Kings. He'd show up and make attempts to learn the business, but Randolph would brush him aside, or put off any effort he made, often in front of the other board members. After a while he stopped completely."

"His father sounds like a real piece of shit. So why did Armand keep bothering? He could have taken his millions and had his fun."

Janice scribbled something on a notepad and slid it across her desk. "Shall I send you to him? You can ask him yourself."

He shrugged as he put the address in his phone. "Sure, why not? It's not like I have anything else on the horizon." His eyes narrowed. "Do I?"

Studying her screen, Janice tapped the mouse. "I'm not sure. It's barely eight. I'll email you with any others when I have the details for your meeting with Armand Winters."

That was his cue to leave. He got to his feet. "I'll be waiting for your email."

She raised a hand and answered her ringing phone.

Outside, he stood gazing at the sky, blinking at the bright sunlight. The crowds streamed past him. People on their way to work. On their way home from the night shift. School children holding hands with their parents, teenagers gossiping or going over their homework.

It seemed like everyone had someplace to be but him. Hayden gritted his teeth and decided to use the time to catch up on everything he'd neglected while working his crazy hours for Boris. He found a coffee shop and settled in to do some work.

After ordering an egg-white omelet, sliced avocado, and coffee, he read through the morning news, checked his emails, and scheduled a haircut and manicure. His leg jiggled as he scanned his most recent credit card statement. A few months of no salary, even with his severance, and he'd be in trouble. A message popped up from his mother.

Hi, darling. Haven't heard from you in a few days, and Dad and I were worried. Call when you get a chance.

He hit the screen. "Hi, Mom."

"Oh, you didn't need to get back to me right away. I know how busy Boris keeps you. Hold on and I'll get Dad." He heard her yell, "Jim, Hayden's on the phone. I'll put you on speaker, honey."

Smiling to himself, he ate some of his omelet while waiting.

"Hayden? How're you doing?" His father's deep voice echoed in the background.

"I'm well. But I wanted to tell you. I got laid off."

"What? What the hell was Boris thinking?" his mother cried out, and he squeezed his eyes shut. Nicole Porter was no shrinking violet and rarely kept her opinions to herself. "How dare he fire you? You gave a thousand percent to that job to the detriment of yourself. Was it—"

"No," he cut her off abruptly. "It had nothing to do with that. Boris never found out. No one will." Past mistakes, though from two decades earlier, hung over his head like a guillotine. He might've been a child in the eyes of the law, but the ramifications were proving to last a lifetime.

"So what happened?" his father asked, always the calm to his mother's storm. If you searched "opposites attract," his parents' picture would be the first to pop up. But through it all, the good and bad times, they had each other. No matter that he'd caused them problems, they never wavered in their love.

"What happened is that Boris is an idiot. That's obvious," she ranted, and Hayden bit his lip to keep from laughing.

"Nikki, please let Hayden explain." His father managed to get a sentence in between her huffs of outrage.

"It had nothing to do with me or my work."

"Of course it didn't," his mother agreed. "Your work is impeccable." Her indignance was sweet, and after that morning's discussion about Randolph Winters's treatment of his son, Hayden felt sorry for all the kids who didn't have the support system he'd had.

"Impeccable or not, Boris got himself married, and his new wife—his very young, very shrewd wife—doesn't want anyone standing in the path to her husband's fortune."

"Meaning you?" Of course his father already knew the answer.

"Meaning me. I received severance, and Janice is busy setting up interviews for me. I'll have something soon."

"If you need—" His parents spoke in unison, as he'd known they would.

"No, no. I know you want to help, but I'll be fine. When I was seventeen and stupid, it was appropriate, and I still royally screwed up. At thirty-seven, my problems are my own. I love you for the offer, but I'm sure I'll have another interview soon and find something."

His phone buzzed with a message from Janice.

Armand Winters will see you today at 12 noon at the Kings' offices.

"See?" His heart kicked up a notch. "I just got an email from Janice. I have an interview today at noon. I'd better get going because I have lots to do before then."

"With whom?" his mother asked. "What company?"

"Sorry. Don't want to jinx it."

"Don't sell yourself short. You're the best. Make sure they know it."

"I will," he promised. "Love you. Talk soon."

"Good luck, we love you," his father replied.

Hayden's throat grew tight. "Love you too."

Imagine getting a call in the middle of the night that your underage child had been arrested for being a cam boy and having sex for pay—and having to come bail them out of jail. Hayden would never forget the disappointment, shock, and pain in his parents' eyes. It didn't matter that in his mind he'd done it for them—so they wouldn't have to drain their resources to pay for college when they could barely make it on their own. In their eyes, they'd failed him, and though the record of his offenses was sealed in the legal system, it lay heavy on his chest. He'd yet to come to terms with the weight of his guilt and foolishness, and he'd never forgiven himself for the problems he'd caused.

But that was for another day. Preferably he'd have a job and income secured. Hopefully this would be the one.

Now that he had the interview set up, he figured it was time to do a little research on Armand Winters. He typed the name into the search bar, and pages of articles appeared. He squinted at the thumbnail pictures.

"Wait a second..." Hayden tapped on Images. Up popped a picture of his pickup from the beginning of the week. "Armi? Holy shit." Remembering, he touched his lips. The guy had started out shy, but his kisses had been demanding, and Hayden had willingly given in.

When he'd woken up and found Armi gone, he'd almost been disappointed, though he was a one-and-done man. That hot mouth on his dick...the blissful expression when Hayden had come all over his face...soft, needy whimpers as they'd kissed. Hayden had wanted more.

He began to laugh and motioned to the server to bring him the check.

What the hell are the odds? The smile faded from his lips as he studied the picture, obviously taken at his father's funeral. His arm was wrapped around the shoulder of an older woman, most likely his mother. Big sad eyes, dark hair, and a soft, full mouth. Hayden recalled Armi being bullied by the asshole at the bar and Janice's words about his father treating him like dirt in front of people.

An unexpected and inexplicable wave of protectiveness burned through him. Armi didn't deserve to be treated like dirt. Hayden wanted this job. And he was going to make sure he got it.

CHAPTER FOUR

"Thanks, Trevor. I appreciate the quick action." His second full week at the office wasn't going any easier than the first. At that first board meeting, as he'd told Russell he would, Armi had requested that their scouts spread out to Division III schools as well as junior colleges and community colleges. He'd seen the looks and heard the grumblings, but despite quaking in his shoes, Armi had stood his ground. Russell had done his job and come to Armi's defense, but Armi hadn't missed the huddles after the meeting and meant to ask Russell about it.

Trevor was saying, "Janice assured me this man is top of the top. She personally recommended him. He was personal assistant to the head of the largest international shipping company in the US and is a whiz at keeping schedules and getting things done without you even knowing he's there."

Barely listening, Armi scrolled through his work emails, trying to keep up with scouting reports, training reports, fiscal reports... His head spun. It was hard diving into the deep end of the company with no life jacket. But Armi was used to going it alone. His father had hardly made the office a welcoming place for him, and as the years passed, Armi came by less and less often, eventually giving up completely. It gnawed at his gut that he'd allowed others to take over. No one questioned his decision to allow Russell to run the team—it was as if people expected Armi to hide, to not show his face and collect a check. After speaking with his mother, who'd proved surprisingly adamant that he could do it with proper guidance and support, Armi had shocked everyone by showing up at the office, intending to work, while enduring condescending expressions from the board when they thought he wasn't looking.

For the fifth time that day, he thought maybe dear old Dad was right and he should give it over to Russell and go grub in the dirt with his roses.

"Yeah? If he's so good, Trev, why is he available?" *Shit.* He'd forgotten about the four p.m. staff meeting. He should order food or something for everyone. He scribbled it on a sticky note.

"Because his old boss got married and the new wife is now his personal assistant. She doesn't want to let him out of her sight. You know how it goes."

Actually, he didn't. As awkward as he was in business, Armi was twice as bumbling and left-footed in his personal life. His few sexual encounters had been brief, unsatisfying, and left him lonelier than before. Except for that wild encounter with Hayden. But he knew it was a one-off, never to be repeated.

It was why he preferred to stay with his garden. The prick from a thorn wasn't half as hurtful as being snubbed, put down, or laughed at behind his back.

"Armi? Are you listening to me?"

He blinked back to awareness. "Sorry, what?"

He heard Trevor's huff of annoyance. "I said, Hayden Porter will be there at noon."

At the mention of the name Hayden, a thrill of excitement tingled up his spine. It would be silly to think it was him. His Hayden.

If only Hayden were mine...

He licked his lips, imagining he could still taste Hayden and see him fall apart as he came. The smell of his come, his hard dick throbbing...God, he was beautiful. A shame they'd never see each other again. He wasn't about to stalk the man's apartment building, and he didn't even know Hayden's last name.

"Yeah, okay. I'll be ready. I'd better go. And thanks, Trev. I appreciate it."

"Anytime. Please, try and come for dinner sometime. Marianne wants to see you. We both do, but she misses you. And your roses."

"Sounds good. I promise I will once things settle down a bit. And I'll bring her something new I'm working on."

"I'm going to tell Marianne, so she'll hound you even if I won't. Now that you'll have a real assistant, I'll make plans with him, and you'll always have to show," Trevor joked.

"You're that positive I'm going to hire him?"

Trevor's sigh filled his ear. "Listen. You need help. And this guy sounds like exactly who you need. Unless he's a serial killer, there's no reason to say no."

In a good mood for the first time all day, Armi laughed. "And how would I know if he was? But I get your point. I promise, if he's as perfect as you say he is, I'll hire him."

"Let me know. Gotta go. Talk soon."

Armi ended the call and wrote on another sticky note: *Make dinner plans with Trevor. Don't forget flowers.*

The next few hours were spent up to his eyeballs in salary negotiation reports from the lawyers, and he took copious notes. Spending was on par with earlier years, so he didn't see any issues there and moved on. Eating his sandwich, he opened the report from Russell on the off-season trade talks. They were in the heart of free agency now, and he scoured the athletes the Kings were pursuing, wondering why they had their sights on some who were plagued with injuries or had trouble off-season with bad behavior. A piece of pickle fell on his suit lapel, and he grimaced at the mustard stain it left.

As he dabbed at it with a napkin, his phone buzzed. "Yes?"

"Your twelve o'clock is here. Hayden Porter."

"Thank you. Bring him in, please."

He blotted the spot with some water, which only made it more apparent, and tossed everything into the garbage. He stood to peer at his reflection in the mirror. A quick knock on his door before it opened.

"Mr. Winters. I have Hayden Porter."

"Please, Josh, call me Armand."

Josh stepped aside, and in walked Hayden Porter.

His Hayden.

The man he'd last seen half-naked and sleeping. The man whose dick he'd sucked and licked. His mouth dried while his face burned. *What the hell?* Trevor couldn't have known...

Hayden closed the door behind him and strolled into the office until he stood in front of him.

"Hello, Mr. Winters."

Armi swallowed hard. "Is this a joke?"

Hayden's smile faded. "What do you mean?"

"You know what I'm talking about," he hissed. They might be alone in his office, but his eyes darted side to side as if someone could overhear their conversation.

"Yes. We met at The Vibe, and you came home with me." He lifted his chin, those green eyes Armi couldn't stop thinking about, cool and determined. "But that has nothing to do with this job."

Somewhat dizzy, Armi circled around to put the expanse of his desk between the two of them and sat. Well, flopped would characterize it better, as his legs trembled.

"You're a personal assistant?"

"I am." Still standing, Hayden tipped his head. "May I sit?"

"What? Yes, of course. Please."

Hayden took the straight-backed chair and sat. The contrast was laughable between this man, beautifully dressed in a conservative suit and tie, almost prim in his appearance, and the wild-eyed, passionate man with the wicked mouth and teasing tongue. Armi grew weak, recalling all the tattoos against his skin, now hidden under his clothes. Hayden opened a leather portfolio and handed him a copy of his résumé.

"I know you're extremely busy and this interview was on short notice, so you might not have had the chance to review my qualifications."

Armi took it and scanned the page. "Impressive. I know of Kunoff Shipping. I've seen their barges."

"I made sure everything Boris—Mr. Kunoff—needed was always in place. I pride myself on being a step ahead so you never fall behind."

"That would be a switch," Armi said, his smile wry. "I'm never caught up."

"I can help with that." Hayden leaned forward, his body language eager and willing. "I'd have your calendar set for the week and make sure you're always up-to-date on what you need to know for your meetings. I may not know the ins and outs of football, but I'm a quick learner."

"Don't worry, I'm not so knowledgeable myself," Armi admitted. "We can learn together." Aware that might sound intimate, he rushed to explain. "I mean, uh, I can do it, and *you*—"

"Mr. Winters," Hayden broke in quietly. "I think we need to get things out in the open and clear the air between us." He chewed on his lip, suddenly vulnerable. "I know this might be embarrassing, but it doesn't have to be."

"No? I'm glad you think so." Their eyes met briefly before he forced himself to look anywhere but at Hayden's face. How could he sit with him day after day, knowing what he looked like naked?

Worst of all, wanting to see him like that again.

Obviously, Hayden wasn't obsessing over him, and Armi listened to his argument.

"Mr. Winters, I can put aside how we first met and chalk it up to a strange New York experience. I'm sure you're feeling as awkward as I am. But I know I can help you, and as a professional, I can assure you, our relationship would be strictly business."

It was a silly fantasy to wish that Hayden had told him he wanted a repeat of what happened between them. It was surprising that Hayden remembered him at all.

"What would you expect your hours to be?"

Hayden brightened. "Whatever you want. In my old position, I would be in the office no later than seven thirty. Boris would arrive at nine, and I'd have everything set up for the day–his meetings, personal appointments, and so on. All documents would be ready for his signature with appropriate copies, and I'd make sure he got to his evening appointments." Hayden hesitated. "I don't mind arranging lunch and dinner reservations, as well as your personal appointments, but I'm more than a glorified gofer. Yes, I'll have your breakfast waiting for you, and lunch as well, but it goes beyond those simple tasks."

A smile twitched up Armi's lips. "I see you have strong opinions about that."

Green eyes blazed fire through the fan of those dark eyelashes. Hayden set his jaw. "Yes, I do. I'm the best of the best, and I'm not modest."

That arrogance was a fucking turn-on. Not that he needed an excuse to lust over Hayden.

"So I see." Armi's shoulders slumped. "I'm not exaggerating when I tell you I'm in over my head here. Way over. No one, least of all me, expected that I'd be sitting in this chair so quickly–or at all. Not a single person thinks I can do the job–one says he does, but I'm not sure. He was my father's best friend." Armi raised his gaze to meet Hayden's. "I have no one completely on my side."

"That would be me," Hayden stated, his voice soft but urgent. "If I work for you, yes, I'm employed by the Kings, but you would be my main and only concern. I'd be on your side, in your corner. Whatever you need."

Whatever I need?

"I-I don't know."

A vision of Hayden in mid-orgasm, eyelids fluttering, body twitching sprang to Armi's mind, and he trembled. Apparently, Hayden could pick up on body language as well.

"You're still thinking about what happened between us."

Armi ran a shaky hand through his hair. "How can I not?"

"Because it's in the past. It was a club hookup. It didn't mean anything, so we can forget about it."

With a sinking heart, Armi realized that what Hayden had said was true. For Hayden. He probably went to clubs and picked up guys all the time. A man as beautiful and sexual as Hayden could have his choice of lovers. Armi had made it easy for him that night. The truth was, Hayden might work for him, but he was way out of Armi's league.

He forced a smile. "Yeah, sure. No big deal. Okay, well, let me call your references, and I'll get back to you in a few days."

Hayden nodded and stood. "Thank you. I think we could work well together." His eyes twinkled. "I have an in with the best dry cleaners in town that can do wonders with lunch spills."

Instinctively, his gaze shifted to his suit lapel and the remnants of his mustardy-pickle smeared into the fabric. Armi sighed. "It's inevitable. No matter what I do, my breakfast, lunch, or dinner lands on me somewhere."

Hayden remained unfazed. "It's very common to keep a change of clothes in the office. I can arrange for a suit, shirt, and tie to always be here, or evening clothes if you have dinner plans, so you'll always have what you need to wear."

Why hadn't he thought of that? "You'd have to include shoes as well. The other day, I noticed—too late—I had on one black and one brown loafer." Russell had pointed it out to him right before the meeting but assured him no one would notice.

"Happens to everyone."

Doubtful. Armi never witnessed his father make one misstep. "I'll walk you out."

He opened the door, and Hayden passed in front of him. His dick twitched, and he closed his eyes. Could he work with Hayden and not think of those wet, hot kisses? Or how his skin tasted and smelled? Who was he to have these insane thoughts? He'd never been a sexual person, yet lust burned in his blood for this man.

Side by side, they made their way through the sprawling space, and with a sinking heart, Armi saw Whitmore approaching him.

"Armand, what the hell are you thinking with that damn fool scouting idea?" The anger rolled off him in waves, and Armi shrank from his rage. That didn't stop Whitmore from getting right into his face, pointing with his finger and continuing to berate him. "Do you want to destroy this team? Is that it? You're finally getting back at your father for speaking the truth about you? I know you're ignorant about sports, but for God's sake—"

"Excuse me, but who the hell are you to talk to him like that?" Hayden snapped.

Whitmore swung around to face Hayden, and Armi put a hand on his arm. "It's okay."

"The hell it is. You're the owner of the company." Hayden turned to Whitmore. "You don't talk to him like that, or to anyone for that matter."

"Who the hell am I?" Whitmore's gaze flicked over Hayden, dismissing him. The man was legendary for his cutting comebacks. Some of the support staff in the common area left their seats to see what the tumult was about. "Who the fuck are you to tell me what to do in my own company?"

"He's my new assistant," Armi heard himself say. "And this isn't your company, Jacob. It's mine. I own it, and you'd better get used to it."

A slight smile kicked up the corner of Hayden's mouth, and Armi watched as Whitmore grew apoplectic.

"Your assistant? And you're going to let him talk to me that way?" Whitmore sputtered.

"Frankly, I don't think he was hard enough. I dislike bullies and mean people."

"Bullies and mean people?" Whitmore laughed in his face. "This is a billion-dollar business, not a toddler playground. If you're not man enough to play in the big leagues, maybe you should step out of the sandbox and let us do the work."

In the past, he would've quivered at Whitmore's nasty words and relented, but having Hayden there gave him courage. Emboldened, Armi drew in a deep breath and folded his arms. "Is there a problem with you taking orders from me, Jacob? I told you my position, and as owner and president, I expect you to follow through."

"What's going on here?" Russell's quiet, authoritative voice cut through the tension, and he joined the three of them and put a hand on Armi's shoulder. "Can I help?"

"I–" Armi began, but Whitmore cut him off.

"Armand's hired someone who was disrespectful to me. I was letting him know I won't tolerate being spoken to like that."

"You've hired someone already?" Releasing him, Russell gave Hayden the once-over, and Armi wasn't sure he liked it. Not for any other reason than one person had no right to judge another by a single look. It told nothing of their character, only appearances, which often proved to be a mistake. "That was quick."

Hayden stayed quiet, but those clever eyes remained watchful, and Armi knew, though his references needed to be checked, that it was mostly a formality. His immediate reaction to stand up to someone as powerful as Whitmore proved what he'd said in the interview: Hayden would be there for him. In his corner. He could lust after his assistant in private. Hayden would never need to know.

"Yes. This is Hayden Porter. He comes highly recommended." His mind made up, he nodded at Hayden. "I was bringing him to Human Resources to get him set up."

"That's good." Russell frowned, contradicting his words. "How many people have you interviewed? I hadn't noticed any other candidates."

"Are you in charge of Mr. Winters's hiring?" Hayden asked.

The question startled both Russell and Whitmore, but Armi appreciated that he'd started setting boundaries.

Brows up, Russell studied Hayden's face. "No. But I'm Armand's friend and second in charge. I'm just looking out for him."

"So am I."

Armi bit back a smile.

CHAPTER FIVE

"It's not too early to treat myself with a glass of champagne, is it?" He'd called Janice as soon as he'd gotten home. After that odd exchange outside Armi's office, he'd spent over an hour in HR getting his paperwork filled out, and he was tired. But exuberant. "I got the job."

"No shit? He hired you on the spot? Must be those pretty eyes of yours. Bastard," she swore. "It's not fair that you have longer lashes than I do."

"Very funny." Hayden decided if he could tell anyone about their odd connection, it would be Janice. Not like she and Armand Winters would cross paths. "But there is something I have to tell you."

"I'm hearing a story," she singsonged. "Spill it."

"I've met Armand Winters before." He ran the tip of his tongue over his lips, remembering those needy, broken sounds from Armi when he'd sucked him off. "Remember you told me to go out and enjoy myself after Boris let me go?"

"Don't tell me..." She cackled with glee.

"Well, I don't kiss and tell, but let's just say, it was an enjoyable night. For both of us."

"And now you're his PA. How deliciously convenient."

Hayden pulled himself out of the fantasy of fucking Armi on his desk. "No. I mean, yes, I'm his PA now, but no, the two of us are not going to be taking it any further. I told you, I don't sleep with my bosses."

He might not ever get the chance to be naked with Armi again, but that didn't mean he liked seeing Russell Anders touching him. Whitmore was a bully and a blowhard, and Hayden had dealt with plenty like him. Anders was another story. Something was going on there, but he didn't know what. Yet. But Armi was vulnerable and sweet, and Hayden refused to allow anyone to take advantage of him.

"Your bosses have all been married and or straight, and Boris was seventy-five. I doubt his wrinkled ass would appeal."

"Come on, Janice. You know that's not me."

Her sigh was one for the martyrs. "Yeah, I know. But a girl can dream, right? I mean, I've seen pictures of Armand Winters. A little bit of a nebbish, but a cutie. I'm surprised he was at the same club as you."

Stung, he sniped at her, "Why, because I'm not good enough?" He already knew Armi Winters was way, *way* out of his league, but it sure as hell didn't feel good hearing it from Janice.

"No, dummy. Because he seems quiet and shy. Not the kind to hang out looking for a hookup, which I know is where you found him. He seems more the piano bar and theater type."

His hackles lowered. She had a point. "Well, yeah. I see that too. I guess he felt like letting go for a night. Seeing how the other half lived." Hayden could write him a book. The conversation had dulled his thrill over his new position. "Anyway, I wanted to let you know how it turned out. Your firm will get its fee, and I have things to learn about football in general and the Brooklyn Kings in particular. Bye."

Before she could squawk her displeasure, he ended the call, and with a glass of champagne in hand, picked up his laptop and googled everything he could find on the Kings.

One hour and two rolls of sushi later, he took a break and stretched out on the sofa. No wonder Armi was a nervous wreck taking over. There were so many rules to learn and complications with agents and players and the unions, it was impossible to learn the inner workings of an NFL team in a week, a month, or even a year. Armi may have grown up in the world of the Kings, but Hayden wondered how much he truly understood.

He logged in to the Kings' network and accessed Armi's calendar, which to his shock was completely empty. He scrolled and scrolled through to the end of the year, and there wasn't a single entry. "That's impossible. He must have meetings, appointments, dinners. This makes no sense at all."

On a hunch, he looked at the schedules of Russell Anders, Jacob Whitmore, and Troy Geiger and saw their days were filled. "Why isn't Armi invited to any of these meetings?" Seething, he searched the directory for Russell's personal assistant and called her.

"Russell Anders's office. How may I help you?"

He winced at the perkiness.

"My name's Hayden Porter. I was hired today by Armand Winters as his personal assistant."

"I heard." Her voice was tinged with amusement. "You put that snob Jacob Whitmore in his place. Wish I'd seen it."

At this moment, he didn't have time to gossip. That could—and would—come later. "I'm looking at Mr. Winters's calendar, and it's totally blank. When I checked Mr. Anders's and Mr. Whitmore's, I see they're full."

"Well, Armand isn't always invited to every meeting. He's the owner but not necessarily the one who makes the best decisions."

Listening to her brush off Armi's position, he bristled. "Mr. Winters is the owner. He should be invited and given the opportunity to decide whether to attend or not." He scrolled back several weeks. "I don't see anything on his calendar to indicate that he was even asked to participate."

"You said your name is Hayden?" Her tone had turned decidedly frosty. "That's not how it works. Armand isn't like his father. He doesn't know anything about the game, the players, nothing about running the Kings. Armand should leave it up to the people who know what they're doing. Now, you'll have to excuse me."

The phone went dead, and Hayden wondered what he was getting himself into. He remembered seeing Armi almost in tears at the bar from the dickhead who'd gotten a drink spilled on him. Now he understood why. Like when Whitmore got in Armi's face and he'd reacted, Hayden's protective instinct burst free.

"Not anymore. Not on my watch."

He found every meeting starting the following week and added Armi to all of them. He waited, and as expected, the phone he'd been given after he'd been entered into the Kings' system began to ring.

"Hayden Porter." He couldn't keep the grin off his lips. "May I help you?"

"This is Larry White, Mr. Geiger's personal assistant. Why did you add Mr. Winters to Monday's budget meeting?"

He lazed back on the sofa. "Well...let me think. Don't you think the owner should know how the team's money is being spent?" He waited a beat. "Unless there's something to hide."

"What? No," he denied vehemently. "Of course not. I'm appalled at your insinuation."

Hayden pounced. "Who said it was an insinuation?"

He repeated, almost word for word, the same conversation with Whitmore's PA and all the others who called with similar questions. By the time he finished, Armi's calendar for the next month was filled, and Hayden took a break for dinner. He picked up a grilled-chicken salad and brought up his dry cleaning from the delivery room in the lobby. While eating, he searched online for more on Armand Winters—both his personal and his professional life.

There was little information aside from the usual pedigree—prep schools, ivy league college. He'd worked at one of the major CPA firms in the city for five years after graduation, then left. After that, not much except...

"Bulgaria? What the hell is there?"

Fascinated, he began to read.

Eight a.m. on Monday morning found him entering the offices of the Kings. He seemed to be the only one there. It was a little later than his usual, but he'd made several stops along the way. He set his bundles on the reception desk and frowned.

"Why does it still say 'Randolph Winters, Owner and CEO'? That should've been changed weeks ago." Annoyed already, and he hadn't even set foot past the entrance, he pulled out his phone and made a note to himself: *Call to have replacement sign ordered for Armand.*

Gingerly, he picked up the packages, and with his shoulder, pushed open the glass doors leading into the office area.

"How is this possible? A huge organization and no one's in at eight a.m.?" He shrugged. "Well, just gives me a chance to do what needs to be done." First thing was to make coffee and turn on his computer. After setting up his desk as he liked—computer monitor on the left, inbox on the right, and all black pens—he started on his tasks. He placed the several dozen roses he'd purchased at seven that morning in the slim crystal vases that luckily hadn't broken during his travels. On his desk, he set the candy-pink Queen Elizabeths, the front receptionist desk held two vases of sunny Michelangelo yellows for cheerfulness, and the last and largest were in Armi's office. Beautiful, lush, peach Peace roses.

Hands on hips, he surveyed his arrangements with satisfaction.

"I thought I'd find you in early."

He turned to see Russell Anders several feet away. Watchful eyes met his.

Hayden turned on the charm. "Good morning, Mr. Anders. Yes, but I'm amazed no one else is. Almost eight thirty, and I'm the only one here. Color me surprised." He said it with an easy smile and took a seat behind his desk to arrange his desk drawers. "Is there something I can help you with, sir?"

"I figured to get in early to help you acclimate."

About to dismiss him, the old adage about catching more flies with honey than vinegar sprang to Hayden's mind. "That's so very nice of you. May I offer you a cup of coffee?"

Anders nodded. "That would be great, thanks. Cream, no sugar." He pulled over a chair and sat. Waiting.

He prepared the cup and handed it to Anders, then took the seat behind his desk, the friendly smile never wavering. "So, tell me what I should be prepared for."

Anders took a sip, grunted with satisfaction, and set the coffee on Hayden's desk. "I like Armand. I really do."

Hayden kept the mug to his lips, listening. He was waiting for the "but."

"But," Anders continued, "he's a little...different."

Hayden raised a brow, allowing what he hoped was an invitation to continue "Oh?"

Perhaps sensing a camaraderie in his willingness to gossip, Russell hitched up his slacks and wheeled his chair closer. "Even as a child, he was...soft. Unable to stand up for himself."

"I think he's very nice. And sweet."

Anders's lips twitched. "He is. A very nice kid."

"Kid? He's close to forty." Anger welled up inside Hayden, but he held his tongue.

"True, but he's a dreamer at heart. We never thought Armand would be taking over—Randolph planned to give Armand a sizable share but not give him control of the Kings. I was to take over as owner and general manager."

"So you feel cheated?" Surprised by Anders's openness, Hayden hoped to glean as much information as possible.

"No, no, of course not," Anders rushed out. "But the team must be protected."

This was getting stranger and stranger. "Why would Mr. Winters do anything to hurt his business? When we spoke, he seemed intent on the Kings continuing on their winning ways. He's grown up in the organization, and he knows what he's doing, at least to some extent. I'm going to make things easier for him. That's why I added him to all the meetings scheduled that I discovered he was left out of. An oversight, no doubt." He kept his face bland.

Was that a flash of annoyance in Anders's eyes?

"That's good to hear. I'll check with Lucy so that doesn't happen again. I can't imagine how that slipup occurred."

I'll just bet. I wonder how many other meetings he's accidentally missed.

"Great. And I'll reach out to everyone as well." His smile was cat-that-drank-the-cream satisfied. "It's always good to have a backup. I'm sure you agree."

"Of course. And I'm very glad Armand has someone in his corner."

Hayden finished his coffee and spied people trickling in. A quick glance at the computer screen showed it to be several minutes after nine. "Well, time for me to get to work. I appreciate the talk, Mr. Anders."

"I'm glad we're on the same page, Hayden."

We're not even reading the same book, Russell, but I know your story.

Russell walked away, greeting people, and Hayden set out to work on Armi's schedule, as well as reading up on the trade negotiations.

"Did you bring the flowers?"

Armi stood in front of him, and this time Hayden's pleasure was genuine. "I did. I know you like roses, and I thought they'd brighten up the place."

Happiness shone from his face. "Thank you. They're beautiful." Almost reverently, he touched the petals of the pink roses.

"I'm glad. There's another bouquet in your office. If you like, I can have them all the time. I'll have the florist deliver them when these start to fade."

Armi nodded. "I'd like that." Halfway to his office, he turned. "Can you come inside, please?"

Confused, Hayden followed him and shut the door. "Is everything all right? Did I do something wrong?"

Armand remained still, gazing at the large bouquet of roses on his desk. "I'm confused. How did you know I like roses?"

"I..." He wet his lips. Did it sound weird? Maybe, but he wasn't going to lie. "I researched you and discovered your passion is roses. You've won numerous contests and have some exotic bushes you're credited with creating in the New York Botanical Gardens."

"I don't know if I'd give myself all those accolades." As was becoming obvious, Armi rarely accepted praise and was more used to self-deprecation. "I experiment by grafting them to try and grow new subspecies." He touched the petals of the roses on the conference table. "Sometimes it works, but often it doesn't."

"I'm sorry." Hayden laced his fingers together. "I hope you're not angry with me."

"Why would I be?" Armi's brow puckered.

"Maybe you didn't want me looking you up online? But I was trying to learn more about you."

"I'm not mad. But you know...you could just ask me." Armi's shy smile was like a warm hug on a cold night. "I guess you discovered I'm not very interesting."

"That's no way to talk. Owner of a billion-dollar franchise sounds pretty damn sexy to me."

A bright-red flush rose over Armi's face. "Okay, now I know you're kidding me. I'm the least sexy person around. Please. Don't think you have to flatter me. I know."

"Know what?"

"That I don't belong here."

Hayden spotted a skipped button on Armi's shirt and he pressed his lips together. He really was kind of a mess, but Hayden thought it was cute. He pointed to Armi's chest. "You missed one of the buttons on your shirt. Right in the middle."

"Dammit. I was rushing because I just saw you added me to meetings, and I didn't want to be late."

"I sent you an email. Didn't you get it?"

Armi's cheeks continued to burn red. "I don't usually check work email on weekends."

Hayden rushed to reassure him. "It's not a big deal. I should've texted you and let you know. You'll be fine."

Clearly exasperated with himself, Armi pulled out his shirt and began to fix it. "I'm going to try and do my best."

"I'm sure you will, and I'm going to be there to help you succeed."

The door burst open, and Whitmore entered. "Armand, why the hell did your PA add you—" He stopped dead, his bugged-out eyes taking in the scene–Hayden standing close to Armi, whose shirt was half-open and pulled from his slacks.

Oh, fuck.

Hayden gave his back to Armi, shielding him and giving him a chance to finish dressing. Of course that didn't stop Whitmore from jumping to the worst possible conclusion.

"I can't believe you're doing this in the office. Is that why you hired him?"

Bright red again, Armi stammered, "Wh-what? N-no. It's not–"

Hayden drew himself up to his full height and glared at Whitmore. "What you're insinuating is highly unprofessional and improper. Mr. Winters is the owner and CEO and deserves respect. And I resent your implication as to my qualifications and work ethic."

He always did have balls. After his arrest and expulsion from college, he'd heard the whispers in town but he'd held his head up and hadn't given a damn what people would say about him. He'd been more concerned with how his mistake had affected his parents, and that had pushed him to show everyone in their small town he could make something of himself. His parents' love and support were the strengths he leaned on and learned from.

Finished with his clothing, Armi stepped from behind him. "What seems to be the problem, Jacob?"

"He"–Whitmore pointed to him as if Hayden didn't have a name, and he bristled but remained quiet–"without permission, added you to meetings."

Armi darted a glance his way, chewed his bottom lip, and Hayden hoped he'd stand up to the bully.

"Uh, yeah, I guess it would've been better had someone said something beforehand. But I think I should be there, don't you?"

Hayden hated how apologetic and hesitant Armi sounded and jumped to defend him.

"It's true. I added Mr. Winters to the meetings without him knowing. But shouldn't he have been on the list to begin with? Do you know why he wasn't?" In Hayden's opinion, it was easy enough to see.

"That's not your business," Whitmore snapped.

"Correct, but it *is* Mr. Winters's business, and his business is mine insofar as the Kings. My loyalty is to him. Now, please let him finish getting ready for the budget meeting in"–he checked his watch–"fourteen minutes."

Whitmore worked his jaw, then spun on his heel and stalked out.

"I can't...wow." Armi's drawn-out breath whistled behind him. "I've never heard anyone speak to Jacob like that."

Hayden wished he'd held his tongue. He was afraid he'd made an enemy of Whitmore, but he couldn't stand there and let him browbeat Armi.

"I hope you don't mind that I added you to the meetings."

"N-no. I don't, but..." He bit his full lower lip. "I didn't have a chance to look at what the meetings were about, and I don't want to look unprepared. Would you mind..."

"Do you want me to come with you? I've read some of the financial reports and made some notes for you."

"You did? You'd do that?"

Armi's stunned expression was confirmation that the stories were all true. No one had ever stepped up for Armi. And that was fucking sad. A wrong that needed to be made right.

"Of course. It's part of my job."

It wasn't part of his job or his nature, however, to want to put his arms around someone to give them a hug, but that vulnerability hit him like a sucker punch to his jaw. He needed to shut that down immediately. He wasn't anyone's pillow to provide comfort.

Armi's eyes lit up, the relief in his body language palpable. "Thanks, Hayden. I appreciate it." A slight flush rose to his cheeks. "I'm really glad you're working here."

Hayden gave him a brief smile. "I'd better go get ready." He escaped to his desk.

This might not be as easy as he'd first thought. Unlike at Kunoff Shipping, where he'd finish his workload and afterward clear his mind of Boris Kunoff until the following morning, Hayden had a feeling he'd be thinking a lot about Armand Winters, day and night.

CHAPTER SIX

Armi glanced at his watch. "Jesus. How did it get to be six o'clock?" Groaning, he sat in his chair and stretched out his legs in front of him. "I've never been so busy in a single day since I studied for the CPA exam."

"And you must be hungry. You didn't eat the lunch I brought you." Hayden stood at the open door of his office. "Again. You've skipped lunch every day this past week."

His stomach growled, and he laughed. "I guess that's your answer. Yeah." He rubbed his now rumbling stomach. "What happened to the food you ordered? I'll eat it now."

Hayden wrinkled his perfect nose. "You couldn't. It was fettuccini from Scarpetta's. I can order you something fresh if you'd like."

"Don't bother." He scratched his head. "I can do it when I get home. I'm exhausted and need a shower and to get out of this suit." As he spoke, he undid the top button of his shirt and loosened his tie. "My brain is fried."

"Would you like me to schedule you for a massage? That could help."

Armand studied his hands. "I don't know. I've never had one."

"What?" He could see he'd shocked Hayden. "How can that be?"

Armi shrugged. "I've just never...thought about it. Relaxing for me means—"

"The garden and your rosebushes?" Hayden filled in for him.

As always, the thought of his garden and the serenity it brought him soothed his jumbled nerves. "Yes. I like to spend at least a few hours a day with the roses and check in on them for any signs of disease...or simply to unwind. Being there, among their quiet beauty, brings me joy."

"It sounds beautiful. How many varieties do you have?"

It was the first chance he'd had to talk with Hayden since his hiring the prior week. He'd been caught up in a whirlwind of meetings and intense trade negotiations. Hayden had written up crib sheets for each team, and who was a free agent, and whom the Kings were pursuing. It all made his head spin, and he was looking forward to the weekend and time with his flowers. There was little he loved more than talking about his roses.

"I have fourteen distinct varieties, but I'm constantly grafting. It's why I moved to Bulgaria for a year. They have the most beautiful roses in the world, and there was no better place to learn about cultivating and growing them. I have hybrid tea, climbing, floribunda, grandiflora, David Austin. I'm trying some older varieties, like Damask and Gallica…" He trailed off, realizing he was babbling, and ducked his head. "Sorry. I'm boring you."

"Actually no. You're not. At all."

Armi made a face. "Come on, Hayden. I know I'm your boss, but you don't have to spare my feelings."

Hayden crossed his arms. "One thing you'll learn about me the more we work together is that I don't lie. If I was bored, I'd leave." To Armi's surprise, Hayden took several steps inside his office. "I'm genuinely interested. My mother has always had roses in her garden, and she takes care of them like they're her babies. I'd love to be able to give her some tips."

His lips twitched up. "I understand." Maybe it was having Hayden in every meeting that gave him more confidence. Or maybe it was their connection from the club that had his mouth speaking before his brain could catch up. "Would you like to come home with me and see them?"

Hayden's eyes widened.

Face burning, Armi stammered, "I-I'm sorry. That was stupid. Of course you have better things to do. I'm sure you're tired from working so hard."

"I'd like that."

"Y-you don't have to say yes just because I'm your boss."

A frown puckered his smooth brow. "Remember what I just said? I don't lie. I say what I mean. And I'd really like to see your roses."

Heart hammering, he nodded. "Okay. I'll just finish up here, then."

The cocky smile he remembered from their night together returned. "You're the boss, Mr. Winters." He left, and Armi rubbed his face.

"I can keep it together. He's just a guy."

Without paying much attention to what the hell he was doing, Armi closed his computer down and left. Hayden was at his desk, fingers flying over the keyboard. Caught up in watching him work, Armi remained silent.

"I know you're standing there," Hayden said as he continued entering information. "I'm transcribing my notes from the last meeting. Should be done in a few minutes. I'll send them to you."

"I-I'm sorry. I didn't mean to make you uncomfortable."

"You're not. And you shouldn't apologize. You're not doing anything wrong." He stopped, pressed a button, and swiveled around to face Armi. "I'm ready to leave whenever you are. I sent you everything so you can review it later." Hayden rose, and Armi couldn't help admiring the strong back and curve of his perfect ass in snug trousers before it was covered by his suit jacket.

"Great."

As they passed by the reception desk, Hayden pointed to the wall. "Just so you know, my first day, I put in an order to change the sign to your name. It should be arriving soon. And all the letterhead, stationery, plus the website still have your father's name as owner and CEO. That must change too. I meant to do it this week, but I've been in meetings with you and didn't have the chance. I'll get to it next week."

Damn. He hadn't even thought about that, and obviously, no one else in the Kings did either. Except Hayden. Who'd only worked for him for a week.

"Thank you. I appreciate it."

Hayden looked at him oddly. "You don't have to keep thanking me. It's my job." He pushed the elevator button.

"I know, but that doesn't mean you don't deserve appreciation or acknowledgment that I recognize the effort you're putting in. It's common courtesy." The doubt in Hayden's eyes was telling, and Armi pressed him. "Didn't your bosses before me ever let you know?"

The doors opened, and they entered the crowded cab. Hayden waited to answer until they stood outside, waiting for their car.

"To answer your question, no. None of my bosses ever said thank you. It's what was expected of me. To go that extra step so they didn't have to think about it."

The car slid to a stop in front of them, and Armi opened the door for Hayden. "Whether that's true or not, that doesn't mean it's right. Or that I'm going to be the same as anyone else you've worked for." The car took off. "Was Kunoff Shipping your only job?"

The air shifted between them, and Hayden's profile tensed. "No. I worked for the head of an international bank and then the CEO of one of the largest hedge funds in the world. Do you want to check my references now?"

"No, definitely not," Armi rushed to reassure him. "You satisfy me completely."

A hint of a smile flickered on Hayden's lips. "I'm glad."

Realizing how that sounded, Armi groaned. "Oh God, you know what I mean. I wasn't–"

Hayden rested a hand on his arm. "I know. I was just teasing."

The car slid to a stop, and Hayden withdrew. For the first time, Armi wished he lived farther away so Hayden could keep touching him. They got out, and

Hayden trailed behind. When Armi opened the front door to the town house, Hayden hung back.

"What's wrong?" Armi asked.

"Nothing." Hayden's response came swiftly, and as in the car, Armi sensed Hayden putting up a virtual wall.

"Follow me. The garden is this way." They passed by the parlor, formal dining room, and the large kitchen. Growing up, he'd split his time between the home on Long Island and the town house, but after his parents divorced, they sold the estate in Old Brookville, and his mother gained sole ownership of the house in the city. She gave it to him upon his college graduation and moved into a smaller apartment off Central Park on Fifth Avenue, claiming she didn't need so much space and Armi could use the garden for his roses.

He opened the door to the solarium, which he'd converted to a greenhouse. It was where he performed his grafting, as well as cared for the roses indoors during the winter months.

"Wow, this is...just wow." Hayden stood surveying the glass-enclosed room, and his admiration was obvious. It wasn't forced or faked. Finally in his element, Armi's chest swelled as he explained what he was trying to accomplish.

"I'm blending hardy roses with those of a more delicate nature to see if I can get healthy specimens. Plus, I'm trying to figure out how to achieve new colors. I love the shaded petals, like the Peace rose you put in my office. How did you know they're my favorite?"

A faint blush tinged Hayden's cheeks. "I didn't. They're my mother's favorites as well. During the summer she always cuts them and has bouquets all around the house."

"She has good taste."

Hayden peered at the cuttings in pots and the buds forming. "Looks like you're getting flowers. What colors are you hoping for?"

Armi smiled. "Almost anything. Come outside with me."

It was a beautiful evening, and the garden was in full bloom after a day of bright sunshine. A riot of colors greeted his eyes—blush to magenta pink, crimson red to coral. Cheerful yellow climbers shared the trellis with delicate, peach-edged whites.

"It smells heavenly." Hayden wandered about, and Armi thought how gorgeous he looked surrounded by flowers. How would it be to have someone special to share dinner with under the stars, surrounded by the beauty and perfume of his roses?

He sighed, and Hayden, who'd leaned in to smell a large hybrid tea—John F. Kennedy—gazed up at him. "What's wrong?"

Forcing a pleasant expression, Armi shook his head. "Nothing. Nothing at all. Everything's fine."

"You have a beautiful home, from what I saw. It's just you alone?" Hayden reached out to run a fingertip over a velvety petal, and Armi had never wished more to be a flower.

"Y-yes. I grew up here, and my mother moved out when I graduated from college. Probably hoping I'd get married and have kids."

"Is that so far-fetched? Marriage and family, I mean." Hayden sat in one of the Adirondack chairs. "Do you want that?"

"Do I have a choice?" The familiar tightness returned to his chest. "It's not as if I have much to offer. Aside from my money."

Hayden's brows drew together. "You're kidding, right?"

Armi leaned against the wooden picnic table. "Come on. Now I know you're blowing smoke up my ass. I know I'm no prize. I'm clumsy and awkward and not quick with the comebacks. It takes me time to process and think things through. I don't care about fashion or the latest trends. You don't have to flatter me."

"Cut it out." Hayden's voice whipped across him, and Armi flinched as if he'd been slapped. "Stop it." Visibly angry, Hayden left his chair and stalked toward him, his face dangerous, and yet Armi was as turned-on as the first night they'd met, when Hayden had been flirty and teasing. "What the hell are you talking about?"

"It's nothing new. Stick around long enough, and you'll see the whole picture of what you've gotten yourself into."

"That's bullshit."

"I'm not looking for pity. It's just how it is."

Hayden stormed off to pace the garden, and Armi watched his long, lean body move with grace. He stopped and strode over again. "I'm telling you, that's bullshit, and I'll prove it. Did I know anything about you when we met that night at The Vibe?"

"No, but—"

"But nothing, Armi. I saw you, and I liked you, and I wanted you. Period. I took you home with me, and we had sex. Intense, fucking awesome sex. Are you denying that?"

"N-no." Unable to bear the intensity of Hayden's piercing eyes, he dropped his gaze. "It was the best night of my life."

Cool fingers tipped his chin up, and Hayden's eyes bore into his. "It was hot as fuck. And you were sexy as hell. Stop thinking you're not enough. You might be everything."

His breath caught as a deep ache bloomed inside him. He wanted...God, he wanted someone to love and hold him and say those words because they meant them. Not because they felt sorry for him, like Hayden did.

"Thanks for the pep talk. I'll try."

A flicker of doubt clouded Hayden's expression, but he dropped his hand and stepped away. "Thanks for showing me your garden. It's beautiful. I'd better be going."

He'd planned to ask Hayden to stay for dinner so they could get to know each other better, but obviously, that wasn't on Hayden's evening to-do list. And the way he was dancing on his toes, he couldn't wait to get away from Armi and out of his house. Armi understood. It was enough to spend the day working with him; Hayden didn't need to waste his night as well.

"Sure, no problem."

With a false smile pasted on his face, Armi led Hayden through the town house to the front. Hayden remained silent, with none of the earlier teasing or sensuality he'd given Armi a glimpse of.

"I'll see you Monday," Hayden said. "You should have the scouting reports that were requested at the meeting over the weekend. I'll start a spreadsheet for you."

"I appreciate it." Armi took out his phone. "Let me call you a car."

"I can walk." Hayden opened the door.

"Please, Hayden. Let me?"

The struggle played out on Hayden's expressive face. "I don't mind walking. It's only half a mile or so."

And before he could answer, Hayden took off. As Armi wasn't about to run down the street after him, he watched Hayden disappear around the corner toward Second Avenue.

With a heavy sigh, he closed the door and leaned against it. "Well, that's that." He returned to the garden and sat in the chair Hayden had vacated, staring at the roses, until the sun set. Why had he been so foolish as to assume Hayden would want to spend time with him out of the office, maybe have dinner? From the first day, Hayden had made a point of stating their relationship was to remain strictly professional. No crossing the boundaries of employer-employee. Armi wouldn't make that mistake again.

CHAPTER SEVEN

What the hell was he thinking?

Hayden used the twenty-minute walk home to clear his head. Because everything inside him was yelling to turn around, go to Armi and kiss the hell out of him. To let him know that his low opinion of himself was definitely unwarranted. But he couldn't.

He slammed into his apartment, and frustrated, undressed and stood under the shower. Hot water streamed over him, but it couldn't wash away the loneliness. Self-imposed exile for sure, but it hardened him from the pain. Except for the night he'd met Armi. From the first, the sweet sadness of the man had struck a chord. One whose tone he didn't recognize.

For him, the music had died long ago.

Dressed and pacing his apartment, Hayden argued with himself. He'd broken his rule of getting too close, but that mistake was easily rectified. No more jokes, no after-work get-togethers or home visits. Strictly business. He couldn't afford to lose this job.

That decision made, he lay on the couch, staring at the ceiling. The perpetual strain of wondering if his past mistakes would pop up weighed heavily on him, but only now did he suffer a twinge of regret.

"Stop feeling sorry for yourself. You've got a great job, a beautiful apartment, and you're living in the city. What more do you want?"

He decided to do a little more digging into the Winters's family history to understand Armi's tense relationship with his father, and the more he read, the more his anger grew. Randolph Winters was never photographed with Armi, and in the Kings' Super Bowl appearances, Hayden didn't even see Armi in the owner's box watching the game or joining in the celebration on the field. Anders, Whitmore, and Geiger were the ones at Randolph Winters's side.

"I think...I need to be a lot friendlier to Russell Anders. He seems to have been the go-between for father and son." With that decision, Hayden pulled up Russell's calendar and began to plan.

"Good morning, Mr. Anders." Hayden waved. "I've brought pastries. Would you like anything?" He figured food would be a good icebreaker, especially on a Monday morning.

"I shouldn't," Russell chuckled. "But they smell good."

"Oh, please. You're in great shape. I'm sure you can sneak a muffin in every once in a while." The sunniest smile he could manage rested on his lips, and he pushed the tray toward the man. "Besides, I hate to eat alone."

He didn't miss Anders's penetrating stare, but he picked out a scone and bit off the end. "Delicious. Thank you."

"Of course. Can I make you a coffee?"

Russell eyed him. "Lucy usually brings me one. She should be here soon."

"I don't mind."

"Hayden, what's going on?"

Shit. Had he come on too strong? "Nothing. I was trying to be nice."

"I know you think you have to protect Armand, but he's an adult. He needs to learn how to manage this new position on his own."

"I'm not protecting him, but I do sense that people don't think he's capable. And I don't understand the negativity directed at him. Not you, of course. You've been very helpful. And I appreciate it."

"I'm here for anything you need. I want the Kings to succeed and be winners." Anders seemed to be weighing something in his mind. "Maybe we can help each other."

Now that was what he'd hoped to hear. "I think we both want the same thing." His phone rang. "Excuse me, please. I have to get that. Hello?...Oh, good. Please have him wait. I'll be right out. Thank you." At Anders's raised brows, he explained, "I ordered a new sign for the front, naming Armand Winters as owner and CEO. Mr. Winters approved it. I think it's time, don't you?" He flashed another guileless smile.

"Of course. Good idea."

"And please, bring Lucy a pastry. There's plenty here."

"I will. I'm glad we had a chance to chat." Anders selected a muffin. "I'll see you later."

He strolled off, and Hayden hurried to the front, where he found the person from the sign company waiting. After giving him instructions, he walked off, only to hear his name called. It was Josh, the receptionist.

"Is something wrong?" Curious, Hayden stopped. He'd hardly exchanged ten words with Josh, though he'd made sure to be approachable. The more friends he had in the company on his side, the better.

"I just wanted to say I'm glad you took the initiative to do this." He darted a side-to-side glance and lowered his voice. "No one here treats Mr. Winters with respect, and I don't like seeing it. He's the only one who always says hello and brings breakfast for all the support staff—not just the inside people. He's really nice. I'm a nobody here, but I think it's good you recognized it and you're doing something about it."

"You shouldn't describe yourself as a nobody. Us support people must stick together. And I appreciate you telling me this." He gave Josh a friendly nod. "Let me know if you hear or see anything I should know. We both have Mr. Winters's best interests at heart."

"I will, and thanks. It can be lonely out here with no one to talk to."

"I understand. I'd better get to work." If Josh was hoping to strike up a friendship, he was asking the wrong person. Hayden had no time for friends. The phone was ringing when he arrived at his desk.

"Good morning, Armand Winters's office. How may I help you?"

"Well, first you can by telling me whom I'm speaking with." The amused voice was cultured and that of a woman, most likely his mother's age.

"This is Hayden Porter, Mr. Winters's PA. And you are?"

"Eloise Winters. I wasn't aware my son had hired an assistant, but thank God." Her laughter was merry, and Hayden's lips twitched. "When did you start?"

"This is my second week, ma'am."

"Maybe you can pop me into a lunch date with him sometime soon, if he's not busy."

As they spoke, he checked Armi's calendar, which, while full of business meetings, was lacking in any personal appointments. "He's free today, if you are."

"Perfect. I'll be by at one."

"Wouldn't you rather I made you a reservation and Mr. Winters meet you there? I can call the Grill or the Regency Bar." He figured those would be safe places close by, where she'd enjoy lunch.

"And miss a chance to meet you? Certainly not. I'll be by around one, probably earlier, and you and I can have a chat."

He blinked. Obviously, Armi didn't take after his mother in the social-skills department. "See you at one, Mrs. Winters."

The office filled up, and by the time Armi walked in at nine twenty, it was humming with activity. Hayden heard Armi before he saw him, as he stopped to greet each person he passed. When he came into his line of vision, Hayden gave him a quick once-over and was pleased to see that his shirt was buttoned correctly and his clothing didn't wear parts of his breakfast. Of course his hair was a bit messy, and while personally Hayden preferred that look, he made a note to suggest a haircut, in case Armi wanted to appear more corporate. Again, as in the club that first night, Hayden was struck by the crystal-clear blue of Armi's eyes and that sweet, disarmingly shy smile that was such a fucking turn-on.

"Good morning, Hayden."

"Good morning, Mr. Winters. Maurice Hadley's agent called, and your mother will be here at one for lunch."

At the mention of his mother, he stopped and stared. "My mother? She called?"

"Yes. I offered to make a reservation, but she insisted on coming here."

"I'll bet she did," he muttered. "Thanks for letting me know." He turned to leave.

"I put the scouting reports for the teams on your desk."

"Thanks."

"And I marked some of the players you might be interested in, based on what you stated in the meetings and from what I've read the Kings are looking for."

Armi cocked his head. "Are you sure you've never worked in football before?"

"Very. My father is the football buff. I don't even watch the game. But I do pay attention."

"So I see." He moved toward his office but stopped again, his cheeks slightly pink. "The new sign looks very nice. Thank you for thinking of it. I probably never would've."

"Part of my job," Hayden said lightly.

"I'm not so sure."

Hayden heard him but didn't respond.

"And thanks for the Danish," Armi called out. "Cherry's my favorite."

Hayden smiled to himself. "I figured," he whispered, having noticed during his visit the box holding a cherry pie on Armi's kitchen counter.

An hour or so passed, during which time he checked on the order for the new stationery and contacted the webmaster to update the website and whatever electronic footprints the team had that still carried Randolph Winters's name. The phone rang.

"Armand Winters's office. How may I help you?"

"This is Martin Price from *City News*. I'm the sports-desk reporter. I'd like to speak with Mr. Winters."

"Hold one moment, please, Mr. Price. I'll check his availability." He'd never put a cold call through without discussion first. He hit the Intercom button. "Mr. Winters? You have a call from the *City News* sports reporter. Do you want to take it?"

"What? I-I can't answer questions off the cuff. What if I don't know the answer? Could you...would you please ask him what he wants, and, uh, maybe he wants to meet in person?" The quaver in his voice made him sound so young and vulnerable.

"I'll deal with him. Don't worry." He clicked on the line where Price waited. "I'm sorry, but Mr. Winters is tied up in meetings all day. If you send me your questions, I'll make sure to give them to him and get the answers to you ASAP."

"I usually don't talk through a third party. Randolph was happy to meet me for lunch so we could speak freely about the team and where he sees it going for the coming season." He paused. "Is there a problem with me meeting his son?"

"Not at all. I'm sure Mr. Winters would be happy to entertain you as well. How does tomorrow, one o'clock at the Grill sound?"

"Like I'm already anticipating the meal," Price chuckled.

"And you'll forward me the list of questions you'd like Mr. Winters to answer, so he can be prepared?"

"Now where's the fun in that? I'll see him at one."

Before Hayden could answer, Price ended the call. A bit of a wiseass, but nothing he couldn't handle. He spotted Lucy approaching, and though they hadn't met face-to-face yet, after their phone confrontation, he tensed, anticipating drama.

"Hi, Hayden," she chirped. "I wanted to introduce myself. We've only seen each other across the table so far. I'm Lucy. Thank you for the muffin. It was delicious. Sorry we got off on the wrong foot over the phone."

Dressed in black and rail-thin, Lucy projected the nervous energy of a terrier, but her smile appeared friendly enough. "Hi. I'm glad you liked it. Nothing like a little sugar and carbs to start the day." He laughed and she joined him. "That's a gorgeous dress. Prada?"

"Yes." She smoothed a hand down her waist and preened. "Thanks. Gotta look good. Russell sets a high standard, and I don't want to fail him."

"I doubt you could. He seems like a great guy."

Her eyes lit up. "He is. The best boss." Her gaze shifted to Armi's closed door. "How is it working for Armand? He's so sweet."

Damn right he was. And he knew how sweet Armi's kisses were.

"Mr. Winters is a very kind person. I think I'm going to like it here. Everyone's been friendly." Whitmore passed by with a scowl, and they both nodded at him, but he didn't respond. "*Almost* everyone." He allowed himself a tiny grin, which Lucy jumped on.

"He's such a jerk," she whispered. "Would you like to have lunch? I usually order a salad from the place across the street and eat in the break room. It's not as bad as it sounds."

"Considering at my old job I ate at my desk, it sounds good to me." Cozying up to Lucy could only help him. Hayden didn't trust anyone, but he'd listen to what she had to say. "I take my lunch at one. I'll meet you there."

Her eyes sparkled. "Great. See you then." She wiggled her fingers and walked off.

"Glad you're making friends here."

He spun around to see Armi at the door to his office. "I'm sorry, did you need something? I didn't know you were standing there."

"I was wondering if you wanted to go over the info you sent me on prospects and why you marked them."

"Sure." He hopped out of his chair to follow Armi. "And Martin Price from *City News* still wants to talk to you. I told him you'd have lunch tomorrow at the Grill." He passed by Armi on the way into his office, and he smelled delicious. Hayden breathed deep, briefly allowing himself to recall their time together.

Hot, wet kisses. Sweat-slicked skin tasting sharp on his tongue. A thick cock pumping out hot, sticky come...

"Hayden?"

A shiver ran through him. He rubbed his eyes and saw Armi in front of him, his brow wrinkled. "Sorry. What did you say?"

"I asked if you know what that reporter wants."

"To find out more about how you're going to lead the team and the organization. I gathered he used to do the same thing with your father."

Those big blue eyes flared with alarm. "What? I-I don't know how to answer that. I'm not sure yet." He paced the office. "What am I going to say? He's going to crucify me, and I'll look stupid—stupider than everyone already thinks I am."

"First of all, no one thinks you're stupid. How about I find old interviews he's done? I'll make up a list of questions I think he'll ask, and we'll go over them today. Don't worry, it'll be fine."

The fear in Armi's face subsided. "Thanks. You're a lifesaver."

"Not a problem. I'm here to help you, remember?"

Armi's smile was faint. "Yeah. But still..." He shrugged. "This is above and beyond, so I truly appreciate it."

"No worries. Do you know what you'd like to order for your lunch with your mother? What are her favorite foods?"

"As long as there's a salad, she'll be happy. And she likes fish."

Hayden nodded. "I'll take care of it. And I'm having lunch with Mr. Anders's PA today. Anything I should know about her?"

Puzzlement creased Armi's brow. "Lucy? I don't know. She doesn't really talk to me. She's like one of those popular girls in school who never speaks to the guys who aren't cool enough."

It pained him to see Armi's lack of self-confidence. "Okay. Let's get to work. By the time you meet with the reporter tomorrow, you'll be more than ready."

CHAPTER EIGHT

"Hello, sweetheart." His mother swept into his office and kissed his cheek. "Where did you find that gorgeous man outside your office?"

"Hayden's my new PA."

"So I've heard." Her eyes danced. "Aren't you smart? Makes coming to work so much more pleasurable."

Cheeks burning, he snorted. "Mom, that's ridiculous. First of all, didn't you divorce Dad because of his affairs with all his secretaries? And second, Hayden is more than just a gorgeous man. He's smart, quick, and–" At her smirk, he realized he'd fallen into her trap.

"All that and he's been here how long? And while your father's eyes wandered, along with the rest of his body parts, his affairs weren't with the women who worked for the Kings. He had a weakness for cocktail waitresses, cheerleaders, and strippers. But back to you. I am glad to see you've decided to get some help. You need it."

A knock at the door saved him from answering, and Hayden walked in with their lunches. "I have grilled chicken and fries for you, Mr. Winters, and grilled salmon over a salad for you, Mrs. Winters."

"It looks delicious, Hayden. Thank you," his mother answered with a smile. "Would you like to join us?"

Hayden shook his head. "Thank you very much for the invitation, but I have a lunch date. Enjoy."

"Thanks, Hayden." Armi took a fry and dipped it in ketchup...which promptly dripped on his pant leg.

"Dammit," he swore. "I'm such a klutz."

"Don't worry," Hayden rushed to reassure him. "I brought stain remover to the office just in case it happens to me. It's not a big deal."

Which Armi knew was a lie. Hayden wasn't clumsy, and Armi had yet to see him less than perfectly put together, even at the end of the day.

Except that night in his apartment. Hayden writhed under him, a sweaty, disheveled mess, his mouth all swollen and his dick out.

Unaware of Armi's filthy thoughts, Hayden busied himself.

"Let's put some club soda on it until you give me your pants after lunch for the dry cleaner." Hayden took a bottle from the refrigerator in the corner of the office, and after wetting the napkin, dabbed at the spot on his thigh. Their faces were close enough that Armi could see the faint shadow of Hayden's stubble and count the constellation of freckles dusting his skin, making him look younger. Softer too, than the tough, hard image he projected.

Electricity sizzled in the air between them. Hayden's eyes met his, and desire smoldered in those green depths. Armi's breath hitched, and his heart thundered. Perhaps Hayden had realized he'd strayed too close to dangerous territory because he jerked his hand away.

"That's good enough for now. I'd better get to my lunch date. Nice to meet you, Mrs. Winters." Without waiting for a reply, Hayden fled.

"Well, that was quite a show." His mother gazed at him thoughtfully.

"What does that mean?" With a napkin fully covering his lap and shirt up to the knot of his necktie, he cautiously cut his chicken breast and ate it.

"It means that your PA is as smitten with you as you are with him."

He started laughing—and he couldn't remember laughing so long and so hard. "I didn't know you decided to become a comedian, Mom. Please, don't lie to make me feel good. Hayden works for me. He's paid to be nice."

Talking about his shortcomings to his mother always brought out her anger, and today was no different. Her eyes flashed fire. "You're a wonderful man who doesn't realize everything he has to offer. You're good-looking, intelligent, but most importantly, you're a kind person who deserves someone who loves him to pieces."

"And you're prejudiced."

"Why, because I'm your mother? I'm happy to list your faults as well." Her eyes twinkled. "You're disorganized, a little forgetful, and too free with your time and affection in the hopes that people will like you."

"Gee, thanks. In other words, a patsy. Don't worry. I already know." His appetite fled, and he set his fork on the plate.

"Not a patsy. It's never a negative to care about people, and don't let anyone tell you otherwise. But a little too trusting and free with your heart? Yes."

"Not lately. I haven't had time for anything except learning the ropes here."

She ate a bit of salmon and salad, before patting her lips with the napkin. "How did you come to hire Hayden?"

"Trevor. He and I talk every week, and I'd mentioned being overwhelmed. He reached out and said he knew of someone who could help me. Hayden became available because his former employer's new wife took over his position. He came with stellar recommendations, so I decided why not?"

"Doesn't hurt that he's fabulous to look at either," she murmured, and his face flamed.

"Mom," he warned. "We have a strictly professional relationship." He averted his eyes, and of course, his mother pounced.

"But there's something else, isn't there? I can tell you're holding something back."

As close as he and his mother were these days, Armi had no intention of revealing what happened.

"No. There's nothing between us. At all. Can we eat our lunch, please?"

"Very well." She picked up her fork, and Armi narrowed his eyes. Eloise Winters didn't give up easily, but she kept to her word, and instead they discussed her charity work and his garden. He spoke of the path he was focusing on for the team, and she listened carefully. "That's very altruistic, but you have to consider the bottom line."

He huffed and tossed the napkin to the table. "Really? I thought you would understand what I'm trying to accomplish."

She remained unperturbed. "I do, and I commend you for it. But you do need to remember that at the end of the day, this is a business. The team needs big names, not only from free agency, but from college players. While I love the idea of giving underserved colleges a chance, the focus needs to be on big names."

"I understand. But there must be unknowns who are doing great in their schools and not getting the recognition."

She thought a moment. "Find them, then. Send out junior scouts to those schools and have them report to you. But don't ignore the moneymakers."

"Father taught you well," Armi noted with a smile. "You sound like Russell."

"Well, they were attached at the hip. I often joked with Russell that he was closer to Randolph than I ever was."

Recalling the odd signals he'd thought Russell had been sending him, Armi decided his mother would know better than anyone. "Let me ask you something."

"What is it? And by the way, those roses are beautiful. Are they yours?"

"No, Hayden read online that I love roses and brought them for the office. Anyway," he hurried on, seeing the gleam in her eyes, "was Russell ever married, or engaged?"

She cocked her head, seeming intrigued by his question. "No, not in the forty years I've known him. He was a serial dater—loved the chase but got bored once he caught them. I think he's a confirmed bachelor."

Which fit with his idea that Russell might be gay or bisexual but too afraid to admit it in the macho atmosphere of professional sports.

"Why?" she asked.

"No reason." It wasn't his place to comment on a feeling or hunch about someone's sexuality. If Russell was in the closet, it was his decision when or if to open the door. "And I'll take your opinion under advisement."

"Oh, my. Such corporate speak. Looks like you're acclimating pretty well to the position after all."

He made a face. "Very funny. I hate to rush you out, but I have an interview tomorrow with a newspaper reporter. I need to prepare for it, plus I need to finish reading through the scouting reports."

"I'll leave you, then." She gathered up her purse and rose to her feet. "Come by the apartment soon."

"We never spoke about you, Mom. Are you getting out? How are you doing?"

"I'm fine. Why wouldn't I be?"

He held his mother's defiant gaze. "Anna."

"Because she was pregnant? I didn't care. Your father and I have been divorced for over thirty years. What he did had no bearing on me."

"I just want you to know that you can talk to me, like you want me to talk to you."

"That's sweet, but I'm fine."

"I'll walk you out."

Hayden wasn't at his desk. Armi couldn't help noticing the surface remained pretty bare of any personal items, and he wondered why.

He kissed his mother at the elevator, and while he wasn't vain, he had to admit it was nice to see his name and not his father's on the wall.

In his office, he dumped the remains of their lunch, and even with all the work waiting for him, he plugged Hayden's name into his browser.

"Two can play this game, Hayden," he muttered to himself. "You're a puzzle I'd like to find all the pieces to."

The usual résumé and connection to Kunoff Shipping popped up, but that was about it. Strange, as it seemed Hayden was a person who should've had a much more vibrant social-media presence. Instead, the opposite proved true. No funny posts or pictures with friends and family.

Nothing.

He searched a bit deeper, looking for public records, and came up with only a high school graduation date. Armi chewed his bottom lip. "Could he not have gone to college? Maybe he dropped out?" His mind worked fast and furious.

"Does it matter if he doesn't have a degree?" Not to Armi. He knew what people called him behind his back, or when he gave money to the homeless on the street—trust-fund baby, bleeding heart, sucker—but he couldn't unsee the great divide and knew how damn lucky he was. Maybe Hayden had climbed that ladder out of poverty and wanted to start fresh and clean.

"He has the right to live his life as he wants."

Armi shut down the computer and picked up his phone. "Trevor?"

"Don't tell me you're calling about getting together for dinner this weekend?"

Dinner? Shit, he *had* forgotten. His gaze lit upon the sticky note on the side of his computer screen. "Yeah, of course," he said a little too heartily, and Trevor snickered.

"That's not what this call is about, is it?"

"Saturday night? How's that sound?"

"Good. So what's up?"

"It's Hayden Porter. The PA you recommended?"

"Yeah, sure, what about him?" Trevor sounded surprised. "He's working out, isn't he? I heard he's one of the best."

"No, he's doing great. Really helpful." How to put this without sounding creepy or stalkerish... "Just, I never bothered to call any of his references because I hired him on the spot. I was wondering how much you knew about him."

Papers shuffled in the background, and he heard the phones ringing. "Not much, actually. I took the info from Janice, whom I trust. Give her a call. Here's her number."

Armand jotted it down. "Thanks. I'm sure it's all fine."

"I am too. See you Saturday night. Seven thirty. Don't forget," he warned.

"I won't. I promise."

The call ended, and he stuck the sticky note with Janice's number into his pocket and wrote one for dinner with Trevor, then tossed the other one out. While waiting for Hayden to return from his lunch, he pulled up articles Martin Price had written, but in the back of his mind, something about Hayden's past didn't sit right.

CHAPTER NINE

"So, Hayden"–big brown eyes peered at him through a thick fringe of eyelashes–"I'm glad you gave me a second chance to make a first impression." Lucy tossed the shining waves of blond hair over her thin shoulders. Her salad lay untouched in front of her.

"Oh?" Amused, Hayden took a sip of water. He was all about redemption. Besides, Lucy was the key to figuring out Russell Anders.

"I kinda bit your head off the first time we spoke, but I was just protecting my boss."

"Which is what I'm doing. So I'm glad we understand each other. It will take me a little time to acclimatize to the culture here."

"Was it different in your previous job?" She scrunched up her nose. "You worked for some shipping corporation?"

"Yes to both. Very different, and no socialization whatsoever."

Kunoff Shipping was a huge operation with offices across the United States, and even after all the years he'd worked for Boris, Hayden hadn't met all the directors of the company. There'd been little time for sit-downs and chats with other assistants, and none of the directors ever acknowledged his existence, aside from asking him if they could speak to Boris.

"Oh, that's not how it is here, at all, so you should get used to it." Her eyes twinkled. "The Kings' organization is very social. Everyone here likes to be in each other's business. It's hard to keep things private."

That wouldn't be the case with him. Hayden had spent half his life hiding and wasn't about to spill his guts to anyone. But in an effort not to alienate Lucy, he forced a smile. "I already know about Mr. Winters. He loves roses and is very kind. What about your boss? Is he married, divorced?" He hesitated. "Seeing anyone from the office?"

Her cheeks pinked.

Aha! Bingo.

"I—Russell's a great boss. He's not married, never has been." She ate some of her salad. "How about you? Do you have a girlfriend?"

He toyed with his fork, pushing the lettuce in the container. "I'm not dating anyone at the moment. The new job keeps me pretty busy. There's so much to learn."

"Well, if you ever need help, feel free to pick my brain. I've been here five years, and I've seen it all."

"I'll bet you have." Not wanting it to seem like an interrogation, he ate a bit more before asking another question. "From what I've seen so far, it's a nice place to work."

"I think so. I love my job, especially the perks. I get to meet the football players, which is really cool. And sometimes I go to dinners at restaurants I'd never have the chance to if I'd stayed in retail. And, of course, all the tickets to the games are great."

"And Mr. Anders and Mr. Winters have a good working relationship, I feel."

"Oh yeah, definitely." She leaned forward as if to share confidences, and Hayden did the same. "Matter of fact, Russell was always nicer to Armand than his own father." Her nose wrinkled. "It was awful, the things I overheard."

A knot formed in Hayden's stomach. "Like what?"

She peered around the room, but no one was near enough to their table to overhear. "Randolph Winters was a bully. He never treated Armand with any respect. I'm sure it was because he's gay. Russell was always telling Randolph to try and spend more time with Armand, but Randolph wasn't interested." Her lip curled. "He was too busy with Anna to spend time with his son. So Russell did it instead. He and Armand have a great relationship—he always encouraged Armand to lean on him and helped him after the plane crash."

"Helped him, how?"

"You know, by taking him step by step through the business plan, scouting reports, the draft and free agency. All that's so overwhelming, and Russell's only too happy to help."

Hmm. I bet he is.

He could play along. "That *is* nice for Mr. Winters. I'm sure he's been a big help. Do you think he felt he should be appointed CEO?"

Lucy lifted a shoulder. "I don't think so...I mean, yeah, we were all surprised that Armand wanted to take over, but the reality is"—her voice dropped—"for the most part, Russell's really running the show. Eventually Armand will bow out and let Russell take over." She collected the leftovers of her lunch and tossed them into the trash bin. "Everyone likes Armand, but you can agree that it would be best for the team that way. You won't have to worry about your job, though. Armand would still keep you. I'd better run. It was great talking to you. Let's do it again."

She click-clacked out on her stilettos, leaving Hayden to ponder their conversation. Part of him agreed that it would be best for the team not to have an upheaval right before the season started. The other part didn't like the behind-the-scenes finagling and sneakiness. He'd yet to determine if Russell truly cared about Armi, or if it was a way to get his hooks deeper into the team, and what Lucy had revealed didn't make Hayden any fonder of the man.

At his desk, he began to make a list of questions he believed Martin Price would have for Armi, and cross-checked with interviews the reporter had held with other new owners. He'd reached number twenty when his intercom buzzed.

"Are you busy?" Armi asked.

"Do you need me? I'll be right in."

"Thanks."

In the years he worked for Boris, Hayden could count on one hand the number of times the man had said thank you to him. He waited in front of Armi's desk.

"What can I help you with?"

"This interview...I don't...I'm not sure..." Armi chewed the inside of his cheek, and Hayden could see he was working himself up into a panic.

"Don't worry," he soothed. "I've got you covered. I've already worked up a bunch of questions from past features I've read. We can practice them this afternoon."

Relief flooded Armi's eyes. "Thanks. I know it's a lot—"

"Not at all," he smoothly interrupted. "It's my job. We can start now. I'll just print out two copies."

"Armi, you ready?" Russell stood in the doorway.

"R-ready for wh-what?" Armi looked to Hayden, but Hayden had no clue. "Do I have a meeting now?"

Hayden searched his mind. "Not this afternoon. Tomorrow is pretty full."

"I told you yesterday," Russell sounded exasperated, which raised Hayden's hackles. "We have a meeting about free agents today at two thirty." He pointed to his watch. "It's two twenty now. I figured we'd chat for a few minutes beforehand, and I'll fill you in."

"It wasn't on the calendar." Hayden pulled out his phone to check. "No. There's nothing."

Russell barely paid attention to him. "I must've forgotten to put it on, but come on. I can brief you on the way."

Fucking slick, Russell. I'm on to you, sneaky fucker.

"Don't worry." Pretending it was no big deal, Hayden waved it off. "We can do the interview questions later."

"Come with me, please, Hayden," Armi turned to him and pleaded.

Russell's jaw hardened, and Hayden responded promptly. "Of course. Let me get my tablet to take notes."

Russell said, "I can help you with anything you'll need, Armand. Hayden will need to answer your phone."

"Will Lucy be at the meeting?" Hayden wanted to know in case he was being deliberately left out.

"No," Russell clipped out. "It's just the board members, Coach Jackson, and the scouts we sent out."

"Oh...I don't know, then...maybe you should stay..." Armi ran a hand through his hair. "I guess."

Unwilling to put Armi in an uncomfortable position, Hayden nodded. "No worries. Mr. Anders is correct. I'm learning, but I can see it's going to take some time, even though I've already picked up so much." He gave Russell a sunny smile and didn't miss the narrowing of the man's eyes. "I'll use the time to prep for the interview tomorrow." As the owner, Armi should have whatever he wanted, but Armi wouldn't push Russell, and it wasn't Hayden's place to do so.

"Interview?" Russell questioned. "What's that about?"

Armi wiped his brow. "Oh, uh, the guy from *City News* wants to talk to me. We're having lunch tomorrow."

"Martin Price?" Russell sounded surprised. "He was a good friend of your father's, and he's a Kings fan. Usually press inquiries come through me."

"Even if they wanted to speak to Randolph Winters?" Hayden schooled his face to remain neutral. "The owner of the team would clear his interviews through you?"

Russell ignored him. "Don't worry about it. I'm sure he'll give the interview a good spin. We'd better go, Armand."

"Hayden—" Armi began.

"Armand, please." Russell hustled him out of the office without another word.

Before Hayden left the office, a large sticky note on the computer monitor caught his eye—*dinner Trevor 7:30 Sat. nite.*

Of course, Armi hadn't entered it on his calendar, so when he returned to his desk, Hayden added it. Several calls came through from other media outlets, and Hayden set up interviews with them, but this time managed to get the questions sent to him and promised that Armi would have them back within the week.

At five thirty the office started to empty out with still no sign of Armi. He passed by the conference rooms but didn't hear any voices.

Where the hell are they?

Hayden spotted Lucy at her desk, fixing her hair and putting on fresh lipstick, obviously preparing to leave. Her purse—a very expensive designer name—sat at her elbow.

"Hi," she greeted him after puckering up and blotting. "Leaving too? We can walk out together."

Not a chance, sister. "No, I'm staying a little while. Going to wait for Mr. Winters to return. Do you know which conference room they're in? I did a walkaround but didn't hear anyone."

"They all left at five."

"Left?" Puzzled, Hayden didn't understand how that happened. "Where'd they go?"

"To Doyle's down the block. The usual hangout."

"Oh, really? I didn't know. I didn't see anyone leave."

"The large conference room has a separate entrance. It allows for big sports names to come and go without anyone seeing them. You know how the press goes crazy when they think a trade might be happening."

No, he didn't, but Hayden supposed he would have to start thinking that way.

"I guess that makes sense. But a bar?"

She rolled her eyes. "So clichéd, but late-afternoon meetings always end up there. I think they're on the verge of signing a big free agent and they're celebrating."

How did Armi feel, surrounded by people he didn't consider his friends? If he was nervous going into the meeting, he might be in way over his head and panicking.

"Thanks for the info. Have a great night."

"You too. Let's do lunch again soon." She picked up her purse and walked around her desk.

"Definitely."

He gathered up his wallet and phone and waited until he figured Lucy had already left, then made his exit. Doyle's was one of those old-fashioned Irish bars fast becoming extinct in the city. No-nonsense drinks, solid pub food, and a dark wooden bar with half a dozen beers on tap. The stools were filled with after-work revelers, whom Hayden skipped over. His gaze lighted on a table in the corner, where he spied Whitmore and Geiger, along with four other men he'd never seen— probably the coach and his staff. The men were laughing and joking together, enjoying each other's company. Armi's back was to him, and Hayden's heart gave a funny bounce.

Damn. He looked so alone. Excluded. Russell put a hand on Armi's shoulder and whispered in his ear, and Hayden's hand balled into a fist. He wanted to punch Russell in his face for touching Armi so intimately.

What the hell was Russell doing?

Hayden's chest rose and fell as the cadence of his breath increased. Russell's hand remained on Armi's shoulder. That was unacceptable to him.

Without thinking, Hayden strode to the table. "Mr. Winters?"

Armi's head shot up. "Hayden? Wh-what're you doing here?" Those big blue eyes were slightly glazed, and a flush stained his cheeks. Russell frowned and removed his hand. Hayden's stomach unclenched.

"How much have you had to drink?"

"Just a couple," Armi mumbled. "The guys ordered."

"Maybe you should get something to eat? You have that interview tomorrow, and we still haven't gone over the notes."

"Are you his PA or his mommy? Let the guy have some fun." Whitmore sneered. "We're celebrating a big signing."

"Who'd you sign?" Ignoring the others, Hayden directed his attention to Armi.

"Darrell Hopkins. The number two rusher in the league last year. And we have our sights on an All-Pro defensive tackle. We'll know more soon."

Hayden eyed him. "You're enjoying it."

"Of course he is," Russell insisted, answering for him. "It's a huge win for the team. See, Armand? I told you the right way to do it. The big names are going to bring us a Super Bowl win."

But Hayden wasn't concerned with Russell's take. Armi smiled up at him. A little crooked and way too endearing. He shouldn't like how much it meant to him. "I kind of am. I like the negotiations. It's all good."

Glittering blue eyes drew him in, and Hayden's heart kicked up a notch, but if Armi didn't want him here, there was nothing left for him to do. "I'm glad. Well, I'll leave you, then. Have a good night. See you in the morning."

He nodded to the others and left, only to hear his name called as he reached the corner. "Hayden. Hayden, wait."

He stopped and turned to see Armi running after him. "What's wrong? Did you forget to tell me something you needed for tomorrow?"

A bit out of breath, Armi put up a finger, and Hayden waited. "Sorry." He rubbed his face.

"What're you apologizing for?" Armi needed to get out of that habit.

"I-I felt like you came for a specific reason, and I didn't appreciate it." That same sweet smile made another appearance. "I might've had a tiny bit too much to drink. That was stupid of me."

Was this man for real? He'd never had a boss talk to him like this. "Don't say that. You were celebrating. And it's okay. I'm fine. You can go back to the others, just try not to get drunk and wind up with a hangover. I'll see you in the morning, and we can work on the interview questions then."

"Wait. Can't we...can we do it now? I, uh, I think I've had enough." Armi hiccupped and swayed, his face earnest and hopeful before he glanced at his watch. "Oh, shit. I'm sorry. It's late. Go home, have dinner, and I'll see you tomorrow."

Dammit. Armi looked like he'd lost his puppy.

"It's no problem if you want to do it now. I'm here for whenever you need me." He didn't miss the flush over Armi's face.

"I-I don't want to make you work overtime. It's not fair."

Hayden grinned. "I did say at my interview that I'll go the extra mile. It's what makes me special. I can meet you at the office and—"

"No," Armi stated with emphasis. "If I'm making you work overtime, I'm giving you dinner. We'll do it at my place. It's more comfortable there."

Once again, Armi managed to surprise him. He'd never been invited to Boris's home, except to pick up his mail when he was away. Now it was the second time Armi was having him to his house. Hayden became flustered. "Are you sure?"

"Absolutely. I'll get a car, and you can decide what you want to eat. We'll order when we get home."

Home.

Hayden allowed himself a brief moment to imagine what living in that beautiful town house would be like, but chased the thought from his mind. Pure silliness. Armi was being...Armi. Kind and considerate. Of course he'd treat him properly. Hayden had to stop thinking of him naked. That thick cock, heavy and delicious. Strong hands gripping his hair as Armi thrust in and out of his mouth. God, he could almost smell him.

Shit.

Hayden rubbed a hand over his face. He needed to get laid–the upcoming weekend for sure. It had been too long, and losing himself in some hot, meaningless sex would do the trick. It would certainly stop him from thinking about Armi. He deserved to treat himself after a long week.

"Hayden? You coming?" Armi stood by the black car waiting at the curb.

"Yep."

He slid into the back seat, and Armi settled in next to him. All he had to do was get through the next day, and this strange desire would be gone and he could concentrate solely on his job.

CHAPTER TEN

"Dinner first, or do you want to go through the questions you have for me?" Armi twisted his hands. The Scotch and few snacks he'd eaten churned in his stomach. "I have no idea what to say." He laughed but was too tense to fake it. "I hate talking to strangers or people I think are out to make me look silly." He met Hayden's sympathetic eyes. "It doesn't take much, as I'm sure you realize."

The horrible vision of grad school reared its ugly head and cleared the fog from his brain. While studying for his master's, he'd taken a few courses in tax law, and part of the curriculum was briefing the cases in class. When the professor would call on him, he'd agonize over reciting the facts of the case, then wait to see what questions would be fired at him. Anytime he was called on, Armi didn't miss the sly smiles and behind-the-hands laughter from other students, knowing his quiet, halting words made him an easy target.

"Oh, I don't know about that." Hayden held up a hand and ticked off his fingers. "In my time so far, you've held your own in the budget meetings, got your ideas into motion for scouting, and tonight the team signed a huge name with maybe more to come. So where's the problem?"

"Old perceptions die hard." He shrugged. "Anyway, maybe we should eat first. I should soak up some of that liquor."

Hayden frowned. "How much did you have to drink?"

Shame flowed through him. "Two and was on the third by the time you arrived. I-I swear I don't normally do this. Hell, I don't even like Scotch, but everyone else was drinking it, and I didn't want to be left out." His gut cramped. "*Ugh*, I don't feel well."

Hayden took his arm and led him to the sofa. "Sit. I'll bring you some water and Tylenol. Be right back."

He watched Hayden move around in his house and liked it. He liked everything about Hayden. He closed his eyes.

"Mr. Winters? Mr. Winters?" A cool hand touched his cheek, and he leaned into it. "I have your water and pills."

He opened his eyes. Hayden held a glass and two tablets and sat next to him. Close but not close enough. "Hayden...can you please do me a favor?" he whispered and watched as Hayden's expression turned wary, but he nodded.

"If I can."

"Please stop calling me Mr. Winters. I really hate it."

The tension receded, and Hayden grinned. "I can do that, sure."

"I liked it that night...you know...when you called me Armi."

"If that's what you want."

"I do." He took the glass of water and Tylenol and downed them. "Okay. What do you want for dinner?"

"Something light in your stomach would be best. How about some pasta and grilled fish?"

"Uh, yeah, sure. Whatever you think is best."

Hayden frowned. "You need to start thinking about what *you* want. What *you* need."

Christ.

Did Hayden even think about what he was saying? He needed more of what happened between them the night they first met. More kisses. More touching. Ending with Hayden inside him. His heart pounded. Hayden remained close, his full lips parted. So tempting. Armi could taste Hayden's breath on his tongue.

"I–I'd better order dinner." Hayden scrambled away, and Armi cursed his stupidity.

Idiot. He already said he doesn't want you. Stop trying to make the impossible happen.

"Do you mind if I go change? I hate sitting around in a suit."

"Armi, you don't need to ask my permission." Fingers moving quickly over the phone screen, Hayden kept his attention down. "Okay, I'm going to order you pasta primavera and grilled salmon."

"What about you?"

"I'm not that hungry."

Armi glared. "Hayden, order yourself something, or I'm not eating."

"Whoa, okay." Hayden's lips twitched. "Now that's what I'd like to see more of at work."

"What, me forcing you to eat?" He undid his tie and popped open his shirt buttons.

"No," Hayden responded, completely serious. "You being assertive." He sighed and ran a hand through his thick blond hair. "You can tell me to mind my own business and I'll shut up, but you tend to apologize to everyone or let other people run the show for you. It's your team, Armi. You're the boss."

"I-I know. And I'm trying. Russell's been really helpful...what?" He paused at the flicker of annoyance on Hayden's face. "Don't you like Russell?"

"I have no reason not to like him. He's been very nice to me."

Like the professional he was, Hayden held off criticizing anyone, but Armi sensed he held back his true opinions.

"He's a nice person—at least he's always been nice to me."

Hayden didn't respond. "If you show me where your office is, I can print out copies of the questions."

"Oh, shit. The printer's broken, and I never bothered to fix it. I just use the one in the office."

"It's fine. No worries."

Hayden's smile reassured him, and he ran upstairs to put on a T-shirt and sweats.

The doorbell rang, and as he descended the stairs, he watched Hayden take the bags, and he again pretended they were a couple, eating their dinner after a day at the office.

"That was quick," he said, and Hayden lifted the bags.

"Let me put these down. Where do you usually eat? Kitchen or dining room?"

He laughed. "I've never used the dining room. I usually grab something from the fridge and sit in the kitchen, or bring home takeout and eat in the living room in front of the television."

"Life of a single guy. Let's go to the kitchen, then."

"Sure."

Hayden followed him and set their meals on the big island. While he hadn't thought he was hungry, Armi surprised himself by eating every bit of the pasta and fish. Hayden, he noticed, had ordered only a salad with grilled chicken and barely touched it, concentrating on his iPad.

"You don't like it?" Armi asked when he'd finished.

"Huh? No, it's fine. I'm just trying to see if I missed anything." Hayden's lips twitched. "You got some sauce on your shirt." He pointed with his fork.

Of course he did. "I swear I can't eat a meal without wearing some of it." Anxiety hit him like a punch in the gut. "Shit. What if that happens tomorrow at my lunch? I'll look like a fool. My father was always impeccable." His stomach cramped. "I can't do this. You'll have to cancel." He got to his feet, and breathing heavily, ran from the kitchen to the one place he found peace. The backyard.

He walked the perimeter, touching his roses, bending to smell them. Footsteps came from behind.

"Armi, you can't think like that."

He faced Hayden. "Why not? You've seen it. I'm a mess, hanging on by a thread. I don't know why I thought I could do this. I've never spoken to a reporter in my life." A thought seized him. "Please come with me tomorrow."

Hayden's brows flew up. "Me? I don't belong there. I'm just your PA."

"Exactly. You'll be able to help me when I get stuck. Which I will."

Hayden frowned. "The first thing you have to get rid of is the defeatist mindset. Be positive."

"Okay." He wiped at the spot but only succeeded in smearing it more. "I'm positive I'm going to screw it up somehow."

"Armi," Hayden warned. "That's not what I meant, and you know it. Come on. Let's go over the questions. I went through the past five years of Martin Price interviews, and he pretty much has a standard script he follows."

"Really?"

Hayden grinned. "Really. Would I steer you wrong?"

He gripped Hayden's arm. "No. I know you won't. It's crazy, but I feel so much better with you in the office."

Hayden stood rigid under his touch. "I'm glad," he replied softly and withdrew.

If ever there was a signal that what happened between them would never be repeated, that was it. Hayden had made his decision, and Armi needed to give up the wild fantasy of the two of them together. It would remain just that—a fantasy he'd only explore in his very dirty dreams.

With dinner finished, they returned to the living room. Hayden pointed to the laptop on the table. "I sent you the questions, so you can use your computer or your phone, whichever's more comfortable."

Acutely aware that Hayden had taken the single chair to sit in rather than the space next to him on the couch, Armi found the document and read through it. "You're right. These are pretty standard questions. Do you think I should tell him about the team looking deeper into Division III or the lesser-known schools for quality players? And what about my long-term goals? What should I say?" He nibbled on his lip.

"*Hmm.* Good question." Armi appreciated Hayden not tossing out platitudes but taking the time to think about the answers. "Maybe say...the Kings are looking into new ways to strengthen the team with quality players, and we're exploring all avenues open to us."

"Ohh, that's good." He took that down word for word and repeated it several times.

"And as for long-term goals, getting into the playoffs and a Super Bowl win is always the right answer, I think."

"Right again. See?" Frustrated, he tossed the phone aside. "It comes so easily to you. I get hung up on feeling like I'm going to look stupid." He stood and began to pace. "It's like college and business school all over again. I hate speaking in public, and every time I'd get called on to answer a question, I'd hear the snickering because I wasn't confident. It's like the jungle where only the strong survive. My oral presentations were a disaster. I never got above a C."

"Whoa, Armi." Hayden joined him and put a hand on his shoulder. "You're doing great. I'm telling you the truth."

"You're saying that to make me feel good."

"No. I'm not." Hayden's eyes blazed fire. "And I had no complaints about your oral presentation. I'd give you an A."

His face burned. "That...that's different."

"It doesn't have to be. Just remember how confident you were with me, and use that."

A shudder ran through him. "I wish...I wish it were that simple."

"It will be. You're going to kill it. Let's go through everything until you feel ready."

Hayden returned to his chair, and Armi missed his closeness. His mere presence gave Armi confidence. He'd have to figure out a way to channel that energy into the lunch tomorrow.

"All right. Let's do this."

Martin Price turned off the recorder. "Now that wasn't so bad, was it?"

It was horrific, but Armi gave him a tentative smile. "I guess not." He gulped his third glass of ice water. "Do you have everything you need?"

"Yep. It's all there. And just in time for dessert."

"I hope you enjoy it."

Price took a big scoop of his *crème brûlée*. "I know I will. Nothing for you? You didn't eat much."

"I, uh, don't usually eat a big lunch." He'd barely managed to choke down a bowl of soup. Hopefully Price didn't notice that a spoonful of it had landed in his lap. At least it was on the napkin this time and not on his tie.

Shrewd gray eyes met his. "I didn't make you nervous, did I?"

"Me?" Armi huffed out a laugh through a throat so tight, it almost hurt. "No, not at all."

Price finished the dessert and blotted his lips. "Always delicious. Thanks so much for the lunch and the interview. It should be in Friday's paper if my editor doesn't have too many changes."

Their server brought over the bill, and Armi signed it and left a big tip. "I'm looking forward to reading it."

"Good luck, Armand." Price left him seated, and Armi watched him walk away, only to see Russell–whom he hadn't noticed sitting at the bar–stop Price. They spoke for a few minutes, then left together. His phone buzzed, and seeing it was Hayden, he forgot about Russell.

"Hi. He just left."

"How did it go?"

"Tell you when I see you."

"Okay. You have a three o'clock conference call, but other than that, the day is free."

"What's that about again? Sorry. I concentrated so much on this interview, I didn't pay attention to much else."

"It's about salary caps. How it'll impact the team if you sign the two big names. Geiger will take the lead, but I have all the stats for you. Don't worry. That's why you have me."

If only that were true in every sense of the word.

It was a brisk, ten-minute walk back to the office, and upon his return, Hayden followed him inside and closed the door.

"So tell me. And here's a green tea and a cool towel for your neck. I figured you might be a little nervous, and this should help."

He sank into his chair and took a sip. "Thank you. It went...okay. I think. He asked all the questions you said he would, and I gave the answers we discussed." The cold felt wonderful against his overheated skin.

"But not too quickly, as if you'd rehearsed, right?"

"N-no, I don't think so. I took my time. But then he asked me some personal questions." His cheeks grew warm. "I wasn't prepared for that."

"Personal? Like what?" Hayden's eyes narrowed.

"Like, am I dating anyone, and do I want to continue with the team, or am I only doing this because of my father?" He took a napkin off the desk and wiped his face. "I-I didn't really know how to answer that, so I said that I don't discuss my personal life and that I'm very happy to be leading the team into the future."

A bright smile lit Hayden's face, chasing away his frown. "That's perfect. Excellent job."

Praise wasn't something he was used to. Never from his father, and though Armi had heard it from his mother, after a while it became like white noise. A deflection of his father's painful words. Hearing it from Hayden stoked his confidence.

"Thank you again for going the extra mile. I know you have better things to do with your time, so I appreciate all your help. I couldn't have done it without you."

"You're welcome, but of course you could. It's all there. Inside you. Have faith in yourself, and others will as well. When you're ready to go over the stats, let me know."

After Hayden left, Armi sat and wondered why the words of a virtual stranger meant so much.

CHAPTER ELEVEN

The trouble began Friday afternoon.

His phone rang. "Armand Winters's office. How may I assist you?"

"Hayden?" It was Josh the receptionist.

"Yes? Do you need something?"

"Uh, no, but Mr. Winters's mother is coming in, and she doesn't look happy."

Hayden thought fast, but there was no appointment Armi had forgotten. At least that he was aware of. "Thanks."

She burst through the inner office doors and made a beeline for his desk. He stood to greet her.

"Hello, Mrs. Winters."

"Is he in?" Unlike the first time they spoke, Eloise Winters's voice held little warmth. Tension rolled off her, and her lips were pinched in anger.

"I'm sorry, but he's in a meeting. May I take a message?"

"How did this happen?"

"I have no idea what you're talking about."

She brandished the newspaper. "The article by that Martin Price. It makes Armand look *awful*. Like a weakling who doesn't know which way to turn."

Fear and shock zinged through him. "I-I don't understand. He came back from the meeting in good spirits and said it went well."

She gave a very unladylike snort. "He couldn't have." She flipped open the pages and started to read.

" 'Armand Winters is the epitome of a nice guy, but you know what they say about nice guys. And I'm afraid if the Kings are being led by him, that's where they'll end up. Last place. His carefully rehearsed answers couldn't hide the fact that he's woefully unequipped to handle the complicated inner workings of a top NFL team, which is evidenced by his insistence on turning away from top-college talent to pursue smaller names with little to no experience.' "

"Jesus," he breathed, stunned beyond belief. That wasn't what Armi was supposed to say. How the hell did Price find out?

She slapped the paper on his desk. "It gets even worse, but I'll spare you."

This was bad. Very bad. Not that Hayden gave a fuck about the team. His concern was the hit Armi's self-esteem would take from a public whipping.

"How did he even know about the scouts Armi has with the Division III teams? Only the inner circle has that information. Someone must've said something. I wonder if Price spoke with anyone else besides Armi?" Hayden mused.

"Armi?" A sly glint lit Mrs. Winters's eyes. "I haven't heard anyone call him that in forever."

Heat rushed through him. *Dammit.* "I—he said I could."

"I'm sure he did. I'll wait for him in his office if you don't mind."

"No, of course not. Please." He opened the door for her. "Let me bring you something. Tea? Coffee?"

"No, I'm too upset. I might throw it against the wall instead of drinking it." He waited until she settled into the chair.

"I'll leave you, then." He withdrew, and thinking fast, went online to read the article in its entirety.

The tragic death of Randolph Winters has revealed a weakness in the team they're so desperately trying to keep hidden. The late owner had football in his blood, but that doesn't seem to have passed down to his only child, who prefers to spend more time with his garden than the game. Kings fans can only hope that the team's strong inner circle and Coach Jackson's excellent skills and players will rise above the limitation at the apex to make the team a contender after this terrible loss.

It was as if Armi had been at a different lunch than Price. "This sounds like he had inside information from someone close to Armi."

"Hayden? What's wrong? You look angry."

Unaware of the storm about to hit, Armi stood by his desk, and Hayden stifled the urge to put his arms around him. There was no way to prevent him from reading the article, and it was best to get in front of it, but Hayden also knew that wasn't his job. Still, he wished he could offer something to soften the inevitable blow.

"Your mother is here. She's waiting in your office."

"Really? She didn't say anything." He checked his watch. "It's late. Go home. You deserve a day off with how much you've helped me lately."

Guilt swept over him, but he managed a weak laugh. "I'm barely here a few weeks, and you're already trying to get rid of me? Plus, it's the weekend. I'll relax then."

"I have no desire to get rid of you, Hayden. I'll see you Monday. Night." Armi walked into his office. "Mom, hi," Hayden heard before the door closed behind him.

He debated for a moment whether he should stay, but when he heard raised voices, he decided it would be humiliating for Armi to find him sitting there, as if he knew and was waiting for him. He closed his computer and left.

Josh stood by the elevator. "Hi. Ready for the weekend?"

Was he? Hayden preferred to keep busy at work, giving him less time to think about being alone. "I always am."

"Sounds like you've got plans. Doing anything interesting with a special someone?"

The conversation was shifting to a more personal level than Hayden felt comfortable with, and though Josh was a nice guy, Hayden wasn't about to share confidences. Still, he didn't want to be rude.

"Yes. My couch. We're in a very committed relationship. But seriously, I have a lot to catch up on, considering I'm still learning the job as I go. It's only my second week."

"Is that all it's been? Seems like you've been here a lot longer," he mused. "Anyway, if you're interested in getting together–"

Hayden was quick to cut him off. "Thanks. But I never get involved with people where I work. Too messy."

Disappointment came and went on Josh's handsome face. "I get it. But I hope we can be friends."

Without answering, he smiled. The less people Hayden let close to him, the better. They took the elevator down to the lobby. "I'm gonna pick up something at the newsstand before I head home. See you Monday."

Josh gave a wave and disappeared into the crowd. Of course, Hayden had nothing to get. He planned to wait until he saw Armi leave. The negativity of the article must be devastating to his already low self-esteem. He picked an inconspicuous spot in the expansive, busy lobby and munched on a chocolate bar, waiting. After ten minutes he spotted Russell Anders, Jacob Whitmore, and Troy Geiger walk out together, laughing and talking. How the hell could those three be so happy when an article had just eviscerated Armi's leadership? Hayden's stomach churned, and he hoped that what he suspected wasn't true. Was Armi's inner circle sabotaging him?

Fifteen more minutes passed, and Eloise Winters strode out of the building. Hayden debated following her but thought better of it. If Armi wasn't okay, Hayden doubted Eloise Winters would've left Armi alone. He tossed the candy wrapper into a bin, hitched his bag over his shoulder, and left.

At home he showered, ate a microwaved burrito, and changed for the evening—a spritz of cologne, a short-sleeved white shirt, slim-fitting beige linen pants rolled up at the cuff, and tan loafers. He drank an iced vodka and soda and slipped a condom in his wallet, putting it, his phone, and his keys into his pockets. Within a five-block radius there were any number of bars he could hang out in and find someone to pass the night with.

Hayden had no idea why he passed without stopping by all the places he normally gravitated to—each spot was hopping, and he could almost smell the fuck-me vibes from the people who spilled out on the streets. Continuing, he walked farther downtown and found himself on East 71st Street in front of Armi's town house. It was natural and only nice to check on his boss after reading an article that destroyed his character. Armi was such a sensitive guy, and the more Hayden thought about it, he most likely wouldn't fall apart with his mother. He'd wait until he came home.

He rang the bell, but no one answered. Pushing the button again he heard the chimes. Nothing. Maybe Armi didn't come directly home. Maybe he wanted to be alone. Nothing more he could do. Halfway down the stairs, he heard the door open.

"Hayden?"

Armi looked...terrible. His shirt was half-open and wrinkled, and his blue eyes were red-rimmed.

"I-I wanted to make sure you were all right."

"You read the article."

The flatness in Armi's voice sent a chill through him, and Hayden retraced his steps up the stairs. "I did. I'm really sorry. I can't believe he said that shit."

Armi bit his lip. "Do you...can you come in for a little while? If you want to."

God, he hated how the little confidence Armi had gained had now been pummeled out of him by that nasty reporter's article. "It's why I came by. I didn't want you to be alone."

He passed by Armi, and the waves of defeat rolling off him were visceral and painful to witness. Armi dragged his feet to the family room, and this time

Hayden sat by his side. He took off his bag and set it aside.

"Why? Why would he do that to me? It was so nasty...so mean. Saying that I'm weak and unprepared to lead the team." His head hung low. "That I'm nothing like my father."

"But you aren't, right?" Hayden wanted to put a different spin on it. "And that's a good thing. From all I've heard, he wasn't a kind person. Especially to you."

"No, but it doesn't matter."

Frustrated, Hayden grabbed Armi, hands curving around surprisingly muscular biceps. "It does matter. Stop saying that. You matter."

"I don't know."

It was the quiver that did Hayden in, and he couldn't stop himself from capturing Armi's mouth with his. The sweet softness of Armi's lips blew Hayden's intention to keep the kiss brief, but his emotions laid waste to that idea. His fingers undid the remaining buttons of Armi's shirt while his tongue demanded and was granted entrance to Armi's warm mouth. Armi sucked it hard.

"Oh God, Hayden," Armi rasped, and that husky growl sent an electric spark straight to his dick. "You taste so good."

Their tongues danced and rubbed slowly, stoking his lust. Hayden teased the points of Armi's nipples, loving how violently he shivered beneath his touch. Armi took Hayden's face between his hands and kissed him as if he needed his breath for life.

"Please, Hayden. Please," Armi begged, and kissed his lips.

"What? Tell me what you want." His heart thundered, drowning out the warning signals from his brain that this was a bad idea.

"You. I need you. Please. Make it better. Make me feel good."

Hayden crushed their lips together while his fingers undid Armi's belt and unzipped his trousers. Desire rose bold and fierce between them, and Hayden's mouth watered at the thick bulge pulsing under the thin fabric of Armi's briefs.

"Lift up," he whispered, and Armi complied, allowing him to pull the clothes off. Armi kicked them away, naked now below the waist. "So fucking gorgeous," Hayden murmured and lapped at the fat head of Armi's cock, teasing the slit, tickling along the ridge underneath. Eyes fluttering, Armi squirmed and panted, his face flushed pink. "You like that?" Hayden did it again, only this time he took Armi's stiff length deep and sucked hard, Armi's cock stretching his mouth to the limit.

Armi's hips snapped hard, shoving his cock deeper into Hayden's mouth. Hayden moaned, loving the pleasure-pain, wishing it could go on forever.

"Oh, oh, fuck. Fuck," Armi cried out, and Hayden played with his sac, squeezing his balls. Armi's eyes rolled to the back of his head as his body arched off the sofa and he came, jerking down Hayden's throat.

Hayden swallowed eagerly, licking his lips free of the sticky fluid.

Chest heaving, face a picture of bliss, Armi lay limp beneath him. "Hayden?"

"*Hmm?*" Hayden shifted and winced, his trapped dick throbbing and painful.

"Fuck me."

Those two words cleared the fog of lust from his brain. "I-I don't—"

Armi opened his eyes. "But I do. I know you think it's a bad idea, but look at us right now. I need you," he whispered, and Hayden's defenses lowered.

"I didn't mean for this to happen."

Armi's smile was sweet. "I know. But after reading the horrible things Price wrote, all I wanted was to be with you. Having you turn up on my doorstep was an answer to my secret wish. I want you." Armi reached out a hand, and without hesitation, Hayden took it. "I need you. Please?" Their fingers entwined, Armi rose and tugged. "Come upstairs with me."

His head screamed that Armi was right. It was a bad idea, the worst, but one glimpse of Armi's gorgeous ass drove all coherent thought from his mind. It would be his fantasy come to life, however briefly. No need to think too hard on it—they'd have this one night, get it out of their systems, and then he and Armi would work to figure out how to counter the attack on his character.

After all, it was only sex. No big deal.

In Armi's bedroom they stood chest to chest. He cupped Armi's face. "I've never done this before. I don't want you to think I make a habit of sleeping with my boss."

Armi's brows flew up. "No. Of course not. You've been nothing but professional with me. But just for tonight...can we forget our roles? I'm not your boss, and you don't work for me. Make it like that first time between us. Let's forget everything except how much I want you. And I think you want me too."

Hayden ran his thumb over the soft pout of Armi's lower lip and along his firm jawline. "You're wrong. I *definitely* want you. I have since that first time." He guided their mouths together, sighing at the delicious warmth spreading through his blood. The tip of Armi's tongue played along his lips, tracing and tasting, and Hayden opened up to dance and tangle his with Armi's. God, he was so fucking sweet.

Together, still holding each other, they moved to the bed. Armi removed his shirt while Hayden stripped off his clothes. Both of them naked, Armi touched him, his hand sliding up his thigh to wrap around Hayden's aching shaft, and Hayden grunted.

"I want this in me." Armi bent and pressed his lips to the wide head. "I need it."

The last bit of hesitation fled, and Hayden pushed Armi down under him, his cock brushing Armi's flat stomach. They kissed, rolling on the bed, hands and lips searching, tongues probing, mouths hot, slick, and wet. His jangling nerves settled, and the red flags faded away. All he could think of was being inside Armi and how fucking fantastic it was going to be.

"Hurry," Armi pleaded, but Hayden shook his head.

"Not on your life." He buried his face where the curve of Armi's neck met his shoulder and savored the hot smell of his desire. Hayden snaked his tongue along the jut of his collarbone to lick a path across Armi's broad chest. Tight, cherry-red nipples beckoned, and Hayden sucked and bit the tips until Armi cried out and beat the bed with his fists.

"Oh fuck, oh God, Hayden," he gasped. "What the hell?"

But Hayden didn't answer, couldn't, caught up in Armi's greedy, desperate sounds and the ripple of his twitching body under him. Hearing Armi's harsh moans of pleasure spurred him on to spread Armi's legs and kiss his once-again rigid cock from tip to root. A hard push to Armi's legs sent them to his shoulders and exposed his ass to Hayden's hungry gaze.

"Perfect. Look at you. Gorgeous. And all mine."

He didn't miss Armi's cock jerking at his words, spilling out precome over his stomach. After Hayden licked it up, he moved lower to press a kiss to the tight, pink hole.

"Ahh, what the hell is happening? Oh, God." Armi nearly levitated off the bed as Hayden continued to slip and slide his tongue in and out of his hole.

"You like this, huh? Like getting your ass eaten?"

"Mmm. Never knew." Armi's head thrashed on the pillow. "Fuck me before I die."

Had no one ever given Armi this pleasure? Hayden's heart pounded at the thought of being the first to taste his virgin hole. "I wouldn't let that happen." Giving a low chuckle, Hayden gave a long loving lick from top to bottom, then crawled up to whisper against Armi's gasping lips. "Where's your stuff?"

Armi shuddered and gasped. "Drawer. Only have lube. I don't have condoms. No reason to." His bright-red face turned away, and Hayden understood it was because he didn't have sex that often.

"I have one. Don't worry." Hayden scrambled off the bed to get his wallet out of his pants and pulled the condom from his wallet. "But not so fast." He knelt by Armi, held his throbbing dick and rubbed the head around the wet rim of Armi's hole, loving the noises Armi made. Jesus, he was going to come just from the touch of skin on skin. He needed all of this man.

Hayden rolled the condom down his aching shaft and slicked himself up. The first nudge into Armi was tight and beautiful. "Oh, yeah. I knew it'd be like this. So hot." He sank in another inch, and Armi released a strangled sound that drew Hayden's balls up.

"Hayden, please, everything. Give me...I need...ahhh." Armi shivered, his words slurring.

"Yeah, baby. I got you." He couldn't stand not moving, and drove in deep. Armi's passage sucked him in, and Hayden lost it. The need to thrust overwhelmed him, and he barely heard the headboard slamming against the wall as he pounded into Armi.

"Oh God, oh God, Hayden," Armi panted and worked his rock-hard length. Hayden hooked one of Armi's legs over his shoulder, giving himself another inch of delicious heat. His dick was squeezed painfully tight, and he reveled in the pressure. All that mattered was losing himself inside Armi.

"Oh yeah, baby, that's it," Hayden crooned, then moaned when Armi grabbed his ass, mashing their lips together. He sucked Armi's tongue as he plunged in and out of his wildly shaking body. Sweat poured off every inch of him, and his vision blurred. The world careened from black to white to gray as he exploded. Armi drained the last bit of sanity from him, and gasping for air, Hayden collapsed, eyes fluttering shut.

He had no idea how long they stayed locked together, covered in sweat and come. Tremors rippled under his skin, and Armi's mouth rested on the cut of Hayden's jaw, his lips curved in a slight smile. Hayden expelled a rush of breath and nuzzled under Armi's ear.

"That was...I don't think there are words to describe it." Hayden licked the tiny lobe, and Armi trembled beneath him, so he did it again. He shifted and groaned. "I can barely move. I should get up."

"I-I know I can't." Armi sighed, his lashes brushing Hayden's cheek. "Do you...are you leaving?"

Hayden blinked, his heart shriveling. "Do you want me to?" He slipped from Armi and tried to sit up but failed, his legs still too shaky.

Armi averted his eyes. "No, but I figured...you know..." He shrugged.

"No, I don't know." This time he managed to roll off Armi but lay on his side, facing him. "Why don't you explain it to me?"

"I know you didn't come here to end up like this. You were trying to make me feel better, and I made it easy for you."

"Okay, stop right there." Hayden's lips thinned. "I do feel bad for you. That article was a disgusting piece of trash, and you didn't deserve to be treated like that." He reached out to stroke Armi's cheek. What the hell was he doing? He didn't do sweet. The right thing would be to get up, make excuses and apologies, and leave. "But that's not what happened here."

"No?" Armi's long lashes hid his eyes, and Hayden leaned closer to brush those delicious, kiss-swollen lips.

God, he was fucking up so badly, but his next words tumbled from his mouth like a torrent of water exploding from a broken dam. "Not even close. I wanted you. Not because you're my boss or because I felt sorry for you. I wanted you because you're the sexiest fucking thing, and I couldn't stand not knowing what it was like to be inside you."

Armi's cheeks turned crimson, and his clear blue eyes met Hayden's. "No one's ever said that to me before."

"Then lucky me, I'm the first."

"So...do you want to stay?"

His lips tugged up. "I thought you'd never ask."

To hell with bad ideas.

CHAPTER TWELVE

It took Armi forever to fall asleep. After they showered, dried off, and flopped into bed, Hayden was out immediately, his breath soft puffs against Armi's shoulder. Maybe he was too afraid to fall asleep, believing everything that happened was a dream, and when he woke up, Hayden would be gone.

But finally his lids lowered, and the next time they fluttered open, bright sunlight streamed in through the windows. He turned his head.

Hayden was still there. Sound asleep next to him. Armi snuggled the pillow to his face, drawing in the scent of Hayden's skin. He could've lain there all day, simply staring at the perfect profile and lusting after the ink covering his arms, but a full bladder ruined his fun. He brushed his teeth and returned to bed, marveling at the sleek lines of Hayden's naked body, ogling the thick cock that rose from the curly golden patch of his groin.

"Look but don't touch doesn't apply." Without warning, Hayden rolled on top of him. "Good morning."

"H-hi." He nibbled his lip. "Did you sleep well?"

"*Mmhm.* Like the proverbial log." He ran his nose down Armi's cheek, ending at his mouth. "You brushed your teeth? I didn't bring a toothbrush." Hayden pressed kisses to his neck, under his ear, and licked inside his ear.

Armi moaned. "I-I don't care. Please. Oh, God." His dick filled, and Hayden hummed with approval.

"I like what's popped up. My favorite morning drink." A firm hand wrapped around the length, and then Armi cried out as his shaft was engulfed in the searing heat of Hayden's mouth.

"*Ahh, ahh.*" Embarrassed by the loud noises spilling from his mouth, Armi clapped a hand over his lips, but Hayden peeled his fingers off.

"Don't. I like to hear you scream. Turns me on."

Hayden resumed sucking his cock and playing with his own. Armi couldn't take his eyes off him, those gleaming wet lips sliding along his rigid length, the slick sound of Hayden's dick passing in and out of his fist.

"Fuck, Hayden. Oh, God. Don't stop."

His belly tightened, and he flung his head back, his hips thrusting quickly. Hayden sucked hard, those sexy, throaty sounds vibrating against his shaft. Armi's eyes rolled and he came, pulsing hard and heavy, filling Hayden's throat. Hayden got off a moment later, his sticky come spurting everywhere.

Chests heaving, they lay side by side, and Hayden's lips quirked up in a slight smile. "The best way to wake up."

A knot formed in the pit of Armi's stomach. Of course Hayden was sexually superior. Armi couldn't even pretend—imagine telling Hayden he'd never had anyone share his bed for the night. Most likely, he'd guessed. No condoms was a dead giveaway. And the fact that Hayden had one in his wallet spoke volumes.

"What's wrong?" Hayden ran a foot up his leg, leaving goose bumps in its wake. "I see the wheels turning."

"Nothing."

"*Mmmhmm.* You know, I may not have worked for you that long, but I do know you're not a liar. You're too nice a guy."

"God, I hate that." He pulled the pillow over his face and rolled away from Hayden.

A warm hand rested on his shoulder. "Why? It's refreshing."

He lifted a shoulder. "Forget it. I'm gonna get up and get dressed. Would you...do you want to maybe get breakfast? If you don't have plans, of course, which you probably do—"

"Armi. I don't." Hayden pressed a kiss to his nape. "I'd love to get breakfast with you."

A warm glow settled in his chest. "Okay. Great. I can look around—I think there's a spare toothbrush."

"That'd be great, but if not, I'll use my finger in the clutch." He grinned. Armi couldn't help but stare at his beautiful body—the broad chest and rippling abs, the artwork of tattoos up and down both arms. A blond happy trail led to his heavy cock. Golden hair dusted muscular thighs and the gorgeous curve of his ass had Armi biting his tongue to prevent himself from whimpering out loud.

"I'll, uh, go shower."

He ran to the bathroom and washed up quickly, almost afraid to be gone too long, as if Hayden might change his mind and leave. But upon his return, Hayden still sat on the edge of his bed.

Armi hurried to the dresser and slipped on briefs and sweats. With Hayden watching, he pulled a T-shirt on. He didn't like his body–he'd been the chunky, unathletic kid, a phase that lasted until his late teens, when he'd sprouted up and dropped the weight. He exercised and tried to eat properly, but that didn't mean the negative self-image had disappeared with the weight loss. Hayden naked and comfortable was in direct contrast to Armi's rush to cover himself. He could never be so free.

"There's an airplane travel kit under the sink that should have a toothbrush and razor."

Hayden's face was a study in puzzlement. "Okay. I'll be right out."

Armi watched Hayden pick up his discarded clothes before crossing the expanse of the bedroom to the en suite. He heard the shower run and wished he'd had the nerve to suggest they shower together. A sigh escaped him at the missed opportunity. If only this wasn't a one-off, but he knew better. They'd have their breakfast; then Hayden would say he had things to do and see you at the office on Monday.

Freshly washed and dressed, Hayden reentered the bedroom. "Ready to go?"

"Yeah, sure."

They left the town house and walked around, passing a few restaurants with huge lines. "Damn," he complained. "Doesn't anyone eat at home?"

Hayden chuckled. "Let's walk farther downtown. It's less crowded."

They strolled through the streets until they reached a little bistro that didn't seem to have too much of a line. Within fifteen minutes they were seated and had coffee. Hayden ordered the *shakshuka*, and Armi the breakfast burrito. When the server walked away, they each took a sip of coffee.

Hayden moistened his lips. "Do you know how you want to respond to Price's article?"

Pain twisted in his stomach. "I have no clue. I haven't even thought about it since last night...when you showed up." He gulped more coffee, and Hayden continued to regard him with a steady, thoughtful gaze.

"Would you like my opinion?"

"Of course."

Hayden hitched his chair closer and leaned in. "Get in front of it. After breakfast, we can work on a statement for you to put out from the publicity team first thing on Monday."

Armi stopped with the coffee cup halfway to his mouth. "We? You want to work on this with me?"

"News flash, Armi." A cocky grin curved his lips. "I'm the best, and we're going to make sure this stupid piece of shit never messes with you again."

Their food arrived, and Hayden dug into his meal, but Armi remained quiet. After a minute, Hayden glanced up from his plate.

"Is something wrong?"

"I-I guess I'm surprised you want to spend your Saturday with me. Doing this."

Hayden's eyes warmed. "I can't think of anything else I'd rather do." He pointed a finger at Armi's plate. "Eat before it gets cold. We've got work to do."

They ate and spoke of Armi's roses—the time he spent grafting and fighting the diseases that ate away at their leaves, leaving black spots and mildew, how he'd constructed the greenhouse to take care of the bushes in the winter. It was a subject he was passionate about, but when he stopped to take a sip of coffee, he remembered how one guy told him it was boring listening to him droning on about flowers. He pressed his lips together and gave Hayden a weak smile.

"Sorry. I'm babbling. I'll shut up."

"What? No, you're not. I told you, my mother loves her rosebushes. She's always entering them in the town garden contests, but she's never won. I can give her pointers now. Maybe you'll write down some of the things you just talked about, so when I go home I can tell her."

"Uh...yeah, of course. Sure." There was so little he knew about Hayden, he decided it was a good time to ask a few questions. "Where do your parents live?"

"Upstate." Hayden finished his coffee.

"Is that where you went to school?"

"Yes." Hayden shifted in his chair.

The clipped answers were such a direct contrast to Hayden's normal easy speech, it was conspicuous. The questions he asked were innocuous. Why did it make him so uncomfortable?

"What made you want to go into PA work?"

The tension of Hayden's shoulders eased. "I'm very organized, and I love spreadsheets. I don't want to be the boss, but I'm happy to help whoever I work for to be the best they can."

"You do a great job."

"Thanks. Are you finished? You should get home and start working."

His heart plummeted. "Oh, yeah, of course." Guess Hayden had changed his mind because he wasn't including himself in their afternoon plans. "I'll get the check." He raised his hand.

"Thanks. I'm going to stop by my apartment first, change, and get my laptop. It shouldn't take me more than an hour."

"Oh, you're coming back?"

Hayden's brows drew together. "Yeah, of course. I said I would."

He lifted a shoulder. "I thought you might've changed your mind."

"No way. We're gonna get this bastard for what he wrote."

They walked out together and parted at the corner. Armi hurried home, and knowing he had nothing to eat in the house, put in an order for sandwiches, drinks, and snacks. He debated for a moment and included a box of condoms. Not that he expected anything more to happen between them, but he should have them. Just in case.

Of course he'd messed up his clothes—a grease stain on his shirt and coffee spilled on his sweats. Hayden was too polite to point it out. He changed into a Kings T-shirt and a pair of gray sweats. The food came, and he put away the beer, sparkling water, and sandwiches, and emptied one of the bags of chips into a bowl. The rest of the snacks he left in the bag on the island. As a kid, he'd come home from school and grab either cookies or potato chips and go to his room, where he'd sit by himself and watch movies or TV or read. It was the only way to drown out the laughs and jeers of other boys in school when he was the last—as usual—to be picked for team sports.

You'd think he'd be good at sports 'cause his dad owns a football team.

Looks like he eats the football instead of throwing it.

Trevor had been his only friend, but he was on the squash team and always had practice. He'd sit in the stands and watch Trevor play, wishing he could be so athletic and have people cheer him on.

Away at college, he and Trevor would go to parties, but once Trevor met Marianne and they started dating, Armi wouldn't go by himself and spent his free time walking around the campus, even in the coldest winter months. The excess weight dropped, and though he'd kept it off, he never got over the stigma of being that chubby kid in gym class, standing alone. Laughed at and last to be picked.

The doorbell rang, and Armi wiped his sweaty hands on his pants. He peered through the peephole and opened the door. "Mother. What're you doing here?"

She breezed inside. "Hello to you too. I was hoping we could have lunch and talk about that terrible article." He followed her to the front parlor but didn't sit.

"I, uh, there's nothing to talk about. I'm working on a rebuttal."

"Oh? What're you going to say?"

"I-I don't know yet. I'm still working it out."

The bell rang again, and his heart pounded. "I'll get it."

"Are you expecting someone?" She trailed after him.

He opened the door, and Hayden strode past him. "All right, I'm ready to get down and dirty." He stopped in the middle of the hall. "Oh. Mrs. Winters. Hello."

Hayden had changed into a dark-blue polo and a pair of black skinny jeans. He carried a backpack and slid it off his shoulder. Armi caught his mother's smile, and his stomach cramped.

"Hayden. Hi. Come in. Uh, my mother stopped by unexpectedly."

"And now she's leaving," she stated.

Hayden frowned. "Please don't let me chase you away. We were going to work on a response to that article."

"Good. But too many cooks and all that. I'll leave it in your very capable hands. I'm sure you know best, Hayden. After all, it's your job. Armand, I'll call you."

And with that, she disappeared.

Hayden closed the door behind her. "Did I miss something?"

"No. My mother's just being funny. Or at least thinks she is," Armi huffed. "I figure we'll work in the family room. I got sandwiches for lunch if we get hungry."

"Sounds good. I'm ready."

Three hours later, Armi groaned and rolled his shoulders. "Oh, God. That was brutal."

"But we did it," Hayden said with supreme satisfaction and hit a few more keys on his laptop before closing it. "This should shut Price up and let other reporters know not to mess with you again."

It all sounded good, but there were still so many unknowns. "What if it backfires and he gets angry? Maybe he'll write an even worse story the next time."

Hayden's smile was grim. "Let him try. As it is, *City News* is banned from any scoops or information about the team. They can fuck off."

Armi's lips twitched. "You're so passionate about an organization you've barely worked for."

"When I believe in something, or someone, I give a thousand percent of myself. You didn't deserve what Price said. I know how hard you're trying." Their eyes met, and Armi's stomach tightened. Hayden set the laptop aside and got to his feet. "How about a beer to celebrate? We've gone through the club soda and the first bag of chips. I'm ready for something stronger and a sandwich."

"Yeah, sure." Armi blew out a breath when Hayden left the room, and cradled his head in his hands.

Why was he doing this to himself? He didn't need the hassle—everything would be easier if he simply did what people expected and wanted him to. Quit and let the others take over.

Strong hands came down on his shoulders, holding him firmly. "What's wrong?"

Hayden's quiet voice broke the dam inside him. "Why am I bothering? I'm not who they want to lead the team. That's obvious. I know they think I'm a failure."

Instead of responding, Hayden began to knead the tight muscles of his neck, and a groan of pleasure slipped from his lips. The tension melted away, and he closed his eyes. For a moment, the pain of all his failings faded away.

"You don't really think that, do you?" Hayden murmured. "I don't."

He turned his head and slanted a tiny grin at Hayden. "You have to say that. You work for me."

But Hayden didn't return his smile, remaining tight-lipped and grim. "I don't have to say anything. You aren't a failure, and it's time you rise above this. You're the owner. You're in control. Of both the team and your actions."

"Are we still talking about the Kings? Or something else?" He blinked and nibbled on his lip. Maybe their night together had awoken a sleeping giant. He'd never been an overly sexual person, but having Hayden so close left him weak with desire. His thoughts weren't on the team, but on what happened between them. He wanted to kiss Hayden. He wanted to be kissed in return. He dropped his gaze to the floor.

"Armi?" When their eyes met, Hayden was holding the box of condoms. "I found these in the bag with the chips."

Oh, God. He'd forgotten to take them out and put them away. "Uh, it's not what you think."

"What am I thinking?"

Armi's heart thundered.

"Uh, well, uh..." His face burned. "You know. That we were going to..." He licked his lips. "You know, have sex again."

Armi waited for Hayden's response. Wishing and hoping.

CHAPTER THIRTEEN

It would be so easy.

He could almost taste Armi's kisses, and every cell in his body thrummed with need. All he'd have to do was give Armi the slightest sign that he was willing, and they'd be naked again.

"I don't want you to be angry with me for saying no."

Armi looked horrified. "Of course not. That would be wrong and illegal, and God, is that what you think?" He pushed his hands through his hair, and even though he was upset, all Hayden could think of was how adorable he was.

What the hell was wrong with him? When had his strict professionalism gone out the window? Why did this man, this awkward, sweet man, capture his attention and make him see a whole different side of life?

"No. I would never think that of you."

"I don't want you to compromise your integrity. You said you don't sleep with your bosses. Last night was an aberration. I understand. I shouldn't have pushed you."

"You didn't push me. At all. I was totally willing, and I consented." The taut lines of his face softened. He wished Armi could explain it because he didn't know what the hell was going on. "But we're adults, and we can keep the business and personal between us separate. I take responsibility for what happened between us last night, but please don't think for a second I have regrets."

"I just don't want you to end up hating me."

"I don't think anyone could ever hate you, Armi Winters." He put a safe distance between them, otherwise he might reach out and touch Armi. Not a good idea. Because once he started, Hayden knew he wouldn't be able to stop. "How about a sandwich?" He grinned, and Armi laughed.

"That's a segue if there ever was one. Sex or turkey club?"

Hayden believed he knew the answer but had to ask. "You're okay with me still working for you, right?"

An almost frightened expression crossed Armi's face. "What? Are you kidding me? Of course I am. You don't want to leave, do you? Please don't."

"No, of course not. I really do enjoy the job. And working for you. I've learned so much already in such a short period of time." Relief spread through him. "I'm glad we can move past this. Now how about I get the sandwiches and beer?"

"Yeah, sure. We can eat in here. I'm not picky."

In the kitchen, Hayden took a moment and braced his hands on the island. It was the right thing to do. The best for both of them. He couldn't have an affair with

Armi. The office was too small and gossipy, and it was incredibly unprofessional and clichéd...

Dammit. I'm such an idiot.

Not for what happened. Never that. Hayden would carry the night with Armi like a precious memory, an heirloom to take out and reminisce about when the loneliness became too much to bear.

He'd hated having to do it, but he'd lied to Armi, saying he had no regrets. Now that he knew what it was like to be inside Armi, how perfect and beautiful making love to him was, he regretted never being able to do it again. It was going to be torture working with him, but he'd faced bigger obstacles before and managed.

And yet...Hayden could imagine himself side by side with Armi as a partner...a lover. Pain sheared a burning path through his chest. A fucking joke if there ever was one. He wasn't good enough for a sweet guy like Armi. Kids made mistakes all the time. That was what he'd heard. You grew from them. But all he'd learned was that the weight of his stupidity followed him wherever he went. Being the kind and sweet man Armi was, he wouldn't care, but the thought of telling him he'd had sex on camera caused his stomach to revolt. He'd never forget hearing his parents' late-night conversations after he was supposed to be asleep. How people in town whispered about him. And them. Listening to his father cry because he couldn't take care of his family and blamed himself for Hayden's actions.

Nothing I can do about it.

He made a platter with the sandwiches, grabbed two beers and a bag of chips. Back in the living room, Armi jumped up to help him.

"Thanks." Hayden set the bottles on the table and poured the chips in the empty bowl. He raised his beer to Armi. "To only good press. And to you as the owner."

Armi shook his head. "To you. For making it possible."

"No, you did. You need to have more confidence that you can and will." But if there was one thing Hayden had learned, it was that pretty words couldn't erase decades of put-downs and criticisms, and Armi's wounds ran deep. "Let's eat, and you can tell me everything you hope to accomplish with the team."

"You don't have to do this, you know." Armi nibbled on the edge of his turkey sandwich.

"What? Eat?" He took a bite, chewed, and swallowed. "I'm hungry." He smirked at Armi's huff of annoyance. He really was cute.

"No. Pretend to want to be here. I know you have better things to do on a Saturday than spend it locked in here with me, talking about work."

Oh, Armi. They did a real fucking number on your head, didn't they?

"But I don't. I'm working because you need my help. I told you when I took the job that this is what I do. I don't have a boyfriend, and I don't particularly want one. So can we cut this out now?"

"Okay."

"I'd like to start with some information."

"Sure." Armi took a bite of his sandwich and chewed it without much interest.

"Tell me about your relationship with Russell."

Armi's head jerked up, confusion clouding his eyes. "Russell? What do you mean, my relationship with him? He's the general manager of the team. I've known him all my life."

Time to tread delicately. "Yeah, I know. He was also very close to your father?"

"Yes. They were best friends."

"And you've been leaning on him and taking his advice on running the team?"

"Yeah. Hayden, where is this going? I don't understand what you're getting at."

Of course he wouldn't. Because Armi was a good and decent person who'd never think of sabotaging someone else for his own benefit. That was why he needed someone like Hayden, who knew all about the ugly underbelly of people and life in general.

"I'm just curious why. Someone who was best friends with your father—a man who wasn't nice to you—why do you trust him? Shouldn't he have stopped your father from talking all that shit? Shouldn't they both have tried to bring you into the team instead of shutting you out?"

With each word, Armi seemed to deflate, and Hayden hated that he'd brought Armi to such a low point. His phone buzzed, and he pulled it out. "Shit," he exclaimed, and Armi glanced at him.

"Plans you forgot? Don't worry. I have plenty to keep me busy tonight." Armi waved him off. "Go ahead."

Hayden's lips twitched. "Not me, Armi. You. I put it on your calendar for today, but I guess with the article, we both forgot. You have dinner with your friend Trevor."

"Oh, shit." Armi shot up from his chair, dumping his sandwich in his lap and knocking over his beer. "I'm such a klutz."

"Stop it," Hayden scolded and took a bunch of napkins to sop up the liquid. Jesus. It wasn't only the father who was to blame. Where was Armi's mother in all this mess? No time to think about it. He had to get

Armi ready. "Leave it to me to clean up. You have plenty of time—it's only four thirty, and dinner isn't until seven. Go get ready. I won't leave before you're finished."

"You don't have—"

"Yes." He pushed Armi firmly out of the way. "I do. Now get out of here and let me do my thing."

Shooting him a guilty look, Armi left him on his knees, picking up lettuce and tomato from the floor. It took several trips to the kitchen along with some cleaning spray to wash away the smell of food and beer, but he finally finished and returned all the food to the kitchen, dumped the bottles in the recycling, and rebagged the chips. Hands on his hips, he surveyed the space.

"Hayden? Are you still here?" Footsteps pounded on the stairs.

"In the living room," he called out and turned. "Wow. You look...really good."

Pink bloomed on Armi's cheeks, and his blue eyes sparkled. A crisp, white button-down with a black stripe was tucked into dark jeans. "Thanks. My razor broke, so I didn't shave." He rubbed the stubble covering his jaw. "Does it look bad?"

Bad? Does Armi truly have no idea how hot he is?

"No. The opposite. Do you have a bottle of wine or something to bring with you? If not, you still have time. I can run to the liquor store for you."

"No, his wife, Marianne, loves my roses, so I promised to bring her some."

"Perfect. Could you show me which ones?" Hayden had no idea why he asked, but it was worth it to see Armi's face brighten.

"I'd love to. I have some beautiful hybrid teas that just bloomed or are about to. Follow me."

Immediately, when Armi started to speak about his roses, his whole demeanor changed. His shoulders straightened, and his voice rang with strength. If he could be like that all the time, there'd be no problem at the office.

They passed through the kitchen to the greenhouse, and Armi picked up a pair of shears before continuing on to a colorful grouping of rosebushes.

"They're beautiful. I've never seen colors like this."

"They smell as delicious as they look. Go ahead."

Hayden leaned forward to the first bush—a lemony yellow with a tinge of red around the edges, which were like velvet under his fingers. "Ohhh, that's a beautiful perfume."

"Now this one next." Armi pointed to the coral blooms with streaks of yellow and white. "What do you think of these?"

"Even sweeter. And the colors...I didn't know you could have so many different ones in the same rose."

"It's what I'm trying to accomplish. I love working with them." He frowned. "My father used to call it 'grubbing in the dirt.' "

As the light faded from Armi's face, Hayden again cursed the man for crushing Armi's spirit. "Well, I think it's an awesome hobby. My mother always corrals my father into helping her with her garden, and he pretends not to like it, but I used to see him on his own, going through the garden to make sure none of the leaves on the bushes had those black spots. He didn't want her to do it herself and get pricked by the thorns."

"That's very sweet. They must love each other very much."

"They do. They've been married almost forty years."

The droop of Armi's soft mouth tempted, and Hayden wished he could kiss all his problems away. And though his dick perked up at the idea, Hayden dismissed the thought from his mind. He'd quickly learned that as quiet and unassuming as Armi was, one touch from him and Hayden was gone. They'd end up naked.

Idiot. That's not the visual you need right now.

He blew out a long, frustrated breath.

Armi pulled on a pair of heavy gardening gloves and picked up the shears. "That's an anomaly in my world. Almost no one stays married. My parents divorced when I was a kid, as did Trevor's." He snipped and picked off the thorns, and even with his hands covered by the thick canvas, Hayden could see the tender care he took with the stems. "Do you mind holding these while I cut more?"

"Of course not." He took the two long stems and smelled the fragrance of their blooms. He watched Armi collect more flowers until he held a dozen roses of different colors. Armi stripped off the gloves and wiped his face with a paper towel.

"Come on. I have to wrap them."

In the kitchen with his flowers, Armi showed none of the hesitancy in his everyday life at the office, moving with purpose and care as he wrapped up the long green stems and fragile petals. There was no fumbling, and Hayden pictured that firm hand around his cock.

Christ, get a damn grip.

"Great job. It looks professional, like they came from a florist."

"That's done. I'd better go soon, so they can get in water. Marianne, Trevor's wife, is really nice."

As they spoke, Armi collected his wallet, keys, and phone. "Can I drop you off anywhere?"

"Yeah, thanks. I need to get home."

"Tell me your address again?" Armi tapped it on his phone screen. "Car will be here in three minutes."

Backpack in hand, Hayden trailed behind Armi, admiring the snug fit of his jeans and the broad set of his shoulders. They entered the dark car, and with Saturday night traffic, it took almost ten minutes to travel three avenue blocks and the streets uptown.

"This is me," Hayden said as the car slid to the curb. "Thanks, Armi. I'll see you on Monday."

"Yeah. Sure. Have a great weekend." Armi met his gaze, and Hayden's heart twisted, the tightness in his chest unfamiliar.

He closed the door to the sedan and watched the taillights blend in with the other traffic.

Up in his apartment, he sprawled on his sofa. It had been hell sitting next to Armi in the car, smelling his cologne, watching his lips move as he spoke, wanting to kiss him and yet being powerless to do anything about it.

"Dammit." His hand balled into a fist. "How could this have happened?"

It wasn't even seven o'clock on a Saturday night. Summer in the city. He should shower, get dressed, and go out. Find someone to ease the nervous tension bubbling through him. He could almost taste the bitter orange of an Aperol Spritz.

Maybe someone out there could help him remember, because once upon a time, he'd been happy.

CHAPTER FOURTEEN

"So the new PA is working out? I did well?" Trevor handed Armi a beer and then a glass of white wine to Marianne.

"Thanks. Yeah, he's good."

So damn good.

Armi always enjoyed spending time with Trevor and Marianne. Trevor was the brother he'd never had, and Marianne understood his awkwardness, never pushed, and treated him with nothing but kindness. Her natural warmth had allowed him the time to accept and trust her, and she'd become as close a friend as Trevor.

"I know he came with great references and is a whiz at organization, so the fact that you were here on time means it's working out."

Armi made a face. "Ha-ha, very funny."

"Well, I, for one, am glad you're here," Marianne said. "Those roses are absolutely stunning. I've never seen anything like them."

Puffed up by her praise, Armi smiled. "And you won't. They're from my latest grafting experiment. If I can replicate it a few more times, I'll give a bush to the Botanical Gardens."

"They'll be thrilled to have it."

With a *thump*, Trevor set his beer on the table. "All right, now that we have the niceties out of the way, what the hell was that article? Why'd that guy shit on you?"

All his good feelings drained away. "I don't know," he mumbled. "Do we have to talk about it?"

"Sorry, but are you going to respond? That was some BS he said. You've been doing a great job."

He hunched over his bottle. "Yeah, well, so you say. You're my friend."

"Which means what? That I'm going to lie? That's ridiculous. I have ears, you know. I hear things. And I like what I'm hearing. I agree that going after lesser-known names can work in the team's favor."

Armi's head jerked up. "How...never mind. Nothing is secret anymore, I swear. Yeah, I think it's a great idea, but others in the organization don't. They want to sign superstars." He sighed. "I'm trying to work with them, but no one's willing to listen to me. They're more likely to agree if it comes from Russell."

"And what does Russell do?" Marianne asked.

Puzzled, Armi met her frank gaze. "What do you mean? You know his position in the Kings."

She shook her head, the dark waves flowing to her shoulders. "Not what I'm talking about. Does Russell back you up, or does he try and persuade you to his side?" She clasped her hands together. "You said it yourself—Russell always thought he'd be in charge of the Kings. But he's not, and it must grate on his nerves and ego to have to take direction from you."

Armi chewed his lip. "I-I don't know. I lean on him a lot, but he and I don't always agree. He doesn't seem to mind."

"Just make sure it's really you in charge."

"You sound like Hayden. He also keeps telling me to be more insistent in what I want and not have it come from Russell. Problem is, they're used to Russell, and they trust him more. And I can't say I blame them."

Trevor said, "Sounds like Hayden picked up on things pretty quickly. You're in charge, Armi. What you say goes. Remember that. As much as Russell was your father's right-hand man, he doesn't have to be yours."

"Can we table this discussion and have dinner?" Marianne stood and held out her hand to him. "Let's eat and talk about something besides football."

Over their shrimp cocktail appetizer, Armi decided to ask his own questions. "I'm curious, Trev. How did you find Hayden? You said something about another agency?"

Trevor nodded. "Janice Butler runs a very exclusive head-hunting agency—personal assistants to the corporate elite. Our family's known her for years, and we share availability of people when they don't match our needs."

Trevor's family ran the largest agency in the country catering to staffing the entertainment world. Personal assistants, nannies, chefs, housekeepers, or anyone they might need. Trevor's agency was the platinum standard in ensuring discreet, highly qualified individuals.

"So you heard about Hayden, how?"

Trevor helped himself to the broiled salmon and handed the platter to Armi. "Janice sent out an email to us and a few other top agencies. She asked us to keep an eye out in case we heard about something that might not fit our requirements but would work for her. I thought of you." He grinned. "You're welcome."

His face grew warm, and Marianne raised her elegant brows. "I'm sensing a story here."

Damn his inability to hide his emotions. "No, I'm just curious. He's really been a godsend. He helped me craft a response to the newspaper article and made sure I got here on time." Eyes downcast, he pushed his salmon around. "You were right. I probably would've forgotten about dinner tonight."

"So what's the problem?" she asked. "He sounds perfect. Exactly who you need."

"I don't know. There's just something...he's cagey about his background. He didn't want to tell me what city he grew up in or where he went to school. I had to look it up on my own."

"And you think there's something big he's not telling you that might impact his job with you?"

Armi hesitated. Did he? Or was he trying to find out more about this man who twisted him up inside and made him feel like he mattered?

"I'm not sure. But I think I should know a little bit more about someone who works for me other than where he worked before."

"So call Janice Butler. I've already told you this. It's your right. You're the boss."

"I don't know," he demurred. "Will she think it's weird?"

"Who cares?" Trevor shrugged. "You're the client. You can ask whatever the hell you want."

But there went that ugly lack of self-confidence again. "Maybe I'm being too nosy. I mean, I'm really satisfied with how Hayden's working out. I should leave it at that."

"You can do what you want, but if you want to find out more about Hayden, call Janice. She's a straight shooter."

"I guess."

He insisted on helping Marianne clear the table and load the dishwasher. She cocked her head and he braced himself, anticipating her questions. "Have you been going out at all?" She sipped from her second glass of wine. "Trying to date?"

He laughed. "No. This is me you're talking to."

She glared at him. "You're a gorgeous, sweet man who shouldn't be alone. You don't have to be."

"I'm sensing this is leading up to something." He shut the dishwasher door. "What've you done?"

Trevor chuckled. "Busted, babe. I told you Armi would see right through you."

Her lips twitched. "Whatever. There's a guy in my firm—he's so nice. Into the arts and theater. Good-looking and funny."

"Yeah? Everything I'm not."

She punched his arm. "Stop that. He's interested in meeting you."

His heart beat faster. "Yeah? I don't know...I'm not good at dating."

Her hand touched his. "Try it. It's only a first date. Meet him for coffee or a drink. I gave him your number, and he said he'd call you."

He forced a smile. "Sure. Why not?"

"I didn't think you'd call so soon." Sunday afternoon, Armi sat across from Brent Taylor at a small bistro on Second Avenue. "Marianne just told me last night that she gave you my number."

Brent was exactly as described. A touch over six feet, with a lean runner's body and warm brown eyes. They'd shaken hands upon meeting, and his grasp was firm and strong. Maybe Brent could make him forget hot green eyes, wicked lips, and messy blond hair that had invaded his dreams for weeks.

"I figured why wait? If we both had no plans, it would be a nice time to meet."

Armi took a sip of his cappuccino. "So you work with Marianne?"

"Yes, I'm in the real estate division of our firm. But I don't want to talk about her. Tell me about you. Marianne said you're the owner of the Kings? That must be exciting. Football is the only sport I watch."

"I guess it would surprise you then that I'm not that into sports, even football. But after my father died, it all came to me, so I'm trying to rise to the occasion."

Brent's eyes turned soft. "I'm sorry about your father. That can't have been easy—losing him and having to step right into his shoes and hit the ground running."

It wouldn't be right to say losing his father didn't have much of an impact on his life, so he shrugged. "It's been a learning curve. But I'm lucky to have a PA who helps me every step of the way and other great people on staff. We'll work it out."

"A good PA is worth their weight in gold. I'd be lost without mine."

A flash of heat hit Armi, thinking of Hayden pounding into him, kissing him, swallowing him whole... He coughed. "Oh, yeah. Hayden's been a lifesaver."

"And Marianne told me about your green thumb."

Brent was saying all the right things to get him to talk. He wished he felt that spark, like he had with Hayden, that made him want to rip his clothes off and get naked.

"I have a greenhouse in my home. It's where I go after work to decompress."

"I don't blame you. I've heard they're very beautiful. I'd love to see them one day."

Armi guessed this was dating. Not a pickup in a bar like he had with Hayden, where they knew the end result would be hot, wet kisses and orgasms that wrecked him. But Marianne was right. Brent was a nice guy. He didn't make Armi feel awkward and seemed to listen when he talked. "I don't live too far. Would you like to come by now?"

Brent's smile was his answer, and he raised a hand to call the server over. "Check, please."

His house was right around the corner, and he brought Brent to the greenhouse. "These are the bushes I'm working on now." He explained his process, and Brent listened and asked questions.

"You have an incredible setup, Armi. The roses are beautiful."

"Thanks."

Turning serious, Brent closed the space between them. "You're pretty incredible too." His hand circled Armi's nape and drew him close. "Can I kiss you?"

Armi nodded, and Brent's mouth covered his. His lips were warm and firm, and Armi tried. The kiss was...nice. He held on to Brent and made encouraging noises. Brent brushed their lips together one last time.

"That was amazing. You're so sweet."

"You are too."

"I have an early day tomorrow, but I'd love to see you again."

"I'd like that too."

Brent's eyes brightened. "I'll call you. Maybe we can grab lunch during the week."

"That'd be great."

He walked Brent out, accepted another brief kiss, and watched until he turned the corner. Sighing, he closed the door and touched his lips. Brent was the perfect gentleman—no pushing his tongue inside Armi's mouth, no teasing touches or licking his ear.

Armi shivered and rubbed his face. *Dammit.* He had to stop thinking about Hayden. He'd made it crystal clear that there could never be anything between them. Maybe if he and Brent started dating, he'd forget Hayden. He didn't want to, but he had to. Armi went to take a shower and get ready for Monday morning.

Blond hair gleaming under the overhead lights, Hayden sat at his desk. Fresh roses filled the vase on his desk—pink again. His smile reached across the distance. "Good morning."

"Hi."

"I'll have your coffee in a minute. There are several inquiries from magazines and newspapers asking for interviews. I sorted them and put them in order of exposure for the team. Plus, *Out in Sports* is looking for an exclusive about being an out gay man as the owner of a football team. I think that could be very good for your image and for the team." The phone rang on his desk, and Hayden reached for it.

"I agree."

Inside his office, the roses were now a striking coral. He bent to sniff their spicy-sweet perfume. "Fragrant Cloud," he murmured to himself.

"That's what the florist told me," Hayden said from behind him. "Do you like them?"

"They're beautiful. And they last. Perfect for an arrangement. Thank you, Hayden. It lifts my mood to come in and see all the roses."

"Not a problem. Now, Martin Price is waiting on Line One."

Armi tensed. "I-I don't want to speak to him."

"Good. I don't think you should." Hayden's eyes twinkled. "I just like keeping him on hold, hoping."

Armi laughed. "You're terrible."

Hayden winked and left. A few minutes later, the light disappeared on his phone. In a better mood, he read through the interview requests, marking the ones that would give his message the most visibility and put *Out in Sports* at the top of the list. Hayden was right—he should use his position to promote normalizing queerness in sports.

He picked up the phone. "Hayden, please call back Steve Fontana from *Out in Sports*. You can schedule the best time to meet."

"You're booked pretty solid this week, but I'll find the first available. How about the others?"

"I looked them over. I'll send you the list."

"All right. Don't forget the meeting at ten thirty to go over the scouting reports from the weekend."

Having spent the rest of his night with his roses, Armi wondered if what he was doing here mattered at all. He propped his chin in his hand and sighed. "Maybe I should just do what everyone expects and take my share and let Russell run the show. What do I really know about any of this? I don't even know what all the positions on the team are yet."

"Don't be ridiculous, Armi. Positive thinking. You're doing great."

Compliments never sat well with him, mostly because he didn't believe them, but hearing them from Hayden had the desired effect of strengthening his resolve.

"Thanks, Hayden."

Feeling more confident, he picked up his iPad and carefully read through all the scouting reports, making notes as he went. With his attention on the screen, he reached for his coffee and took a sip. Some of the hot liquid missed his mouth, dribbled down his chin, and dripped on his shirt.

"Goddammit," he yelled, and his door bounced open.

"What's wrong?" Hayden scanned him, his gaze lighting on the collar of his shirt. A grin kicked up the corner of his mouth. "Oh. Well, it's your lucky day because I have a stain remover pen that'll fix that up right away. And you should bring in a wardrobe change to keep here. I'll be right back."

He disappeared for a moment and returned with the stain remover. "Here." Hayden uncapped the pen, and Armi took it. He tipped his chin up. "I can't see it. Am I there?"

Hayden's fingers brushed his aside. "Let me do it."

Having Hayden this close was disconcerting. Dangerous. The smell of his light cologne left Armi reeling and breathless. Hayden's body heat surrounded him, and Armi's eyes fluttered closed as Hayden worked on his shirt.

"All done," Hayden murmured, and Armi drew air deep in his lungs to steady himself. "Good as new."

"Th-thanks."

They stood, staring at each other, Armi damning himself for lacking the courage to press his lips to Hayden's.

For the first time, Hayden looked hesitant and uncertain. "I'd, uh, better get to work." But he made no move to leave, his green eyes glittering.

"Yeah. And I have my meeting." Armi licked his lips, and Hayden's nostrils flared.

"Don't want to be late."

Every cell in his body yearned for Hayden, but he nodded. "I'll see you later."

Hayden stepped aside to let him pass.

Armi stopped at the door. "Uh, do you want to have lunch with me?" At Hayden's raised brows, he rushed to explain. "We could go over what happened at the meeting and..." Realizing that meant having Hayden work through his lunch hour, Armi corrected himself. "Never mind. We'll do it after lunch."

He walked away, wishing things could be different.

CHAPTER FIFTEEN

Hayden hoped the meeting was going well. It was getting close to one, and Armi still hadn't returned. No way would he leave until he saw Armi and heard from his lips that he'd held his own. His phone rang with the inter-office line.

"Yes, Josh?" Out of the corner of his eye, he watched a man in a suit approach.

"This guy blew past me, stating he was a friend of Mr. Winters."

"I've got it. Thanks." He set the receiver in the cradle. "May I help you?" He rose to his feet, facing the man. He was tall and well-dressed with a square jaw and neat haircut. Brown eyes scanned him and warmed.

"Hi, you must be Hayden."

Confused as to how this stranger knew his name, Hayden blinked. "Yes. And you are?"

"Brent Taylor. A friend of Armi's."

"Brent?" Armi came over and stood between them. "What're you doing here?"

Instead of answering, Brent kissed Armi.

He fucking kissed him.

Hayden's hands balled into fists, and he saw red. Visions of him pulling Brent off Armi and tossing him into the wall flashed before his eyes. Who the fuck was this Brent person who was touching Armi? Worst of all, why was Armi smiling back at him?

"Hayden? Hayden."

He pulled himself out of the visual of Brent sailing through the air. "I'm sorry?"

"Brent and I are going to have lunch. I'll see you in about an hour or so, and we can discuss the meeting."

"Yeah, sure. Of course." He seethed, watching Armi walk out with Brent. He didn't miss the smug bastard taking Armi's hand and lacing their fingers together, like they were a couple.

When the hell had Armi met this dude? They obviously weren't strangers, as Armi had let him kiss and touch him. More than let him, as Armi hadn't seemed to pull away.

If the world had been a different place, maybe it could've been him sitting across a table, sharing lunch and a drink. He stabbed his fork into his salad.

"Hayden? Where's Armand?" Russell gazed down at him.

"Out to lunch. May I help you with something?" He put on his most pleasant smile.

"Out to lunch? With whom?" Perplexed, Russell frowned.

"A friend." Despite his annoyance with Brent the Beautiful, Hayden wasn't about to give Russell any info. "What can I do for you?"

"I wanted to talk to him about the response to Martin Price from *City News*."

"I can help you with that. Mr. Winters and I worked on it together."

His brows drew together. "Over the weekend?"

Thank God he'd learned to perfect a face that revealed nothing but bland indifference. "Yes. I'm his personal assistant. Whenever he needs me, I'm available. The hatchet job Price did on him deserved a quick and decisive response. I told Mr. Winters it would best to get in front of it by putting out a statement this morning that disputed the incorrect information Price was attempting to peddle."

Russell's laughter boomed. "Are you sure you weren't a politician at one point?"

"Never." But he knew how the world worked.

Russell's gaze turned thoughtful. "What did you say to Martin when he called this morning?"

Instantly on alert, Hayden kept that neutral facade in place. "Why would you think he called?"

Unless you knew.

But Russell wasn't a newcomer at this game either. "I've known Martin Price for years. I know how he operates."

"Well, I told him that Mr. Winters was tied up in meetings for the rest of the day and couldn't talk to him. And between us, I'm screening Mr. Winters's calls. If someone deliberately sets out to be hurtful, they don't deserve to benefit from it. As far as I'm concerned, Martin Price should be *persona non grata* here."

"The guard dog has a bark and a bite, I see." Amusement gleamed in Russell's eyes.

"I won't allow anyone to harm Mr. Winters. And I thought Price had a good relationship with Randolph Winters."

"They did. But Armand isn't Randolph, and Martin knows it. He's trying to make sports editor of *City News*, and he figured an exposé would bump it."

"Is that why he did it? To hurt Mr. Winters? Why would he try and take down the Kings by making people believe the team isn't going in the right direction?" Hayden widened his eyes. "I would've thought you'd be livid over how bad he made Mr. Winters look."

"I am. I planned to call him up and let him know how unhappy the Kings are—"

"But we beat you to it." Hayden cast his eyes to the floor, playing the part. "You're not mad, are you, Mr. Anders, that I helped Mr. Winters with his response? He was very upset. I didn't think it should wait."

Russell put a hand on his shoulder. "Don't worry, Hayden. We both want what's best for Armand." He gave him a hard squeeze and left.

"I know I do. I'm not so sure about you," he muttered to himself.

It was almost two by the time Armi returned from lunch. Brent, flushed and gazing at Armi as if he hung the moon, released Armi's hand. "I had a great time. I hope we can do it again soon." Without asking, he lifted a rose from the vase on Hayden's desk and presented it to Armi. "Next time it'll be a whole bouquet, but this'll have to do."

What a fucking sap. Who would fall for cheesy crap like that?

Apparently Armi, as his blue eyes glowed like twin sapphires. Hayden noticed a spot on Armi's tie but decided against pointing it out while he and Brent made goo-goo eyes at each other.

"Mr. Winters, you have a conference call at three with the head of United Sports Network." Hayden arched a brow, and Armi turned to Brent.

"Sorry. I need to prep for it. I told you, that's why I couldn't have that drink."

Brent captured his hand and lifted it to his lips. "We'll have to make up for it at dinner one night. I'll call you." He directed a blinding smile at Hayden. "Bye, Hayden. Don't let this guy work too hard."

And Brent actually fucking winked at him, like they were in cahoots to get Armi in his bed.

Not fucking likely, champ.

Armi watched Brent walk away, and Hayden's jaw ground tight. Yeah, the guy had a nice ass in that thousand-dollar suit. He'd give him that.

"Hayden?" Armi waited by his side.

"Sorry." He grabbed his iPad. "I'm ready." Once he was seated across from Armi, he couldn't help himself. He had to know. "How was lunch?"

Armi shrugged. "It was nice."

"Nice? Is that it? Your date looks like he's in love." Armi blushed. "When did you two meet?"

Did he sound accusatory? Screw it.

"Last night. He works with Marianne, Trevor's wife." Armi fiddled with the papers on his desk. The roses had fully opened, their fluffy petals huge, the sweet and spicy fragrance perfuming the air.

"Last night? Damn, he works fast."

"He seems nice. We talked, and he was interested in what I had to say when I talked about my roses."

"Why wouldn't he be? You're a great guy."

Armi's dark lashes fanned down over his cheeks, hiding his eyes. "I know you've said so, but it was good to have someone I don't know pay attention and not fake interest. That doesn't happen often. Ever, really."

The implication being that Hayden acted the way he did because Armi was his boss and he had to. Hayden didn't know whether to be angry or hurt.

"Do you think I was faking it?"

Turning red, Armi ducked his head. "No, of course not," he whispered. He finally met Hayden's eyes. "But since we can't be together, there's no reason for me not to see people."

His gaze was surprisingly challenging and momentarily left Hayden speechless. Armi was right—Hayden had told him no, and that should be the end of it. It wasn't fair to Armi.

"You're right," he clipped out. "How did the morning meeting go?"

"It was okay. The scouts have found some good talent to concentrate on, and we're also close to signing Milo Masterson, the All-Pro receiver. There's a meeting tomorrow with him and his agent that we hope will wrap it up."

"Oh, wow. Even I've heard of him."

Masterson's face had been plastered everywhere after last year's Super Bowl win—you couldn't turn on the television without seeing him hawking a product, or pick up a magazine that didn't have his face on the cover.

"Yeah. I think we've reached a good compromise—they got their heavy hitters with these last two signings, and I get to shine the light on some names who might never have gotten noticed."

"A win-win. Good for you. I knew you could do it. Now about the conference call later on, don't mention Masterson until you have it all signed, sealed, and delivered. You can talk about Hopkins."

"Yes, I know. Russell made sure to give me the script."

Of course.

"Did anyone mention your response to Price's article?"

"Yeah. Whitmore asked who wrote it. Obviously, no one thought it came from me because...well, you know." He shrugged, a lifetime of hurts in that gesture. "My father and Russell always worked on statements to the press together." Armi eyed him. "Did anyone say something about it?"

"Mr. Anders came by, and we chatted briefly. I told him you wanted to make sure that your response would be in the papers first thing on Monday, so that's why we worked on it over the weekend. Together."

Armi's cheeks grew pink, just as his personal phone rang. "Excuse me a sec. Oh, hi." His eyes grew soft. "Yeah, I really enjoyed it too. The food was delicious."

Hayden pretended to be engrossed in his iPad and not listening.

"Tonight? Uh, I guess. Sure... Yeah, I can meet you there... No, I've never been, but I've heard it's very good." Hayden sneaked a glance and caught Armi's eye. Armi quickly looked away.

"I'll leave you alone." Vibrating with annoyance, Hayden slipped out of the room and closed the door behind him. At his desk, he had emails to answer for Armi and notes to type up. He prided himself on perfection at the job, and the fact that Armi was doing exactly what he should—dating and breaking free of his shyness—shouldn't affect him at all.

Armi buzzed him. "Yes?"

"Please come in."

"Be right there."

He saved his documents, sent one to Armi, and took two pages from the printer.

"I'm sorry, Hayden. I didn't mean to make you feel uncomfortable."

"You didn't. It's your office, and you have the right to take personal calls." He handed the papers to Armi. "These are a copy of what I just sent you in an email. It's the usual question-and-answer sessions they do with every owner before the season starts, *but* because you're an out gay owner, there will most likely be questions about that. I've worked up some questions and answers, but of course, feel free to substitute with your own words."

Armi started reading, and Hayden's heart went out to him as he saw his fingers tremble. "I really don't understand why my personal life has to be the subject of an interview about my ownership of the team." He chewed his lip.

"It shouldn't be, but it's the world we live in. I've kept things surface and vague. When you talk to *Out in Sports*, then you can discuss it more in depth."

"Thanks, Hayden. I appreciate everything you've done. This is amazing, and I'm sure the call will go smoothly because of you."

He forced a smile. "Just doing my job. You'd better go to Conference Room B, and I've got to finish those scouting notes for you and coordinate your calendar."

They walked out together, and Hayden watched as Armi disappeared from sight. Breaking his rule of no personal time at the office, he did an incognito Google search of the perfect Brent Taylor. Andover Prep School, Harvard undergrad where he graduated *magna cum laude*, then Yale Law School, Law Review, and went to work at one of the biggest white shoe firms handling the major real estate deals.

"In other words, the perfect guy with the perfect background for someone like Armi."

He gave a vicious stab to the X at the corner of the screen and squeezed his eyes shut. Obsessing over a man he shouldn't want and couldn't have was getting him nowhere fast. Time to do the job he was hired for and forget about Armand Winters.

The rest of the day passed quickly, and though he waited for Armi to return after the conference call, he never reappeared. At seven, Hayden shut down his computer and left, figuring to walk off his bad mood. By the time he reached home, he'd sweated through his clothes, and in the shower decided to hell with staying home and brooding. He needed to get laid to wipe the memory of Armi from his brain cells.

He dressed in a casual outfit, ate a protein bar, and headed out. He walked along Second Avenue and picked The Factory, a place he'd previously had success in. With a Tito's and soda in hand, he scanned the crowd.

"Looking for someone in particular?" a voice purred in his ear. A heavily muscled guy in a band T-shirt that smelled as if it, and him, hadn't washed since Woodstock, stood way too close in his personal space.

"Yeah. And still am."

"Ouch. Come on, sweetheart. Don't play hard to get—just hard." He snickered, thinking his joke was funny.

"Do you mind?" Hayden slid off the barstool and walked to the opposite side of the room. The music was hopping, and he swayed his hips as he sipped his drink. He used to have no problem losing himself in someone, but tonight found him picking out all the faults of everyone he saw.

Too drunk.

Too underdressed.

Too overdressed.

Too loud.

He finished his drink and walked out. He tried another bar with the same result. Everyone's laughter was forced. He didn't want to be standing in a bar, trying to make eye contact with a potential bed partner he'd never see again.

Maybe he was too old for this shit.

At home, he got into bed and stared into the darkness. Wondering what Armi and his date were doing. His stomach cramped as he thought of the two of them kissing. Maybe doing more.

He punched the pillow, lying alone in his bed, thinking about a man who could never be his.

CHAPTER SIXTEEN

"I'm glad you didn't have plans tonight." Brent swirled the wine the sommelier poured into his glass. "This is very nice. A good bouquet."

Armi fidgeted with his hands in his lap and forced a smile. "I'm not much of a wine connoisseur. I drink mostly beer."

Brent wrinkled his nose. "I haven't had a beer since college. You'll learn to love it."

Presumptuous much? Shouldn't he respect Armi's likes and wishes? Armi doubted he'd ever enjoy wine, but he didn't want to start off the evening disagreeing, so he nodded. "Sure."

The server stopped by their table and recited the specials. "Do you know what you'd like?"

Armi opened his mouth, but Brent cut him off. "We'll do the Caesar salad to share and the porterhouse for two with mashed potatoes and grilled asparagus." Finally, Brent looked at him. "Sounds good, right? It's their specialty."

Armi didn't particularly like Caesar salad, and he rarely enjoyed eating large meals at night that would sit heavy in his stomach. Should he say something?

"I, uh, was thinking of the salmon."

Brent's brows rose high, and a spark of annoyance flashed in his eyes. "Fish? At a steakhouse? I mean, sure, if that's what you want..."

"No, it's fine. You're right. Steak it is."

The taut lines on Brent's face smoothed out. "Great. I'm sure you'll love it."

He ate little of the salad and a few slices of the steak while listening to Brent go on and on about the big real estate deal he'd closed and how he was going to look for a house in the Hamptons. What happened to the charming man he'd had lunch with?

They were having coffee and tiramisu when Brent said, "Maybe you'd like to join me there for the summer? We'd have a great time trying all the wineries and restaurants."

"The whole summer? I don't know...it's kind of fast, don't you think?"

Brent slid a hand over his. "I really like you, Armi. You're sweet and kind and gorgeous. I'm hoping to get to know you better." The server appeared with the bill, and Brent took it. "My treat. You can get it next time."

Armi sighed with relief. That was the charming Brent from lunch. Maybe he was just trying to impress him. Armi was willing to give him another chance.

"I'd like to know you better too."

Brent's eyes lit up. "How about a drink at my place?"

Armi's heart fluttered. "Sure, but I have morning meetings, so it'll have to be an early night."

"That won't be a problem. Let's go."

Brent's apartment was done in neutral tones of beige, brown, and black. The kitchen was open to the living room, and Armi sat on the sectional couch while Brent poured him another glass of red wine and joined him. They clinked glasses.

"To us."

Armi should be thrilled. He had a gorgeous man interested in him, and he was head of a company. His roses were doing well.

So why was he so unsettled?

Maybe because he'd expected the wild passion he'd experienced with Hayden from a simple kiss. Brent's kisses were...nice. It probably would take some time.

"How was the rest of your day? Did your call go well?" Brent set his glass on the coffee table, and Armi did the same, happy not to have to force himself to drink it.

"Yeah. The conference call was good, and now that we've signed Hopkins and we're about to sign Masterson, it'll really help the team and get us that much closer to the Super Bowl."

Brent's eyes widened. "Whoa. Seriously? The Kings are gonna get Masterson? That's crazy. I didn't know he was leaving the Kickers."

Oh, shit. He wasn't supposed to have said a word until the deal was done. *Dammit.*

"No one does. And it's not a done deal, so please don't repeat it. Tomorrow is the day, so fingers crossed."

"Go Kings," Brent murmured. "And us. Let's celebrate." He leaned in and covered Armi's mouth with his. Again, Armi waited for that hot, overwhelming passion to sweep him away like it had with Hayden.

"You're so sweet," Brent breathed, his face flushed. "I can't stop wanting to kiss you."

Armi allowed him to push his tongue into his mouth, but at Brent's hands, first on his hips, then to the button fly of his slacks, he stopped him. "I'm sorry. I don't have sex so quickly. I hope you understand."

Chest heaving, Brent shook his head. "Honestly, I don't. Kissing on the couch is for kids, and we're not kids anymore. I thought we were hitting it off. This is the next step."

"Not for me. I don't get physical with people I barely know, even if they do buy me dinner." Heart hammering, Armi got to his feet. This was why he didn't date. Being in a position like this made him feel like he should say yes even though no was the right answer for him. "It's how I feel."

Brent's scowl turned his handsome face ugly. "Are you screwing your assistant? The blond?"

Shocked, Armi stared at him mutely, his body growing cold.

"Hey, he's hot as fuck, and the way he glared at me when I kissed you, if you're not getting any, you could be."

"You...you're ridiculous. Hayden works for me." But Armi couldn't help the thrill at hearing Hayden might have been annoyed over seeing Brent kiss him. Was it possible he was jealous? Not that it mattered. They'd agreed to be professional.

Brent rolled his eyes. "Please. Lots of PAs are into it. They like to keep their bosses happy, and they think it's a way up the corporate ladder." A lazy smile tipped up the corner of his lips. "For us, it's a way to let off some steam at the end of a stressful day. If we both want it and it's not on company time, no harm no foul, you know?"

"So you've..." He left the sentence open-ended, and at Brent's shrug, his decision was easy. "I-I—this is a ridiculous conversation. I'm going home." Armi walked away, and Brent followed him to the door.

"Marianne said you were quiet and not into the party scene, but I didn't think that meant at home. It's okay to let loose, you know. Sex is a natural part of life."

"I'm aware. Thanks for dinner, Brent."

Once out on the sidewalk, Armi wiped the tears of frustration burning his eyes. Time to go home and spend time with his roses. They were the only thing left that brought him joy. Brent lived less than a mile away, and Armi decided to walk home, enjoy the nice weather, and hoped it chased away the disappointment at how the date ended. He checked his messages and found one from Trevor.

You don't even give your best friend the scoop on signing Masterson?

Shit. How had Brent already spread the news? It was less than half an hour since he'd left his apartment. He'd told him not to say anything.

Nothing's signed yet. I mentioned it to Brent and told him to keep it quiet. How did you hear?

Afraid that ship has sailed. I'm friends with a couple of guys from his firm, and we're in a fantasy football league. He posted it in our group chat.

Shit. What the hell was he supposed to do?

When he reached home, he undressed and went to the greenhouse to forget about Brent and their date. A new graft he was working on didn't take, and he had no idea how to proceed. Sort of like his life—on the surface all looked well, but if you dug a bit deeper and peeled back the layers, it was rotting away and he was stuck, spinning his wheels.

Frustrated, he pulled off his gloves and left the warm confines of the greenhouse for the cool, air-conditioned kitchen. He pulled out a beer but only drank a bit. Was Brent's gossiping going to kill the signing? But it was all his fault. Why was he so stupid? He should never have said anything. He barely knew the man. He should never have gone on the date. He'd screwed that up too, like everything else.

He picked up his phone, and after debating a moment, sent Hayden a text.

Sorry to bother you, but I think I messed up badly.

Immediately, Hayden responded.

What's wrong?

About to type up the story, he stopped. Hayden couldn't help him. He needed to talk to Russell.

Never mind. It'll be fine. See you tomorrow.

But Hayden wouldn't be put off.

Please tell me and let me help you.

You can't. It'll be fine.

Armi scrolled to Russell's number and texted him what had occurred. Not even ten seconds passed before Russell called.

"Armand, what the hell?"

"I'm sorry. I didn't mean to. We were just talking and—"

"And you revealed sensitive, inside information about the team? Didn't I warn you not to say anything to anyone?"

"Yes, I know. I didn't think—"

"That's the problem. You didn't think. Were you so excited to be on a date that you couldn't keep your mouth shut?"

Russell had never spoken to him like that. Those hurtful words stung as if he'd been slapped in the face. "I didn't do it on purpose. I'm sure everything will be fine."

"Yeah, sure, unless another team gets wind of it and makes him a better offer tonight and we lose him. I have to talk to our lawyers. Hopefully we can do damage control and I can fix this mess you've made. How many more will there be this week? This is number two. Third time's the charm, right?"

Without another word, Russell ended the call. Armi hadn't felt this low in months. He trudged up the stairs to his room, brushed his teeth, and went to bed, but there was no rest to be found.

At dawn, he showered, dressed, and having no appetite, decided to head to the office. He knew it was early when he arrived and Hayden's desk was empty. He yawned and stood in front of the coffee machine, waiting for it to make a cappuccino to kickstart his brain. Hayden walked in, his face filled with concern.

"Armi? What's going on? What time did you get here? I went by your house this morning, but no one answered."

His smile was wry. "I couldn't sleep. I've only been here a few minutes. About to have my first of what will be multiple coffees."

Hayden proffered a large cup. "Here's another. Extra-large cappuccino."

"Thanks."

"Now what the hell is going on?"

"I had a date with Brent last night..."

Hayden's lips thinned, and his green eyes narrowed. "Did he do something? He was pretty slick."

"He was fine. Pushy because when we got back to his place, he wanted to...you know..." He lowered his voice. "Have sex."

A growl escaped Hayden's lips. "The fuck he did."

Hayden getting a little caveman was sexy as hell, and Armi watched as he continued to rant.

"Yeah. It made me kind of sad—I thought he wanted to get to know me, but he said we weren't kids and made it sound as if having sex right away was the norm."

"Not for you. You're different. I knew he was a player with that fake-ass grin. All he wanted was to get in." The fact that he and Armi met as a hook up wasn't the same to Hayden. He wasn't about to explain his reasoning—mainly because he couldn't—but that was his story, and he was sticking to it.

"Hayden, calm down. Nothing happened except a few kisses. I told him no and walked away."

"You don't deserve that. You just met the guy." When Armi raised a brow and crossed his arms, Hayden backtracked. "Okay, but what happened between us was not the same as this. We met at a club and hooked up. You and Brent were on a date." Hayden put a hand on his arm, and Armi swore he felt the pressure of his fingers all the way to his toes. "That's not why you texted me last night. What's upsetting you?"

"I opened my big mouth, that's what," Armi answered, miserable again. "And it could jeopardize the team's signing of Masterson." He recounted what happened and gulped his now cool cappuccino.

A grim-faced Hayden drummed his fingers on his thigh. "What time is the signing?"

"The meeting is at nine thirty."

Hayden's lips thinned. "Here's what we're going to do."

Masterson was probably the biggest man Armi had ever seen up close—at six foot seven and two hundred seventy-five pounds of pure muscle, he barely fit into the chair at the Mark, where Hayden knew the *maître d'* and got them a table for breakfast with less than an hour's notice.

God only knew how Hayden had managed to coordinate this, but he'd had a car pick up Masterson from the Mandarin Oriental hotel. A pitcher of freshly squeezed orange juice and a basket of fruit pastries sat between them.

"This is cool, man. Thanks." Masterson selected a cherry Danish. "Comin' from a small town in Texas, I never thought I'd see New York City, much less eat at these kinds of places."

"Well, I thought it would be nice to treat you to breakfast and welcome you to the Kings organization personally. I heard you recently got married?" God bless Hayden for doing a deep dive on the Internet.

Masterson's brown eyes lit up. "Yeah, Erin never liked being out west, away from her family in Westchester, so when the Kings made the offer, I knew I was gonna accept it. We had a little wedding at her family's house, and in a coupla months we'll go down to my family's house near Dallas and have a big party." His smile was sweet, and Armi could see he loved his wife very much. "Right now she's house huntin'."

"That sounds perfect. It's beautiful up there. As a wedding gift, I'm gifting you and your wife a half dozen of my exotic rosebushes—special ones that I've personally grown from grafting. It's a hobby of mine."

Masterson's eyes grew wide. "Really? Oh, wow, cool. Erin loves roses. All she could talk about was having a garden and planting flowers."

"I hope this is the start of a wonderful life here. We're looking forward to having you on the team, and we know you're going to make a huge difference in our run for the Super Bowl."

"I hope so. You know...my agent called me late last night and again early this mornin'. Other teams have made offers."

Armi winced. "I wasn't aware, but I'm sure they have. You're an excellent player. The best." God help him, he was so nervous, he didn't even remember what position Masterson played.

Masterson chuckled. "You're not like the other team owners I've met. They're throwing all kinds of gifts at me—trips, jewelry, cars, shopping sprees. Plus droppin' hints that having a gay owner might hurt the team. I read that *City News* article. They said maybe you aren't ready to lead the Kings. And some of the guys were talking in my ear. Saying it could be a liability for me."

Armi's stomach dropped, and though his face burned, he spoke from his heart. "I can't change people's prejudices, however ugly or wrong they are. All I can do is be the best I can for the team and for myself."

Their breakfasts came, and Masterson demolished his eggs, turkey sausage, and home fries, but Armi still wasn't sure if the deal was secured. He paid the bill just as Masterson's phone buzzed.

"That's my agent. Hold on. Willis, how's it going?" He walked away, leaving Armi standing there, feeling a little lost. His phone had vibrated numerous times during breakfast, but he'd ignored it and didn't want to look now.

Masterson returned. "Thanks for the breakfast and the rosebushes. I'll see you at the Kings headquarters for the signing announcement. Gonna go back to my room and change. Erin picked out my outfit." He glanced at his plain T-shirt and track pants. Not the usual attire allowed at the Mark, but when you were a famous athlete, you could get away with it. "She said I'd better be cleaned up for the press."

His heart leaped. "You're still going to sign with us?"

"I'm a straight shooter, and I don't like people trying to put others down. Plus, you're the only one who went out of your way to do something special, not just for me, but for my wife. It's easy to sign a check, and trust me, I like money as much as the next guy, not gonna lie. But I've already made more than I ever dreamed possible, and you giving Erin something close to your heart, like your rosebushes, was what did it for me." His eyes twinkled. "See, I read up on you too, Armand, so I know how much the roses mean to you."

Armi held out his hand. "Welcome to the Kings. Call me Armi."

CHAPTER SEVENTEEN

Standing at the signing, Hayden felt like a proud parent. Not that he'd ever know what having kids would be like, but seeing Armi next to Masterson, his face bright with that sweet smile, made Hayden so damn happy. His stomach fluttered.

They'd done it—Masterson was signed, and the papers had forgotten all about the nasty article. Today the sports pages couldn't heap enough praise on the Kings and their leadership. The press crowded into the space, and with satisfaction, Hayden saw Price not up front in his usual position, but at the far edge of the room, his face granite-hard with anger.

"What the hell did he expect?" If it were up to Hayden, Price wouldn't have been allowed at the press conference at all.

"We'll take some questions now," Russell stated, and Hayden frowned.

Why the hell did Armi allow Russell to take over? But he kept his eyes and ears open, planning to take notes on who treated Armi well and who was there for a hatchet job.

"Yes, Morty Unger for *Sports Today*. Do you think that with the addition of Masterson and Hopkins, the Kings have enough power to overcome the other deficiencies in their roster?"

Armi frowned, and Hayden started his fuck-off-and-die list of press people.

"I think—" Armi began, but Russell cut him off.

"We're stronger than ever now, and these two new superstars are only going to make us more tenacious as we make our run for the Super Bowl."

"Dorothy Harwood for *USA Sports News*. This question is for Milo Masterson. Why did you pick the Kings when we heard you had bigger and better offers from other teams, including last year's Super Bowl champs?"

The big man stepped forward and adjusted the Kings cap. "Well, see, I've had my Super Bowl wins already. I wanted a team that gave me a feeling of family. Not to say I don't like a fat bank account because I do. Momma didn't raise no fool." He waited for the laughter to die down. "But after meetin' with all the other teams, I felt a connection to the Kings and their owner. Armand Winters might be new at this, but I think he's got his heart in the team." His eyes twinkled. "Plus, he's made my bride very happy, and that means everythin' to me."

Armi's cheeks turned pink.

"What did he do? Mr. Winters, do you care to let us in on your secret?"

Armi stepped forward. "Well, I took the old adage 'Say it with flowers' and turned it up a notch."

Hayden snickered and nodded to himself. Armi was learning.

Russell leaned in. "We're making sure Milo has whatever he needs to be happy here." His gaze searched the crowd, and a hand shot up.

"Jack West from *Team Rainbow*. This question is for Mr. Winters. Have you received any negative feedback from being an out gay owner of a football team, and to follow up, do you think being a gay owner of a football team is going to hurt or help the Kings?"

"Asshole," Hayden swore. "What the fuck does that have to do with the signing?" His eyes narrowed as Russell spoke.

"I don't think this is the appropriate venue for a question like that."

But the reporter wasn't about to give up. "I'd like to hear that from Mr. Winters."

All eyes shifted to Armi, and Hayden could see how overwhelmed Armi was. He hated all the attention on him, and Hayden ached that he could do nothing to help.

"I-I don't mind answering, but this is a press conference for Milo Masterson and the great addition he'll make to the Kings." He paused, and Hayden willed him to meet his eyes from across the room. Hoping to get Armi's attention, he coughed, and their gazes locked. Hayden smiled and nodded.

"You can do it," he whispered. "You've got this."

As if he'd heard Hayden, Armi straightened his shoulders and lifted his chin. Goddamn, he was so proud of him.

"In the coming weeks, I'll be speaking more about it, but for now all I can say is I'm not the one playing, and you should be thankful for that." A few chuckles went around the room. "The team is only as good as the sum of its players and the respect they have for the coaching staff. I'm merely the conduit to get the Kings the best roster of players to achieve our goal. My personal life should have zero impact on the team's efforts on the field. That's all. Thank you."

"Next question for Milo?"

"Dixon Beyard, USPN. Milo, how do you feel about what Armand Winters just said? Do you think it will have any impact on the team?"

"Listen. I'm just here to play ball, not get involved in any political statement. What the owner just stated sounds good to me. I'm gonna give a thousand percent to the team and the fans so we can bring back a Super Bowl win to New York. I wanna have a parade down Broadway, and I'm gonna do my damnedest to make sure we get it."

"That's all for today, everyone." Russell took the microphone as Milo left the staging area with his agent. Hayden kept an eye on Armi, who shook Milo's hand and then slipped away. "Thanks for coming, and we'll see you for the first home game in September."

With the crowd dispersed, Hayden took off after Armi, knowing the introvert in him had been through enough for the day. But still, this called for a celebration. Upon his return to his desk, Armi stood waiting.

"Take the rest of the day off, Hayden. You deserve it. Everything you did today to help me worked out perfectly. Thank you."

God, he was so fucking sweet and sincere. "I'm good. I don't want the day off." He laughed and rubbed his chin. "I wouldn't know what to do with myself.

Besides, I'm expecting a call back from the guy from *Out in Sports* for that interview."

"Then let me take you to dinner, at least. I want you to know how much I appreciate you."

"You don't have to." He could picture them together. A small table. Candlelight. Intimate conversation. *Dammit.* He wanted it. Yearned for it.

"I know," Armi said with an almost cocky grin. "But I'm the boss. And I insist. I'll let you know when and where."

He blinked, that teasing side of Armi wholly unexpected but so enticing.

"Uh, okay, thank you."

All laughter aside, Armi put a hand on his shoulder. "I owe you, Hayden. Masterson loved the rosebushes for his wife. That personal touch sealed the deal."

"I'm happy if you're happy." The phone rang, but Armi's hand still rested on his shoulder. "I'd better get that." He reached over and took the phone. "Mr. Winters's office. How may I help you?"

"This is Steve Fontana with *Out in Sports*. I think I spoke with you last week?"

"Yes, Mr. Fontana. I'm Mr. Winters's assistant, Hayden. We were waiting for a call to schedule your interview."

"Yes, I'm sorry. Things got out of control here for a few days. I'd hoped to come do the interview myself, but that won't be possible now, so I'm going to send my second, Shane Daniels, in my stead. I hope that's okay."

"Of course. Mr. Winters is looking forward to speaking with your magazine and telling his story."

"Especially after today. That was quite a *coup* to grab Milo Masterson. I watched the press conference."

"Then you'll hear more of the same from Mr. Winters."

Fontana's laugh boomed in his ear. "How is next Monday at noon?"

He checked Armi's calendar. "I'll put you in and make it a lunch meeting."

"Shane will be happy."

"We aim to please."

"I have to say, you're a great cheerleader for your boss. Maybe we should interview you as well."

He met Armi's eyes. "I am when I believe in someone. And I'm pretty boring. There's nothing interesting about me."

The week sped by, and Hayden found himself busier than he had ever been while working for Boris. He and Armi sat together with the publicity team and came up with sound bites and quotes they could send out to the media and national press. There were phone calls with other owners, which Armi asked him to be present for. An appearance with the team, which had started pre-season practice, and more interviews with the press. Hayden could see Armi's confidence growing with each day, but still, whenever he came face-to-face with Russell and the other members of the Kings' inner circle, he wilted like a week-old rose.

Saturday, lying on his couch, checking social media for any mention of the Kings, he received a text from Armi.

Do you have plans for dinner tonight? Sorry it's spur-of-the-moment. I've been meaning to ask you all week, but it's been so busy.

That was so like him. Always apologizing.

Sure. What time and where?

Le Bernardin at 8?

Hayden's breath caught. One of the best restaurants in the world and the hardest reservation to get—near impossible on the same day. Unless you came from the world of Armi Winters, where money and status talked.

Hayden? U there?

Yeah. Meet u there.

No. I'll pick you up.

Hayden scrambled to his feet. He'd sent all his shirts to the cleaners along with his three suits, and they weren't supposed to be delivered until tomorrow. He needed to make a clothing run and fast.

"Next stop, Bloomies."

He managed to find a decent suit on sale, and he could always use another white shirt. His one splurge was a nice tie, and he dug through the designer sale rack and picked out a bright-green silk.

"Just like your eyes," the sales associate cooed. "Such a pretty green."

"Thanks." He took the shopping bags from the man.

"Hot date?"

He thought for a moment. "No. Dinner with my boss."

"Could be the same thing." A knowing grin tugged at the salesman's lips.

"No. It's definitely not."

Hayden rushed home, dropped off his shopping bags, and left immediately to get a manicure. No handling the forks and knives with scraggly cuticles. He might not've come from much, but he did have some standards.

At seven thirty Armi texted him.

I'm downstairs.

He gave one final glance in his mirror and laughed at himself. Hadn't he already told the salesperson he wasn't going on a date? Shaking his head at his foolishness, he left the apartment.

Armi opened the car door for him.

"You look nice." Armi gazed at him, and Hayden couldn't help his own lingering gaze. Armi had tamed his tumbling waves, and his freshly shaven face glowed. He smelled delicious.

"So do you."

Traffic wasn't a complete snarl, and they made it downtown in less than twenty minutes. The restaurant was as hushed and beautiful as Hayden had imagined. They were seated at a corner table, a small floral bouquet in the center of the snow-white tablecloth. A few moments after they were seated, a waiter approached with a bucket and a bottle of champagne. Hayden spied the label–Dom Pérignon–and then the cork popped.

The most magical evening of his life began.

And when dinner was over–a never-ending tasting menu of fish and seafood–Hayden floated on the rarefied air of incredible food, atmosphere, and conversation. Armi talked about growing up on Long Island and discovering his love for plants. Hayden spoke of his dealing with being gay in a small town. He wished the night never had to end. They left, Armi's hand in his, and walked to the car. It stopped in front of his apartment, and he wished nothing more than to invite Armi upstairs, but as wonderful as their dinner had been, taking that next step was a bad idea.

"This was so unexpected and amazing. Thank you doesn't seem like enough."

Armi's eyes sparkled. "I had a great time too. I wanted you to know how much I appreciate everything you do for me."

Maybe he was a little drunk from the bubbles. That was his excuse, and he was sticking with it. He closed the gap between them and settled his mouth over Armi's. The sweetness of their dessert couldn't match the delicious taste of Armi's tongue, and Hayden sucked it until spots flashed and his vision spun. Armi sighed and shifted closer. With regret, Hayden pulled away, and Armi gazed at him with hazy eyes.

"Thank you for the best night of my life," Hayden whispered, then fled before he did something stupid, like grab Armi's hand and pull him upstairs to his bed.

"Shit."

Monday morning. Another rough night, blaming himself for past mistakes and stupidity. Hopefully a shower would clear the cobwebs from his brain.

He'd spent the entire day Sunday in his apartment, preparing for the week ahead, but it was tough going. All he wanted to do was relive the evening with Armi.

And that kiss.

What was it about Armi that turned him inside out? Armi wasn't his usual type—partying guys who knew better than to think sex meant anything more than a good time.

Who was he kidding?

Armi's innocence and vulnerability were huge turn-ons. Not to mention his gorgeous face and body. Watching his self-confidence grow was hot as hell, but Hayden still had the urge to protect him whenever that inner circle surrounded him like sharks scenting blood in the water. He'd never had a man overwhelm his senses to the point where the thought of him kissing or being touched by someone else made him want to punch a wall.

Hence, his isolation and sleepless nights. It would take some time to learn how to calm his exterior, because forgetting a man like Armi Winters didn't happen overnight. Maybe ever.

The fresh bouquet had arrived for Armi's office, and that week the roses were John F. Kennedy, which boasted rich white petals. Hayden made sure to fill the vase and arrange them properly. For his own desk, he decided on bright yellow—God knew he'd need something to cheer him up.

He finished his first coffee and set out Armi's cherry turnover. It had taken him three pastry shops to find Armi's favorite.

"Those are beautiful, thank you."

Armi stood waiting in the doorway, and Hayden's cheeks grew warm. Christ, he never blushed. What the hell was up with that? He cleared his throat.

"You're welcome. If you tell me what else you like, I can make sure to have it for you."

Armi set his Kings duffel bag on the table. "I'll like anything you give me."

Hayden blinked, the double entendre not lost on him. He didn't banter back but hurried from the room.

"Okay, so maybe bagels tomorrow. You'd better get ready for the weekend scouting report. I summarized the notes, sent them to your email, and printed them out."

"Thanks, Hayden."

"Not a problem. Don't forget, lunch today with the *Out in Sports* guy, Shane Daniels. I sent you the questions I think he'll ask, as well as points you'll probably want to get across."

"I seem to be constantly thanking you."

Hayden gave him a brief smile. It hurt.

"You don't have to. Like I said, it's my job."

And said job kept him busy as hell, answering calls from news outlets and coordinating with PR for press releases. With the signing of Hopkins and Masterson, Armi had become something of a media darling. His star, which only a week ago had been sputtering, now was on the rise and burning bright.

When the phones quieted, Hayden gulped his now-cold cappuccino and made a face.

"Hayden?"

Cold washed through him, and he froze. Twenty years had passed since he'd last heard that voice, and he'd hoped he'd never have to hear it again.

Today, his luck had run out.

"It is you. I'd recognize that gorgeous face anywhere."

It couldn't be. It couldn't fucking be him.

Hayden raised his gaze to meet the knowing smirk of Shane Michaels, a.k.a. Shane Daniels. The man who'd seen him naked and having sex. The man who held all his secrets.

CHAPTER EIGHTEEN

Could this meeting go on any longer? Armi tried to concentrate, and for the most part he was able to keep up. The first hour had been the team congratulating themselves on the signings and Coach Jackson laying out the groundwork for the team's upcoming season. They faced a tough first half, but with the addition of the two new players, their chances to make the playoffs were better than ever, barring any injuries.

Russell brought up the next slide of the scouting report. "Jason, you want to give us the rundown?"

"Sure thing. Division I schools, we have eyes on several kids."

The stats were overwhelming, and his mind wandered to the weekend and the dinner with Hayden. He hoped it hadn't backfired on him. Bringing Hayden to one of the best restaurants in the world was meant to show him appreciation for everything he'd done. He'd stepped into the job as seamlessly as if he'd been there longer than Armi.

But was it too much? Did it showcase the differences between them and make him feel less than? Armi's lips tingled as he recalled the kiss in the back of the car. God, he could still feel the rush of heat searing through him. More than anything, he wished he'd had the nerve to follow Hayden to his apartment and make love to him.

He rubbed his eyes. Make love? Where had *that* come from?

"Armand? Armand, are you listening?" Russell's voice broke into his reminiscing.

"Sorry. I-I—"

"Never mind. What do you think?" Russell knew he hadn't been paying attention, but Armi had read the notes Hayden had sent.

"I think we need to think of the future, and with our quarterback approaching thirty-five, it's good we're looking at that position. Plus, I'd like to beef up our special teams." Eight sets of eyes stared at him. "What? Is something wrong?"

With a smile on his lips, Coach Jackson nodded. "Damn good thoughts, Armand. I was telling Russell that your father's one weakness was not paying enough attention to special teams."

Obviously, Coach Jackson hadn't ever had the pleasure of being berated by Randolph Winters, who enjoyed finding faults and pointing out inadequacies. That was saved for his only child.

"How about our Division III players and the other schools? Any kids you've spotted with potential?"

One of the scouts raised his hand. "I've been covering the Southern schools for the past few weeks, and from what I've seen, there are some diamonds in the rough."

"Seniors?" Russell asked. "Any other teams show interest?"

"Both seniors. And no other teams that I've seen, but you never know. Not like we're broadcasting doing this. One's in Georgia and the other in Alabama. My suggestion is for someone else to go see them practice and play this coming weekend for a second look."

Russell tapped some notes on his tablet. "I'll go. Armand will come with me."

"I will?"

"Randolph and I would often take trips to check on scouts' picks. I think it would be good for you."

Maybe a change of scenery would be best. It would take away the temptation of wanting Hayden so badly, he might do something stupid. Like show up at his apartment.

"Fine."

"Good. I'll make the arrangements."

Armi checked his watch. "I have a meeting with *Out in Sports* in less than five minutes. I have to go. Thanks, everyone."

Hating that he didn't have much prep time, Armi hustled to his office but stopped dead. A tall man stood over Hayden's desk but it was Hayden's face that concerned him. He was as pale and stiff as a store mannequin. Armi quickened his steps.

"Everything all right?" He passed by the man to stand next to Hayden, who didn't move. The stranger met his gaze.

"Mr. Winters? I'm Shane Daniels from *Out in Sports*. Nice to meet you."

"Y-yes, you too. Would you excuse us a moment? Have a seat in my office, please. I'll be right in." He pointed Daniels to a chair at the conference table and closed the door behind him. "Hayden, what's wrong? You look sick. Are you okay?"

Hayden wet his lips. "I'm fine."

"Did that man say anything to you?"

"Daniels?" Hayden's jaw worked. "No. Nothing. We barely spoke."

But for the first time, Hayden couldn't meet his eyes, and Armi was certain he wasn't telling the truth.

"Did he say anything inappropriate? I won't talk to him if he did."

"No. He didn't do anything. Forget about it, please? You'd better go inside."

"Are you sure?" He wanted so badly to touch Hayden's face and soothe his obvious fear, but they were out in the open, so he curled his fingers into his palms.

"Yeah. I'm gonna go to lunch. Is that all right?"

He'd wanted Hayden to sit in with him, but instinct told him that wouldn't be a good idea. "Of course. Go ahead."

Hayden took his phone and strode away but turned and retraced his steps. "I'm sorry. Do you want me to sit in?"

"No. It's fine. You've been all alone here at the desk the whole morning, and you deserve a break."

"I'm sorry," Hayden whispered and left.

Armi stood outside his door for a second, then opened it. Shane Daniels was on his phone and looked up when Armi entered. "Hello again."

"Sorry to keep you waiting. Please feel free to have something to eat." He'd called in for sandwiches and salads.

"Your assistant won't be joining us?" Daniels asked as he filled a plate.

Armi took the seat opposite Daniels at the table. He was a big man, well-muscled and broad in the shoulders, in his early fifties. Thick blond hair turning silver at the temples. A strong nose accompanied an angular jaw and thin lips. Harsh lines scored his face. A hint of a hard life played in his pale-blue eyes.

"No. Hayden's at lunch. So, what would you like to talk about?"

Daniels finished chewing and steepled his fingers under his chin. "How did you meet Hayden?"

Armi's eyes narrowed. "What does that have to do with the interview?"

Daniels waited a few beats. "Nothing. You're correct. Let's start. How has it been, as the only out gay owner of a professional football team? Do you feel people treat you differently?"

"Because I'm gay? I'm not so sure that's the reason. More than likely, it's because I'm not a sports fanatic, and I was never involved much with the team."

"I see. But you do *feel* different?"

"I think people aren't sure how to treat me. But it hasn't been all negative. My organization doesn't discriminate in who we hire–that would make me pretty damn hypocritical, don't you think?"

"Well, people do things without realizing the consequences."

"My team–my inner circle–has been nothing but supportive. Yes, there's been a learning curve, but that's only natural. I have excellent support."

"From whom?" Daniels's eyes were on his tablet as he took notes.

"Russell Anders, Jacob Whitmore, Troy Geiger, and of course Coach Jackson and his staff. We've all been working well together."

"And no one's had any problems with your sexuality? No jokes or comments?"

"I think you're hoping that something nefarious is going on, but I can assure you it isn't. Are people homophobic? Of course. But the point I'm making is that here in the Kings organization, I haven't come across that problem."

Daniels finished typing and met his eyes. "Not even because of your assistant?"

His heart swooped and fell. Had someone seen them together at dinner? Or maybe kissing in front of Hayden's apartment building? Heart thumping, Armi gathered his wits.

"Hayden's been a valuable member of my team and nothing but helpful to me. Anyone's sexuality is none of my concern."

Shane Daniels regarded him thoughtfully, and then an enigmatic smile tipped up the corner of his mouth. "I agree. Do you think you'll be staying with the team long-term?"

"Yes. I will."

"It's been rumored that you and your father had a contentious relationship and he never planned to make you the team owner. Did he accept you? Or were you at odds because you're gay? What's true?"

One-two punch.

"I'm not sure what that has to do with me leading the team into the future." His gaze was steady. "I'm not interested in dwelling on the past. Nothing good can come from that."

"But has it put you in a bad place with the other members of the organization who may have had different ideas as to how to run the team?"

Three weeks ago, Armi might've stumbled his way through and given Daniels enough ammunition to make him look the fool. Not today.

"We're all dedicated to making the team the best it can be. Our scouts are all over the country, looking for superior talent, our coaches are the best in the game and future Hall of Famers, and we're hungry for another Super Bowl for our fans. We have the best quarterback in Devlin Summers. The quickest tight end in Brody Martin. Now we've added Milo Masterson to our roster. New Yorkers expect us to be number one, to be winners, and we plan to give it to them."

"Now for the personal side of the interview. Are you married, single, or dating anyone?"

"I'm single, and I'm not seeing anyone."

"Do you want a relationship, and how do you think this new position might affect that?"

"I'm not averse to meeting someone, but they'd have to understand that this job is pretty all-encompassing. It doesn't go away at six p.m."

"Are you afraid someone might want to date you only because of who you are?"

Armi shrugged. "I suppose so, but I'll never know if I don't take a chance."

"Could you ever see yourself dating a Kings player?"

"That would be a conflict of interest for me. You'd have to ask a player if they'd ever want to date an owner."

"Thanks, Armand. This has been a very enlightening interview."

"I'll walk you out." Armi opened the door, noticing Hayden wasn't at his desk. He ushered Daniels to the elevator. "Nice to meet you, Mr. Daniels."

"You as well."

The elevator door opened, and Daniels stepped into the cab and was gone.

When Armi returned, he saw Hayden, head down, trudging to his desk. At his approach, Hayden put up his hand. "Please, can we talk later? Not now. But I need to tell you things."

Confused, Armi cocked his head. "All right. Later."

But that time never arose. He had to sit in on a conference call with the players' union and then join Whitmore and Geiger on financials and new contract negotiations.

It was almost six by the time he escaped from the conference room, and he saw Hayden's desk was empty. It was the first time since he'd started working that Hayden had left before him or before seven. Armi ran to his office, grabbed his stuff, and left. He called for a car to take him to Hayden's apartment. The doorman rang and rang, but no one answered.

"I'm sorry, sir, but he's not answering."

"Armi? What're you doing here?"

From the entrance, haunted eyes met his.

Armi decided the hell with keeping away. That was a stupid idea. "You wanted to talk, right?"

Hayden didn't answer but also failed to tell him to leave, so Armi kept close to his heels as he walked inside. They didn't speak until he sat opposite Hayden on the sectional sofa.

"Shane Daniels."

"The interviewer from *Out in Sports*. That's what this is about?" He wasn't wrong. Those remarks about Hayden had been deliberate.

"I—there are things I haven't told you. About me."

Armi clasped his shaky hands. "I'm not going anywhere."

"Did..." Hayden licked his lips, all that self-assurance gone, his face pale. "Did Shane say anything about me?"

"No. Why would he?"

Their eyes met, and Armi's heart pounded at the absolute defeat and misery in those brilliant green depths.

Hayden hung his head, his gaze on the floor. "When I was in college, I was on a webcam, having sex. I got paid for it. Daniels ran the website."

Armi's stomach tumbled. "Why?"

"Money," Hayden whispered. "My parents were on the verge of losing their house—my father's company went bankrupt, and he lost his pension. Starting over at his age wasn't easy—they'd rather hire people right out of school and pay them less. Now he works at a big-box store and has a weekend job at the mall."

"I'm sorry. That must've been really hard on your whole family."

"Any job I could get wouldn't make a dent in my expenses. I couldn't let them sacrifice their entire savings for my college tuition..." He jumped up from the couch, crossed the room, and stood staring out the window. A solitary figure Armi longed to hug. There he sat with all the money in the world, impotent to do anything.

"So you found another way."

"I told them it was an acting gig I auditioned for. At first it was only me in front of the camera...jerking off or using toys...just stuff to get people to pay. I earned enough to make up for whatever the loans didn't cover and then some." He shrugged, his face flaming red. "I didn't think I'd have to have sex with anyone, but Shane told me I'd get paid triple if I had sex on camera."

"I'm so sorry." He had no idea what else to say.

"I did it once and hated it, but the money was so good." He covered his face. "The next time, the police raided the place where Shane had us perform. They caught us in the act, with the cameras going. I was seventeen, so even though I'd signed a contract, it was void, as I was underage. The college kicked me out, and Shane went to jail because he was selling videos of me on the Internet." His voice caught, and all Armi could think of was Hayden trapped, forced to do something he didn't want to, but not seeing a way out.

"What a bastard. I'm livid I did the interview with him."

"My parents were called. It was the worst night of my life, having to tell them what I'd done. It was the only time I ever saw my father cry. I let them down in the worst way. After everything they'd done for me, all I did was disappoint them."

"I'm sure they understood why it happened. It wasn't your fault."

"They said they did, but I know how badly I hurt them. I never returned to school. I would've been the first in my family to graduate from college, but I was too ashamed to apply and have to explain why I'd gotten expelled. I got odd jobs, took online courses in office management, marketing, human resources...finally got that college degree. I left home for my first job in the city with a law firm—I was a temp filling in for the partner's personal assistant who was out on maternity leave. They kept me on when she returned, and then I met Janice Butler, who took a liking to me. She was dating one of the partners and told me if I worked with her headhunting firm, she'd hook me up with top businesspeople—New York's elite. I told her everything about my past, and she said it's hard to find someone who's gotten far in life without suffering some kind of adversity. My first PA job was with an international banker, but he moved to Europe and I didn't want to leave the country. My second was with the head of one of the largest hedge funds in the country. He went to jail." A slight twitch of his lips. "Then I went to Boris."

"Janice sounds like a smart woman."

Surprising him, Hayden returned to the couch to sit by his side. "I'm sorry. I didn't want you to know because I was so ashamed." He shook his head and made a fist on his knee. "I hate that you had to find out. I didn't want you to think less of me."

There wasn't a chance in hell he could ever think less of Hayden. But to know that his cocky confidence had all been an illusion and that for years he'd walked a tightrope of doubt and fear, that hurt. And it hurt more that Hayden could think he'd be the one to push him off, toppling him to the ground.

"I couldn't, Hayden. I don't. You're an amazing PA. I couldn't survive in the office without you." Armi decided to hell with keeping secrets. "But you're so much more than someone who works for me. I care about you. You're my friend."

"I was afraid you were going to fire me."

"For telling me the truth? Never. You're not going anywhere."

CHAPTER NINETEEN

It was out. At last. The secret he'd carried, chewing him to pieces like a parasite living inside him, had been exposed, and he remained standing. And employed. Hayden allowed himself to breathe and finally looked Armi in the face.

"Thank you."

"Did you really think I'd fire you? I think you're so brave for telling me. Thank you for giving me your trust."

An indefinable yearning filled him, and Hayden wrapped his arms around himself. "I didn't know what to think. I was so busy being scared someone would find out."

"Like your friend Janice said, there isn't a person in the world who hasn't made mistakes or done something they never wanted anyone else to find out."

Hayden snorted. "What have you ever done that was so terrible?"

"I should've tried harder with my father and insisted on working with him. Maybe he might not've died being so disappointed in me. And I shouldn't have tried to change who I was and hope people would be my friend. Because it didn't work. No matter what I did, people still didn't like me."

Hearing Armi's confession crushed Hayden's soul. "No. That's impossible. You can only go so far and try so hard. You're beautiful, inside and out, and you shouldn't have to twist yourself into knots trying to prove it to people. If they can't see it for themselves, they're not worth your time." It hadn't occurred to him that Armi was trying to prove his father wrong, which only made it sadder, knowing it was a battle he could never win.

"So are you, Hayden. I hope you realize it. You have so much light inside you to give. Don't let anyone dim it by bringing up what's no longer important."

In their short time together, Hayden had learned that Armi's eyes reflected his emotions, and the yearning in their blue depths was unmistakable. It matched his own. He wanted Armi, and it would be so easy to lean in and kiss him, merge their breath and bodies and fall into each other to wipe away their collective pain. His heart pounded, and every cell in his body screamed for him to do it. Take and claim what he knew he could get. But he resisted, despite how his blood burned. Nothing had changed. Armi was his boss and a friend. Sleeping with him would ruin the bond they'd forged, and Hayden refused to do anything to jeopardize it because once it ended, he'd have to leave.

And he didn't think he could bear that.

"Thank you for caring so much and for coming by." He moved from the couch to the kitchen, putting space between them, and while it didn't lessen his desire, it was safer. Disappointment flashed in Armi's eyes, and he nodded.

"I'll see you tomorrow." He got to his feet and headed to the door.

"How did the scouting meeting go?"

Hand on the doorknob, Armi stopped. "Fine. Russell and I are going to head down south this weekend to watch some of the prospects play." Armi opened the door. "Night."

"Bye." He leaned against the door and closed his eyes, listening to the footsteps on the opposite side fade away. Damn, he hated doing the right thing.

Hayden had tons to do in the week before Armi left for his road trip—and he was glad for it. It kept his mind off Armi and Russell being away together for a whole weekend. It nagged at him because he suspected Russell of orchestrating something that would somehow get Armi into his bed.

Not that there'd been any overt signs of Russell's intent, but Hayden was laser-fucking-focused on everything Russell Anders did when it came to Armi. Like the frequent touches, innocuous to all but someone who'd spent time watching and noticing he didn't do it with anyone else. That canny bastard was after Armi.

The thought made him sick to his stomach.

"Not your goddamned business," he muttered to himself. "You're not a couple."

"Hayden? What's wrong?" Armi approached his desk, face screwed up with concern. His tie lay askew, and there was a suspicious stain on his shirt that might be butter from the bagel he'd eaten that morning. God, he was cute.

"Nothing." He smoothed his face into neutrality. "Just made a typo and had to correct it."

Armi smiled. "You're such a perfectionist. Don't beat yourself up about it. Can you get us some waters, please? Russell and I have a few last-minute details to go over. He should be here any minute."

"Yeah, sure."

Half an hour passed, and Russell hadn't shown. Armi stepped out of his office. "Still nothing?"

"No. I'll call Lucy."

He buzzed her line, but she didn't pick up either. More curious than concerned, he left his station to check with Josh at the front.

"Did you see Mr. Anders or Lucy around by any chance?"

"Yes. They went to lunch about noon." Josh glanced at the computer screen. "Oh, wow. That's not like him to take a three-hour lunch. I hope nothing happened."

"Thanks." He returned to the office and knocked on Armi's door. "No one's seen him or Lucy since noon."

Armi's brows shot up, and he grabbed his phone. "That doesn't make sense. I'm going to call him on his cell." He waited. "Hello, who's this?...Lucy? What's going on? Where's Russell?"

Hayden stood waiting, unable to hear the other side of the conversation.

"Shit. Is he going to be okay?...*Ugh*, that's awful. I'm glad you were with him. Make sure he gets set up okay at home and tell him not to worry about anything... Yeah. I know, but we can do it another time... Six weeks? Ouch. Well, it's not his concern. I can handle it myself... Yes, let me know how it works out."

He ended the call. "Russell broke his ankle. His knee buckled stepping off the curb after getting out of his car. They're at the hospital. He needs a screw and will be in a cast and on crutches for six weeks."

"Damn, that's rough." Hayden didn't like the guy, but he didn't want to see him hurt.

"Yeah. And we have that trip planned for the whole weekend."

"Are you going to cancel it?"

"Not sure." Armi drummed his fingers on the desk. His phone rang. "Hold on, it's Thomas, the scout. Hi. Did you hear about Russell? Yeah... You think? I'm not sure... That's not the issue... I'll let you know." He ended the call and stared at his desk for a second. "Tom thinks I should go and see the players for myself, since this was all my idea." His face was a combination of fear and insecurity, but Hayden could see something else too. A spark in those eyes that wasn't there when Hayden first started working for him.

"I think that's a smart move. This idea is your baby, so you should get to see the kids you want to help. They'll appreciate the owner of an NFL team coming to see them play."

"You think?"

Hayden smiled. "I know."

Armi narrowed his eyes. "I want you to come."

"Me?" Hayden laughed. "In case you don't remember, I know less about football than anyone here. Including you."

"You might not know football, but you know me," Armi responded quietly. "I need someone I can trust. Plus, with your attention to detail, you'll pick up and record everything Tom says that I might miss or forget. You have good people instincts that I don't. Please?"

A trip to watch college football games in Georgia and Alabama wasn't high on Hayden's list of things he'd wanted to do that weekend, but then again, he had no other plans. And spending the weekend with Armi was a perk he hadn't anticipated.

"Okay. If you're sure."

Like a kid, Armi bounced in his seat. "Great. Our plane leaves at seven. Better go home and start packing. I'll pick you up at four thirty. Traffic's gonna be a bitch out of the city."

"Yes, sir." In a better mood than he'd been in since he'd seen Shane, Hayden threw Armi a salute on his way out.

"Very funny. And Hayden?"

He stopped in the doorway and pivoted to face Armi.

"Thanks."

"Not a problem."

He finished the open tasks on his computer, saved all the documents, and shut it down. Any information he'd need from the scouting reports had already been downloaded to his and Armi's saved files. He decided to splurge on a cab, and once at home, tossed T-shirts and shorts into a carry-on. His travel toiletry bag was still intact from a work trip to Cancun the year before, and he tucked it inside the zippered pocket. On that trip, he'd slipped out after Boris had gone to sleep for the night and partied at the clubs in the hotel zone. He'd gotten no sleep, but it had been worth it.

Funny, but he had no desire to see what clubs were around the hotels where he and Armi would be staying. Armi hadn't even told him what cities—Russell had made the reservations. It wasn't a party trip. He was there for Armi.

As Armi had predicted, the traffic was nightmarish, and it took over an hour to get to Teterboro and on the team's private jet. The flight to Alabama was quick and uneventful, and a car waited for them at the airport to take them to their hotel.

"Montgomery is a pretty city," Hayden remarked, looking out the window.

"Good thing y'all got reservations. Coupla big conventions this weekend means there ain't a room to be found from here to Mobile."

"Yes, I've got the confirmation number right here." Armi pulled it up on his phone as the car slid to a stop and dropped them off at the hotel. At the front desk, Hayden waited to the side while Armi checked in, but joined him when he saw them in a deep discussion.

"I'm sorry, sir, but that's what the reservation says. One deluxe room with a king-sized bed. All our suites were booked by the convention."

"But...but that's impossible. There must be some mistake. Check again, please. Either under Russell Anders or Armand Winters."

"Yes, sir."

Hayden sidled closer. "What's wrong?"

"They say Russell only reserved one room for the two of us. That can't be true."

Sure it can. Just like I suspected.

"Let them check. Maybe it's under another name? Like the Brooklyn Kings?"

The clerk shook his head. "No. Nothing. Just that one room. And we're completely sold out."

"We heard it's a busy weekend."

The clerk's face shone with sweat. "Yes. It's a madhouse. I'm sorry, sir. If something pops up, I'll let y'all know." He paused. "Two keys, gentlemen?"

Armi nodded and took the envelope with the key card. "I'm sorry," he said as they walked to the elevators. "We'll work it out. Maybe there's a pull-out sofa."

But when they opened the door, there was only one king-sized bed with a club chair in the corner and a reading lamp hanging over it. Hayden shut the door behind him and wheeled his suitcase to the opposite side of the room.

"I'll take the chair. I don't mind."

"No," Armi stated with emphasis. "That's not right. I will."

"Armi, I can't have you sleeping in a cramped chair." Hayden eyed the bed. "There's plenty of room, don't worry. I'm sure we can keep our hands off each other."

Cheeks an adorable shade of pink, Armi ducked his head. "Okay, but I really don't mind the chair."

"But I would mind."

They unpacked, and he changed while Armi sat looking on his phone, although Hayden did catch him taking a couple of sneak peeks. "The reviews say that the hotel restaurant is pretty good. Unless you want to go out."

"Maybe tomorrow night. It's been a pretty hectic day. I could just go for a quiet night. A drink and a meal here sounds fine to me."

"I agree. I'll just change." Armi picked up his shorts and T-shirt, standing awkwardly for a moment.

Hayden grinned and held up his hands. "I promise not to peek."

Armi rolled his eyes. "I think that ship has sailed." But he changed as quickly as he could. "Ready?"

"Yep." Hayden followed him, and as they had to wait ten minutes for a table, they got a drink at the bar. "So tell me," he asked Armi, "what are you looking for tomorrow?"

Before answering, Armi drank some of his beer. "Honestly, I'm not sure. That's what Tom is here for—to point out what we're looking for and how they'll fit with the future of the team. You're right in that I should know what it is I'm directing the scouts to do. If I'm going to do this, I have to learn from the field up."

"Why do you still keep saying if?" Hayden frowned. "You're doing a great job from my point of view."

"Which might be a little biased?" Armi teased, and Hayden liked him this way. Relaxed and comfortable in his skin.

"No, I don't think I am. On my first day, you were hesitant and tentative, almost afraid to give an opinion. In the past few weeks, you've given multiple interviews, gotten one of the top running backs to sign with the team, and now here you are, at a scouting."

"None of which I could've done if I didn't have your support." Armi finished his beer and signaled for another. He caught Hayden's eye. "It's the weekend, and we're away from the office. I'm entitled."

Grinning, Hayden held up his hands. "Hey, I'm not saying anything. Go for it. You deserve it."

"And so do you." Armi called over the bartender. "Bring him another, please."

When Hayden received his Tito's and soda, Armi held up his bottle. "To a great weekend. May we accomplish everything we need and want."

"I'll drink to that."

But Hayden knew that wasn't going to be the case. He wanted Armi. He needed to hold him, but that wasn't going to happen. They'd agreed to be friends and nothing more.

Anything else would be a very bad idea.

CHAPTER TWENTY

As they ate, Armi feigned interest in his grilled fish but studied Hayden instead. After revealing his startling secret, Hayden had continued his exemplary work as if nothing had happened. Almost. But Armi, who was used to spotting the tiniest beginnings of disease in his plants, noticed what most people wouldn't—occasionally Hayden would stare off into space, or his fingers would tremble when he held the phone or took notes. Hayden could pretend he wasn't affected by the revelations of his past, but Armi knew better because he now knew Hayden. There was so much hurt from the supposed damage to his parents, and so much anxiety, years of always looking over his shoulder and wondering if that would be the day his secret was exposed.

There had to be some way to convince him that it didn't matter, that his mistake wasn't an unforgivable sin. Armi had always wondered what was behind the shadows waiting in his eyes. And now that he knew, he couldn't rest until they'd been erased.

"Something wrong with your meal?" Hayden pointed to his plate.

"No, just thinking of something." He took a forkful and chewed.

"I'm thinking of something too. Like why the hell Russell would pull shit like that."

Armi swallowed. "I hadn't said anything before, but he's been giving me strange vibes for months."

"Strange vibes meaning what?" Hayden set his fork down.

Armi shrugged. "Sometimes he'd say things that made me wonder if he was interested in me...or he'd get in my personal space. Initially I brushed it off because, I mean, it's Russell. I never would've suspected him of trying to use sex to influence me to run the team his way, but now with this room mix-up...I guess it makes more sense."

Hayden snorted. "Come on. You guess?" His eyes darkened. "He was going to use this weekend to get to you."

Armi choked and grabbed the water glass. "What the hell does that mean?"

Hayden laid his fork on the table and leaned in close. "You know." The flickering candle between them failed to hide Hayden's serious expression. "Russell was going to try and sleep with you."

It hurt more than it angered him that another person in his life he'd looked up to had only pretended to care. He should've listened to his gut. He'd suspected something was off about Russell's eagerness to help guide him.

Hayden continued. "Don't you see? Once you and he are together, he'd use his influence to get the team to do what he wanted. Maybe he'd even talk you into making him the CEO."

With each word Hayden spoke, Armi grew angrier. His appetite gone, he threw down his napkin. "So that's what you think of me? That I'm some damn patsy who's so desperate to have a man in my bed, I'd roll over for him because he pays attention to me?" He left Hayden speechless at the table and found the server. "Put the tab on my room, please. I have to leave." Without looking back, he walked away.

His eyes burned as he entered the room and tossed his key aside. Nothing would ever change. Here he'd thought he and Hayden were friends, and yet Hayden thought he was a stupid, desperate fool who'd do anything to have someone care. The saddest thing? It was Hayden he had those feelings for, not Russell or anyone else.

"Screw it. I'm taking a shower and going to bed."

He kicked off his sneakers and pulled his shirt off, when the lock clicked and Hayden walked in. They stared at each other in the semidarkness. Armi waited to speak because he was too hurt.

"I'm sorry, Armi."

Armi lifted his chin. "Don't apologize if that's how you feel."

"I don't think you're a patsy or that you'd say yes just to have someone." He sank onto the bed and hung his head. "I-I shouldn't have said that."

"But you did. Why? It was hurtful."

Hayden's shoulders slumped, and he rubbed his face. "I–because I was jealous."

Armi's heart pounded so loudly, he could barely hear. "Of what?"

Finally Hayden met his eyes, and Armi's breath caught at the combination of fear and lust glittering in those green depths. "That he would be with you and I couldn't."

"Who says so?"

Hayden shook his head. "We decided. Plus..." He shrugged.

"What? Plus what?"

Hayden huffed out a sigh. "You're really gonna make me say it? For fuck's sake, I was a cam boy, Armi. I was naked on camera for guys to jerk off to. I screwed online, shoved toys up my ass for people to get off." He turned away. "I'm not the right guy for you."

"Why?" Armi demanded.

"Are you kidding?" Hayden sputtered. "Imagine if— no, not if, *when* someone finds out because I'm sure they will, if we ever started seeing each other. You don't need my name attached to yours and damaging the team's reputation."

"For something you did twenty years ago? That's ridiculous. No one's perfect."

"This is beyond some stupid school prank." Frustration poured off Hayden. "I'm trying to do the right thing here."

Armi had always done the right thing. He'd tried to please his father, feigning interest in sports. He'd kept his sexuality quiet and stayed away, burying himself in his flowers, rather than have relationships. He tried to make his father love him.

And where had it gotten him? Nowhere. With no one by his side.

He was tired of being the outsider. The clumsy one. The nice one.

The plus one.

"The right thing would be following your heart." He pulled Hayden up by his elbow and nuzzled into his neck.

Hayden shivered. "I can't," he whispered but swayed into him. "I lose control whenever you touch me."

"Tough." Armi bit his ear, and hearing Hayden moan, knowing he gave him pleasure, was the biggest fucking turn-on of his life. "Come on, Hayden. One step at a time. We have the whole weekend together. Do you really want to spend it talking football?"

"You don't play fair," Hayden mumbled, but he didn't pull away and Armi cheered.

"Haven't you heard? I play to win now."

Hayden ran his hands up and down Armi's body. "What happened to that mild-mannered man I met in the club?"

"He didn't have anything in his life he wanted badly enough." Armi cupped his jaw. "Now he does."

Hayden's forehead touched his, the tips of their noses brushing, and Armi wondered how he was able to stand with his bones melting. "Just the weekend, then. We can have that."

It was impossible to argue because the moment this man touched him, all thoughts faded away and he became a quivering bundle of need. "Please," he murmured. "Please."

Hayden undressed him, fingers brushing the bare skin above the waistband of his shorts, and he stepped out of his clothes, now fully naked.

"Fuck, you're beautiful." Hayden sank to his knees, and Armi cried out at the searing wet heat of Hayden's mouth enveloping his cock. That velvety tongue was as wicked as Armi remembered, and he flung his head back as Hayden played with his balls but never stopped sucking him. His hips pumped wildly, and Hayden cupped his ass to slow him.

"God, Hayden, I can't..." The beginnings of his orgasm tingled in his groin.

Hayden released him and sat on his heels. "You will. Come to bed with me."

Hungry with desire, he watched as Hayden stripped, revealing all those beautiful tattoos. Hayden stood before him, his dick hard and huge, lust blazing from his eyes. "Like what you see?" His hand trailed past his pecs and flat abs to grip his shaft, and he began to pump.

Armi panted as his body throbbed, empty and needy. "Fuck me. All I've thought about every night since the last time was you inside me."

Hayden's eyes widened. "Yeah? That's funny." Hayden pushed him to the bed, caging him under those muscular arms, and Armi nearly swooned. Hayden traced the pout of his lips with his tongue, hot breath gusting along Armi's cheek. "You've fucking ruined me for anyone else. I haven't thought about anyone but you since we've been together."

Knowing Hayden hadn't been with another man stunned him. "I-I didn't know."

"Me either." Hayden brushed his lips to Armi's. "But now that I do..." He covered Armi's mouth and plunged his tongue between his lips.

"*Mmm*," Armi hummed with pleasure as they sucked and teased and played. Their rigid cocks brushed together, adding to the electricity playing havoc within him. Hayden transferred his kisses to Armi's neck and ear, sucking and biting until Armi writhed under his touch and moans poured from his lips.

"You like that?" Hayden nipped at his lobe, then licked a wet path from the curve of his neck to the tips of his aching nipples. "And that?"

"Yessss, God," he groaned, and Hayden's lips brushed his.

"You're so gorgeous when you're turned-on, baby."

Armi's dick pulsed out precome at Hayden's words, and he grasped himself. "Fuck me already."

"Uh-uh. We have a whole weekend, and I'm not rushing anything." Hayden put two fingers to Armi's lips. "Suck," he demanded.

Armi snaked his tongue around them, shivering at Hayden's knee between his thighs, pushing him open. Hayden's fingers breached his hole and Armi panted, digging his heels in, trying to take in more of him.

"Not enough. Need everything."

"I know, baby. Just gotta get you ready for me." Hayden kissed him over and over as his fingers moved. "Can't wait to get in you." When he withdrew, Armi cried out.

"No." He was aching and empty again.

"Just a minute. Gotta get the stuff." He scrambled off the bed, returning a minute later with condoms and lube. With avid eyes, Armi watched him prepare, wondering when he'd become so desperate and greedy for sex.

Hayden teased his rim for a moment with the head of his dick, watching him. "I could do this all night."

Armi glared. "You're not funny—*ahhh.*"

Hayden thrust up and in him, and all thoughts fled but how to stay like this forever. Stuffed full of Hayden. Hayden began to move, his dick dragging in and out, creating a friction so intense, stars exploded behind his eyes, and Armi grabbed his own aching cock.

"You're sucking me in so deep, I might not be able to leave." Hayden leaned down to kiss his gasping mouth, his words heated, voice smoky with desire. "And I don't want to."

Armi moaned. "Don't. Don't ever stop." His ankles locked behind Hayden, and tremors racked him head to toe as his climax ripped through him.

"I can't." Hayden's movements became harder, hips snapping, thrusts penetrating, and Armi knew he'd never been alive before Hayden touched him. "Fuck, you're everything."

Armi's world narrowed to holding on to Hayden's sweat-slicked shoulders, Hayden's dick pulsing as hot come spilled into the condom. A sense of completion, of belonging, swept over him with Hayden lying on top of him, lips nuzzling his hair.

"Are you all right?" Hayden whispered, and he nodded, still overwhelmed. "You're so special. Do you know that?"

He lifted a shoulder, and Hayden rose. "You don't believe me?"

Armi winced as Hayden slipped from him. He hated the emptiness filling the space where Hayden had been. "It's not you. It's me." He rolled away, but Hayden, who'd left the bed to get rid of the condom, returned to him.

"What do you mean?"

Grateful the dim room hid his blush, Armi cast his gaze to the pillow. "I've never felt special. I've never been enough for anyone—definitely not my father. My mother loves me, and though we've gotten closer, I'm not sure she thinks I have the strength to do the job."

"To hell with the job. I'm talking about this." Hayden drew a finger along his cheek, and Armi's breath stopped. "Yeah. You feel it, and so do I. But you do the same for me."

A faint smile touched Armi's lips. "You're saying it, but I don't believe it."

"You think it's always like this?" Hayden's fingers continued their teasing, and despite being completely wrung out, Armi's nerves leaped to life. "If you do, you're dead wrong. Even now, when I can't think of moving because you wrecked me, I want you again. Being inside you is the home I never had. Holding you is having my arms around the world."

Afraid he would become too emotional, Armi trembled and turned away from Hayden.

Hayden sighed. "I'm sorry."

He blinked hard to see through the hot tears. "Why? What for?"

"I said the wrong thing, didn't I? Too much?"

"No, the exact opposite. You said everything right. I just have to figure out why me. The one no one's ever been interested in before."

"Maybe they didn't look hard enough to see who you really are. Gorgeous, sweet, and so fucking sexy." Hayden smoothed the hair from his face. "Their loss is my gain. You were so busy hiding in your flowers because they couldn't hurt you by talking back. But you can have both. The roses *and* be the owner of the Kings."

"And you?" he dared to ask.

Hayden's smile threatened to overtake his face. "You've already got me. There's no other place I'd rather be than next to you."

CHAPTER TWENTY-ONE

Hayden couldn't sleep. Armi lay beside him, snuggled into his shoulder. Every instinct in him screamed to not let this go further, that it could only end with him getting hurt.

What he'd said was the truth—no one had ever touched him like the man beside him. Whether it was that special, gentle sweetness that cracked Hayden's tough shell or that sexy, newly discovered confidence, Armi Winters had encircled his heart and held it in his hand. But Hayden had no illusions. What did he have to offer a man like Armi? A bank account that grew modestly every two weeks? A past to worry about? No matter what Armi said, Hayden knew the truth.

He rubbed his stinging eyes. This was what he'd feared from the first. Before Armi, there'd never been a problem. Sex hadn't been anything other than *that was fun* and *see you* as he walked away. But not with Armi. Each time left Hayden craving more. Addicting kisses, soft skin he couldn't help but touch, and eyes like the bluest ocean, leaving him drowning in their depths.

He shouldn't have given in to the desire licking through his blood that had him hungering for one more time. Because he could no more walk away from Armi now than he could stop breathing.

"What's wrong?" Eyes blurry with sleep, Armi yawned and rubbed his face. "It's three a.m. Why are you awake?"

"Why are you?" He liked Armi rumpled and rough-voiced next to him in bed.

"Really? We're going to play Twenty Questions in the middle of the night?" Blinking, Armi sat up. "What's on your mind?"

"You." He pushed a hand through his hair. "And what's happening between us."

"Which is what?"

"If I knew, I'd be sleeping." He chuckled, but Armi didn't fall for it. Damn the man, he was too smart.

"Maybe you don't want to think about it."

"You sound like you know."

This time Armi did smile at him. "Well, I was sleeping. And having a nice dream, too."

"You're mixing me up." Frustrated, Hayden glared at Armi, who annoyingly remained unperturbed. "It's not supposed to be like this. We were only going to have a good time."

"We did." Armi shifted closer. "The best time."

That husky tone undid him, and before he knew it, Hayden's hands were in Armi's hair and he was kissing him until he swooned. Armi moaned under him, his rigid dick pushing into Hayden's stomach.

"Can't get enough of you." Hayden panted, his fingers already teasing Armi.

"Me either. Hurry," Armi urged. "Now."

Hayden grabbed the lube and a condom, sheathing himself and slicking up in record time. Inch by glorious inch he eased inside Armi, burying himself fully, but instead of thrusting, he rested and leaned down, capturing Armi's lips in a heart-stopping kiss. The thought of leaving Armi and going back to seeing him date some loser ate away at Hayden's guts. Did he have a right to feel this way? Armi was his boss—and so far out of his league, they were in different solar systems. But Armi's lips were soft, and his sighs of pleasure echoed in the silent room. Hayden couldn't resist asking.

"You want to be with me? Do you really want to be together?"

Armi held him by the nape. Their eyes locked, and Hayden's heart pounded at the intensity of Armi's gaze.

"I thought we already were." Armi nipped his lower lip and tugged. "I don't want this to end after the weekend."

Joy leaped through him, and the gnawing anxiety eased. "I don't either."

"I'm not going anywhere. I want to be with you, Hayden. Only you."

Throwing caution to the wind, Hayden couldn't deny the wildness that sprang up at Armi's touch, and he finally conceded. "I only want you too." He began to move faster and faster, driving into Armi, possession and hunger his companions. "Only you. No one else gets to touch you. No one else can have you. Only me."

"You." Armi's head thrashed on the pillow. "Only you."

Lips clinging, they rolled on the bed, Armi ending on top. Moonlight streamed in through the open curtains, highlighting the naked desire on Armi's face.

"God, you feel so good wrapped around my dick." He palmed Armi's shaft and rubbed him from root to tip while digging the fingers of his other hand into the creamy white skin of his hip. "Hot and tight."

Armi rode him, and Hayden lost himself in the fiery brilliance of Armi's eyes. The sheer force of his climax lifted him off the bed, and he jerked and twitched as Armi squeezed his throbbing cock. Armi followed a minute later, his release spattering across Hayden's abs and chest. He cuddled Armi close, still inside him, and kissed his cheek.

"Mine," he whispered when he could gather his breath to form words. "You're mine."

"Well, that was a day and a half," Hayden joked as they boarded the plane for home. Even though he'd become accustomed to flying private with Boris, he still got a thrill that this was his life. Even more so now because it was with Armi.

They'd spent the weekend working, watching the game in Alabama, then heading to Georgia right after for the game the following afternoon. As he'd suspected, Russell had booked a single room with a king-sized bed at that hotel too. Not wishing to get into a discussion with Armi about it while they were busy with football, once they'd settled in their seats for the flight to Teterboro, Hayden couldn't help but bring it up.

"Are you going to say anything to Russell tomorrow?"

Armi had been gazing out of the window as they sailed past puffy white clouds. He had a strange, almost wistful expression on his face.

"I don't know. He's got a lot more on his mind than the hotel rooms."

Was he really going to make excuses? "I mean...yeah, but it's a broken ankle. He'll heal. What he tried to do to you was wrong on so many levels."

"I know. But does it matter now?"

"Why wouldn't it? He tried to take advantage of you." A question he hadn't thought of sprang to his lips, and before he could think, Hayden blurted it out. "Would he have succeeded?"

Brow furrowed, Armi turned a confused face to him. "What're you talking about?"

"Forget it," he mumbled. "I didn't mean it."

But Armi was persistent. "You did. Do you still think I would've slept with him, that I'm so easily manipulated, I would've done anything he wanted? I thought we settled that."

Tension crackled in the air between them as they stared at each other. Hayden broke the stalemate. "No, I'm not saying that. Really. But I hope now you see how devious he is. He planned this whole seduction thing to get you into bed."

"But I don't want Russell. I want you."

Those three simple words hit him so hard, they left him breathless.

Armi reached out his hand, and Hayden took it. It was all so new to him, this feeling of belonging, of caring for another's emotional well-being as much or even more than his own. Knowing how kind and nonconfrontational Armi was, how he didn't like hurting anyone, Hayden was ready to step in and guard Armi from abuse.

"I want you too."

Armi's smile lit his face. "Then there's nothing to worry about."

Hayden knew that was being overly optimistic. He needed to be on guard at so many levels–his past, Russell's manipulations, and Armi, who remained frustratingly optimistic and generous with his time and heart. Hayden was happy to play the watchdog.

Once they landed and were in the car on the way home, Armi seemed nervous. "Uh, do you want to stay the night? With me, I mean?"

Damn, he was sweet. "As much as I'd love to, I need to go home. I don't have clothes to wear. I can't show up to the office in shorts and a T-shirt." He leaned in close to kiss Armi. "But ask me another time, and I'll be prepared."

"You can come anytime."

He grinned. "Only with you."

With a roll of his eyes, Armi groaned. "God, that was bad." The car stopped in front of his apartment, and he kissed Armi again.

"I'm going to miss sleeping with you tonight. I like having you next to me."

"I like it too."

The trunk slammed shut. "I'd better go so your driver doesn't have to wait. See you tomorrow."

"Yeah."

Another quick brush of their lips, and he left Armi. He stood on the sidewalk, watching the car roll away. It had taken every bit of his strength not to agree to stay, but he needed some space to process the weekend.

Or so he thought, because he'd only had time to walk inside his apartment and set his mail and keys on the counter when his mother called.

"Hi, Mom." He shuffled through the advertisements and was grateful he'd moved all his other accounts to online billing. He was also starving, since he hadn't eaten anything on the plane but a couple of cheese cubes, so he opened his laptop and ordered sushi. "What's up?"

"I'm putting you on speaker so your father can listen too. You haven't called in a while. We've missed you."

"Ah, sorry. Things have been crazy." Guilty, he sat and put the laptop aside. "I was away for the weekend."

"Business or pleasure?"

His lips twitched. The pleasure had sure outweighed the business. "Both. I went with my boss to scout college players."

His father laughed. "No offense, Hayden, but what do you know about football?"

I know a tight end, and Armi's got the best.

Of course, he couldn't say that out loud. "I was there to help Armi by taking notes on everything the scout said. He needed me there, so of course I went."

"So the job's working out? You're enjoying it?"

"Yeah. I really am."

"And the benefits are good?" his father asked.

You have no idea.

"Uh, yeah. They're very generous."

"That's good. I'm glad you landed on your feet. We know how tight the job market is, especially in New York, and how expensive it is to live there." His mother's worry always triggered guilt over what he'd put them through.

"It's fine. It worked out. You don't have to worry about me. I'm thirty-seven. I'm not going to make the mistakes I made at seventeen."

"Who said you were? But news flash, sweetheart. We're never going to stop worrying about you. We're your parents." His mother sniffled. "All we want is for you to be happy."

Having seen how Armi's father had destroyed his self-confidence, Hayden knew he was so damn lucky to have them in his life. "I am, I promise. I have my apartment, and a new job that's working out. What more could I want?"

"Someone to share it all with?"

That hopeful note in her voice caught him in a weak moment, or maybe it was the lack of sleep from the weekend, but he slipped. "Maybe I've got that covered too."

"You do? You're seeing someone? Who? Who?"

"Are you my mother or an owl?" he joked. "Seriously, though, it's new. I don't really know how it's going to play out." Not the truth because Armi was his and no one else was going to have him. When he'd turned into this overprotective, possessive person, Hayden had no idea, but that's the way it was.

"But this is the first time you've told us about someone. So he must be special."

In the mirror he caught himself wearing a dopey smile, but he didn't care. "Yeah. He is. Totally not the type I thought I'd ever be attracted to, but I think that's the way it goes in our family."

"Very funny," his mother said, and his father laughed.

"You're correct, my boy. But your mother has held my heart for close to forty years, so I'm thinking it was the right move on my part. So is this like father, like son?"

"Could be." The buzzer sounded. "My dinner's here. I gotta go."

"We'd love to meet him. Maybe we can come for a visit."

"Sure, come visit anytime. Talk to you soon." He ended the call and hit the buzzer. The doorbell rang, and he opened the door to see a grinning Armi standing there, holding a delivery bag and his duffel.

"Dinner?"

His jaw dropped. "What? Is that my sushi?"

Armi held out the bag, and Hayden took it. "Yeah. I told the guy I was going to your apartment and gave him a fifty, so he was happy to let me personally deliver it."

"Uh, come in." Armi passed by him and sat at one of the barstools by his countertop that doubled as an island and his table. He'd changed from the plane, and his damp hair curled at his neck. He smelled and looked fucking delicious, and Hayden's defenses, already weakened, crumbled. "I can't believe you're here." Hayden set the bag down and leaned on the counter, looking at Armi, who flashed him a nervous smile and blushed.

"I got home and showered and thought it was stupid, you being here and me in my big house alone." He clasped his hands. "I hope...you don't mind. Do you?"

The man was too adorable. "You're kidding, right? I was just going to eat my dinner while typing up the notes I took over the weekend for you."

Armi frowned. "You shouldn't be constantly working. Dinner is for eating, not working."

As Armi spoke, Hayden unpacked the food. "I have three rolls here. We can share. And I don't mind. I always work during dinner."

"Even when I'm here?" A tiny grin curved Armi's lips. "Are you sure?"

"Mr. Winters, are you flirting with me?" Hayden slipped his arms around Armi. He bent to kiss Armi by his ear, loving the sharp intake of breath.

"Would you mind if I was?"

"Does it look like I mind?" Hayden continued kissing him, and Armi hummed his appreciation, arching into his touch like a contented cat. "I like it. A lot."

"Sooo, do you still have to work through dinner?" Armi toyed with the chopsticks. "Or is there any way I can talk you out of it?"

He picked up his chopsticks and the tray of sushi. "Come. I watched a show where someone ate sushi off a naked person." Armi turned bright red, but Hayden didn't miss the spark in his eyes. Hand in hand, they walked into the bedroom.

CHAPTER TWENTY-TWO

Russell didn't come in for the entire week, and while at first Armi struggled at meetings to make his voice heard, with the help of Hayden's superior notes and studying every night together, his confidence grew every day. He'd never been happier—coming home to eat dinner, working side by side in the greenhouse and garden with Hayden asking questions and even helping him. He'd never dared to dream of a future before, but he couldn't deny watching it unfold in front of his eyes.

"Look at this." iPad in hand, Hayden walked into his office at close to five p.m. on Friday. "That article in *Out in Sports* just released." His eyes twinkled. "You made the cover. See how hot you are?"

Armi rolled his eyes. "Oh, for God's sake. You're just saying that because...you know..." His face grew hot.

Hayden closed the door behind him and put the tablet on the desk. "Because you are?" He hesitated. "Gorgeous and sexy and insanely hot. And all mine."

Then why did it feel like all this was a dream? "I like hearing that. I've really enjoyed being with you every night, even if you do leave in the morning without me."

"You know why."

"Yeah, but I wish you didn't have to," Armi challenged him.

Unfazed, Hayden leaned against the desk. "You're cute when you pout," he teased.

"Stay with me this weekend? Please?" Having Hayden in his house would be the bow on the present of the week they'd shared since coming home from the scouting trip.

Hayden's eyes dimmed. "I can't. I haven't been home the whole week. I have mail and dry cleaning to pick up, and I have to check out what died in my fridge."

"Okay, so go tonight after work, and then you can come home to mine."

Hayden cocked his head. "Or you could stay at my place. Would you mind?"

Puzzled, Armi felt as if it were some kind of test. "Why would I mind? I don't care where we stay. I want to be with you. But it sounds like you might have a problem with that?"

Hayden pointed to the ringing phone. "I have to get that. We can talk later." He picked up the receiver. "Armand Winters's office. How may I help you?...Oh, yes, Mr. Anders. He's right here. One moment, please." His pushed the hold button. "It's Russell. I think you need to confront him on his little plan that failed."

"I know I do," Armi scowled. "But I want to do it in person, not on the phone. Maybe I'll go visit him, and then after, stop by my house to pick up clothes for the weekend. Meet you at your apartment. How does that sound?"

"Sounds good. I'll leave you to your call." Hayden walked out.

Armi picked up the receiver. "Russell?"

"What's going on? Why are you screening my calls?"

"I'm not. That's part of Hayden's job—to answer my phone. How are you feeling?"

"Like shit. I thought I'd have seen you by now."

"I was planning on coming over this afternoon, if that's okay. I want to talk to you about some things."

"About time. It's been a whole week," Russell grumbled. "I saw the scouting reports. Those two kids might have some promise."

That reluctant approval was about what Armi expected. "Yeah. I'm going to leave now. I should be there in less than half an hour, depending on crosstown traffic." Russell lived in a pretty town house on the Upper West Side. "Can I bring you anything?" It must be hard for an active man like Russell to be alone and laid up.

"Lucy has me covered. You'll stay for dinner. We can talk then."

It sounded like a command rather than a question. "Uh, I'm sorry. I have plans."

"Plans? Like a date?"

"Russell, I have to go. There's someone here to see me. Be there soon."

He hung up and pulled up the article from *Out in Sports*. He was less concerned about how he was portrayed than if Hayden was mistreated. He read through it twice and called Hayden. "Could you come here, please?"

Hayden opened his door. "Something wrong?"

"Did you read the article? The *Out in Sports* one."

"Not the whole thing. I've been doing the weekly reports."

"There was no mention of you. And it was pretty favorable to me. I mean, a little of the what-does-he-know-about-football nonsense, but on the whole, it was positive."

"Really?" To say Hayden looked relieved was an understatement.

"Yeah, really. I think both of you have gone on to have productive lives. Mistakes happen. You're not that desperate seventeen-year-old kid anymore. We all grow and learn to move on."

Hayden left his chair and kneeled by his side. "Don't ever think about changing who you are for me. I like you exactly the way you are."

The air between them sizzled, and pressure built inside him to say what had been tumbling around in his chest. He'd never imagined he'd be in this position, but he couldn't do it in the office. Hayden deserved so much more. Armi swore he could feel the blood beating in his veins.

"I'd better go. I'm seeing Russell, and then I'll come to you."

Armi gathered his things and closed down his computer. He waved good-bye to Hayden, who was typing away and on the phone with the press office, checking quotes on the article they were planning to promote. In the car, he contemplated how to handle Russell, deciding to face the problem head on. The housekeeper let him into Russell's home. "Mr. Anders is in the library."

Armi smiled at her. "I know the way, thank you."

The house was a testament to Russell's life in football—memorabilia in every room and photographs of him as a college player and pro. Armi recognized his father in many of the pictures. Several large-screen televisions took up wall space, and Armi knew his father would often spend afternoons or evenings here, watching tapes of the games. He could count on one hand the number of times his father had invited him to join them.

Russell reclined in a club chair with his leg raised and crutches by his side.

"Damn ankle," he groused. "Have a seat. You want a drink?" He tipped his head to the array of bottles and glasses.

"No, thanks, I'm fine. Do you want anything?"

"Scotch. There's ice in the bucket."

He fixed the drink and handed Russell the tumbler. "How're you feeling?" Reflexively he winced as Russell, in obvious discomfort, shifted in his chair. "Can I get you a pillow or something?"

"No. Tell me about the weekend."

Heart pounding, Armi sat opposite him and crossed his arms. Confrontation wasn't in his DNA, but Hayden was right. If Russell had planned on seducing him, he deserved an answer.

"No, first I think you have something to tell me. Don't you?" Meeting Russell's eyes, Armi had expected some kind of remorse or apology. Instead, Russell remained unconcerned.

"What?"

"You've got to be kidding me. Are you going to play dumb?" It was a struggle to keep his temper. "You booked us one room. One bed. What was that about?"

A slight smile tugged at Russell's lips. "Surprised? I've watched you for years. Could never do anything about it because of Randolph."

"You're...gay?" He'd gotten the vibes right, but hearing Russell—whom he'd known all his life—say it still sent shockwaves through him.

"I'm bisexual. I figured the weekend would've been perfect for us to explore the attraction."

Armi didn't know whether to be flattered or annoyed as hell at Russell's presumptuousness. "So let me get this straight. You figured we'd hook up over the weekend—that because we'd share a bed, I'd be open to fucking you?"

Russell's eyes gleamed. "Oh, no. I do the fucking. Trust me, you'd be begging for it."

His face burned. "I can't believe this."

Russell leaned forward, his face urgent, his voice soothing. "Come on. You can't tell me you didn't notice things were different between us in the office since your father's been gone."

"You were helping me get on my feet with the team. At least that's what I thought."

"I was—still am. Think of it. You and me running the Kings...it's perfect."

A sudden thought came to Armi. "And you would've come out? To the team and the league?"

Russell blinked. "What? No, of course not." His smile turned slightly feral. "Just you and I would know. There's something to be said about secret relationships. Makes it hotter. Tell me you haven't thought about it. You and me. Together."

Armi's stomach turned. He needed to leave. "No. I haven't. Sorry. I'm not attracted to you. But I know what this is all about. It's the team, isn't it? That's all it's ever been for you and my father. You think by getting me into bed, you could influence how the team is run. And soon you'd be running it completely. Tell me, did you think I'd sign my ownership over to you?"

The lunch in the restaurant with Martin Price came to mind, and he recalled Russell being there.

"You talked to Martin Price after my lunch with him, didn't you? You wanted him to write a hit piece on me. It was you. You were the one sabotaging me all along."

It shocked him to the core that Russell wasn't in the least fazed by his question and had no shame. "Come on, Armand. What did you expect? You have no idea what you're doing. Randolph never meant for you to inherit full ownership. Sure, you'd get some percentage of the Kings, but he wanted me to have the majority share and run it. I'm the logical choice."

"So you figured to get both—me and the team."

"A win-win."

Russell's snide tone disgusted him, and Armi couldn't wait to get the hell away. He rose. "You're the loser this time. Because you don't have me, and you'll never own the team. You know what's funny? At one point I was thinking it was all too much and maybe you should take over. Then Hayden told me to prove everyone wrong and show what I could do."

Russell snorted. "That little bitch?"

"He's more of a man than you'll ever be." Armi regretted the words the moment they came out of his mouth. The last thing he wanted was to give Russell any ammunition against Hayden.

Russell's eyes lit up. "You two are fucking, aren't you? I knew it. He's been sniffing around you since he first got here."

"Don't be ridiculous. Hayden is a professional." But his face grew hot, and he damned his lack of self-control and how easily he blushed.

"He went with you this weekend. Is that who replaced me in the bed?"

Armi lifted his chin. "I don't have to explain anything to you. I hope you heal quickly. I have to go."

Later on, in Hayden's apartment, they lay on the couch, and Hayden fumed when Armi relayed the conversation. "That bastard. I knew it. From the first I didn't trust him. He wants the team, and he figured he'd get it through you." As if realizing what he'd said, Hayden stopped ranting. "I didn't mean that he couldn't want you anyway. You know that." He sat up and pulled Armi close. "I'd want you even if you had nothing."

Armi cupped Hayden's cheek and brushed their lips together, loving how Hayden's breath grew short at his touch. "If I have you, I have everything."

For a second, Hayden rested his brow to Armi's. "I never meant for this to happen."

Armi didn't speak—he couldn't. Hayden's damp hair hung over his brow, and Armi pushed away the strands to see his eyes. They stared back at him, full of longing and disbelief. As if they held a secret he was on the verge of revealing. Armi traced the generous pout of his lips, the cut of his cheekbone, then lightly trailed his fingers down Hayden's neck to follow the patterns of all the tattoos on his shoulders and biceps. Hayden's chest rose and fell rapidly, and Armi moistened his lips.

"You're so beautiful." Armi pressed his lips to the curve of Hayden's shoulder, licking a path along his collarbone. Hayden sighed, his dick hardening, and Armi continued, teasing the tight point of his nipples poking through the thin fabric of his shirt. Armi hiked up the shirt to reach his bare skin, while rubbing the bulge at Hayden's crotch.

"Fuck, that feels so good. Harder."

"Not so fast." Armi kept up a steady but light motion on Hayden's dick until he squirmed.

"Goddammit, more." Hayden moaned. "Need you."

Armi slid his fingers past the elastic waistband to grip Hayden's straining cock. The smell of Hayden's desire rose around them, sending Armi spinning into a lust-filled haze. He started to inch the shorts past Hayden's hips, when the buzzer from downstairs sounded.

"Fuck it. I'm sure it's nothing." Hayden lifted his hips. "Suck me. I need your mouth on my dick."

Armi pulled the shorts to Hayden's knees, his hungry gaze latched on to the sticky, leaking head of Hayden's erection. The buzzer had stopped ringing, but Hayden's cell phone vibrated over and over.

Hayden flopped back on the couch. "Shit. I have to get that. It won't take long. Get naked."

Armi shucked his shorts and pulled up his shirt, but he heard Hayden's panicked voice and stopped.

"Mom?... What?... Here? Now?... You're in the elevator?"

Reversing course, Armi frantically pulled on his clothes with fumbling fingers.

"Okay. Yeah. Be right there."

"Someone let them into the building." Hayden fixed his shorts. "Nothing like hearing your mother's voice to drive all thoughts of sex out of your mind." With a rueful smile, he pressed his hand to his rapidly softening cock. "We'll have to wait until later."

A little shaky, Armi smoothed his hair. "Do I look okay? I've never met anyone's parents before."

Hayden kissed him. "You're perfect. My parents will love you."

Armi wasn't so sure why that would be the case. His own father barely acknowledged he existed.

CHAPTER TWENTY-THREE

He loved his parents.

Really.

But why now?

The doorbell rang.

Hayden brushed his hair back, checked that he'd gotten himself under control, and counted to five.

"Hi, you two. How come you didn't let me know you were coming?"

His mother kissed his cheek. "Well, you did say come visit anytime, and since it's been so long…oh." She spotted Armi, and Hayden watched her face light up. "Hi. I'm Nikki."

Armi darted a glance his way, then held out a hand. "H-hi, I'm Armi."

"Armi Winters? Hayden's boss?" His father extended a hand. "Hi, I'm Jim."

"Hello, sir." They shook.

Hayden had stepped over to Armi's side, knowing how nervous he must be, and received a grateful smile. "So yes. When I told you I was seeing someone, it was Armi."

His father sat on the couch. "You were so adamant about not getting involved with your boss. What happened?"

"I don't know, Dad. I guess you can't stop what feels right. I know I said it was a bad idea, but nothing that feels so right could be wrong."

His mother waved a hand in the air. "We should all chat and get to know each other. Obviously, Armi is important to Hayden. He's never introduced us to any other man."

His hand in Armi's, they sat together. "He is. Very important. I never planned this, and Armi and I talked about it. We tried not to follow through on our feelings, but it just didn't work out that way."

"So far, we've only heard from you, Hayden. Armi? What do you have to say?" his father asked. He and his father had always been extremely close, and Hayden knew he was acting out of love, but at the moment his main concern was Armi's state of mind. Only he truly knew the extent of Armi's hurt over the cold and tense relationship with his father and how that affected him in his everyday life.

"Maybe we should—"

"No. It's fine," Armi cut him off, quietly but firmly. "I've never been in a real relationship, mainly because I didn't think I was good enough for anyone to want. It's what happens when you grow up with a father who constantly belittles you and makes you feel less than."

His eyes met Hayden's, who was cut to the core by the fierceness of his gaze. "From the first time I met Hayden, he made me feel equal. Important. Like what I have to say matters."

"It does," Hayden said softly and squeezed his hand. "You matter."

"And I know you might be concerned that I'm his boss and very wealthy, but all the money has done for me is make me less secure that someone could want me for who I am. Hayden didn't know who I was the first time we met, and that made me trust him, which isn't easy."

"Why?" his mother questioned, her eyes brimming with sympathy. Hayden could see she was touched by Armi's words and wanted to hug him.

Armi clasped his hands. "Like Hayden, I've never had a boyfriend, but not for the same reason. No one's ever been interested to find out who I really was. Except Hayden."

"That's very sweet. And I'm sorry you had a tense relationship with your father." His mother reached out and gave Armi a pat. "Just to warn you, we're not like that. The opposite, in fact."

Hayden took advantage of the goodwill between them. "What my mother isn't saying is she likes to be involved. Expect phone calls and visits. She has a need to know."

Armi's smile was shy and sweet. "I think that's nice. I wouldn't mind. I love my mother, but she's always been busy with her charity work and friends. I didn't see her much when I was growing up, but we're trying harder now."

Unwilling for Armi to get dragged under by unpleasant thoughts, Hayden slipped an arm around his waist. "Why don't we go out to dinner?"

"First we have to find a hotel and make a reservation, but sure." His father took out his phone. "We should be able to find something nearby, don't you think?"

While his father checked for reservations on his phone and his mother used the bathroom, Armi whispered in his ear, "I think your parents should stay here, and you come home with me."

Hayden grinned. "You do, huh?"

Armi's smile was unexpectedly wicked, and Hayden wished he could drag him into the bedroom and finish what they'd started earlier. He was outrageously delicious, and Hayden was crazy about him.

"It makes the most sense. I know you wanted to stay here, so the other alternative is to give your parents the bedroom, and we stay out here."

Alarmed, Hayden shook his head firmly. "Oh, hell no. I can't spend the night next to you without being inside you. I need to hold you."

"Then come home with me. We can do whatever you want with them—breakfast, lunch, dinner, museums...I can get tickets to a Broadway show if there's a play they wanted to see."

"Dad," Hayden called out, and his father glanced up from his phone. "Forget it. Armi has a better idea."

They had a great dinner at an incredible Michelin-starred restaurant, where his parents were impressed by not only the name, but the fact that the owner himself came out to greet them.

"My mother is a favorite and frequent guest," Armi explained, and Hayden could see his parents were touched by the personal service they received. After they finished their dinners, they sat with their cappuccinos and dessert.

"We don't do this every night, in case you were wondering," Hayden explained. "Most nights we order in sushi or salads."

"It was very nice of Armi to go to all the trouble," his mother said. "We may be from upstate, but we know about restaurants like this, and we never imagined eating here."

"My pleasure. If you want to see a show, let me know, and I'll see about getting tickets."

"We'd rather spend time with the two of you," she stated with a nod toward his father, and Hayden chuckled.

"That I could've figured. Breakfast tomorrow around ten at Armi's? Does that sound good?"

"It does, but can I make a request?" his mother asked.

"Sure, anything." Armi looked to him, but he shrugged.

"Not a clue."

"I'd like to make my special breakfast. It was always Hayden's favorite when he was little, and I don't get to have us all together that much anymore."

"Say yes, Armi." He sighed and rubbed his stomach. "My mom makes the best bananas foster French toast and candied bacon." Hayden groaned. "Oh God, I thought I was full, but just thinking about it, I'm already hungry for it."

"Who could say no to that?" Armi joked. "Of course. Tell me what you'll need, and I'll make sure to have it for you."

While Armi paid the bill, Hayden called a car for his parents.

"He's adorable. And so sweet. You couldn't have found someone better to love you."

"What? Who said anything about love?"

A snort of laughter escaped her. "Oh, sweetheart. You're cute." She patted his cheek and kissed him. "We'll see you in the morning."

Armi returned, and his mother hugged him tight. "Thank you so much for tonight. This was the best dinner, and we're so happy you're with Hayden."

His father squeezed Armi's shoulder. "It was terrific, thank you. And I agree with my wife. I had some reservations in the beginning, but I can see you're a good man, and that's all we want for our son."

"I'm happy you enjoyed it. I had a really great time getting to know you."

"And don't be late for breakfast. I'm still thinking about the French toast and bacon." Hayden licked his lips.

"Oh, you." His mother nudged him as the car drew up. "Go home and kiss your boyfriend."

He blinked and kissed her cheek, then hugged his father. "Thank you," he whispered.

Side by side, he and Armi watched the car pull away. He took Armi's hand and laced their fingers together. "That's the first time anyone said out loud that you're my boyfriend."

The second car drove up, and he and Armi slid in. "How do you feel about it?"

Hayden pulled Armi by the tie and kissed him firmly on the mouth. "I like it. I like it a lot."

Inside Armi's town house, he pushed the suit jacket off Armi's shoulders and undid his tie, all while they were frantically kissing.

"I was dying during dinner. I want you so much," Hayden rasped, his hands flicking open the buttons of his shirt. Armi mimicked him, and soon they were naked and still in the entrance hall.

"I can't wait." Armi pressed kisses to his chest and neck.

"If we don't get upstairs now, I'm gonna fuck you right here. Against the front door. People might hear you scream for me when they walk by."

Wild-eyed, Armi licked his lips. "Do it."

His cock jerked.

"I have to get the–"

"No. Do it bare. Fuck me bare." Armi gripped his own dick, and Hayden was mesmerized by his hand moving up and down the thick, reddened shaft. "I need to feel you, Hayden. All of you. Skin to skin. Heart to heart."

"I-I've never done it that way," he confessed, but the thought of nothing between him and Armi was blowing his mind, and his cock ached with need. "I have no lube. I don't want to hurt you."

"There's some in the living room, remember? From the other night?"

They'd been watching reels of Kings games on the couch for hours, and he'd decided Armi needed a break, so he'd sucked him off, then fucked him on the couch.

"Yeah." He swooped in and gave Armi a hard kiss. "I'll go get it."

He grabbed the bottle and ran back to him, skidding to a stop. "Face the door," he commanded, and Armi did as told, his legs at a wide stance.

Hayden had every intention of keeping his promise and taking Armi hard and fast up against the door, but now seeing him, so beautifully open and ready, he wanted it to last.

His hands smoothed over Armi's white ass cheeks and spread them open. Armi shivered.

"What're you—*ahhhhh*," he moaned as Hayden licked a wet path around his hole. "Fuck, oh God, Hayden. *Hayden*," he cried out but stuck his ass into Hayden's face. "Please," he panted, shamelessly begging for more.

"*Mmm...*" Hayden licked the rim, then speared in past the tight ring. Feeling Armi go wild under his tongue, hearing him groan with pleasure, had him working harder and faster. "You love getting eaten, don't you? Love my wet tongue shoved up in you?" Armi twitched and shook, his hand moving fast on his erection.

Hayden's dick throbbed and leaked, and with one last suck to Armi's hole, he stood and stuck two slick fingers where his tongue had been. He worked them in and out for a minute, then with his shaft lubed and ready, he nudged past the opening and filled Armi in one hard thrust.

"Fuck, oh fuck," Armi screamed and stiffened, his come spraying the door. Hayden caught him by the waist, hips snapping rhythmically as he pounded into him.

"Mine. You're mine. Aren't you?" He licked Armi's ear and bit the lobe, loving how he quivered and whimpered in his arms. "Say it. Tell me."

"Yours, I'm yours. Always. Forever."

Hearing that, Hayden thrust deeper, pinning Armi under him as his orgasm roared through him. "I love you. I love you." Hayden pressed gentle kisses to Armi's neck. "And I'm yours."

Armi stiffened at his words and turned his head. "What?"

Wishing he could stay this way forever, Hayden placed a messy kiss on the corner of Armi's full and trembling lips. "I said I'm yours."

"Before that." Armi's lips tugged up, and unable to resist, Hayden kissed him.

Reluctant to leave the warm clasp of Armi's passage, he slowly eased out, not caring that he was a sweat-and-come-soaked mess. He needed to see Armi's face when he spoke those words.

Hand to Armi's shoulder, he turned him around. "I. Love. You. I've never said those words to anyone. Never thought I would."

Armi's blue eyes glittered and filled. "I can't believe I'm hearing them. You love me?"

"Baby, why are you crying?" Hayden kissed the teardrops off his lashes. "Of course I do. Why do you sound so surprised?"

Armi buried his face in Hayden's shoulder, and he held him tight, feeling Armi's heart beat a rapid tempo. "I didn't think I'd find anyone who'd want me. The way I am. Clumsy, awkward Armi who was always picked last for everything."

"I pick you first for my heart." Hayden pressed his cheek to Armi's wet one, soaking in Armi's heat, wrapping himself in the man's sweetness. "Is that corny? Yeah. Do I give a fuck? No. Finding you that first night was the luckiest thing to ever happen to me."

"For me too. I never thought a beautiful man like you would be interested in someone like me."

"Someone like you—kind and loving, good-hearted and always thinking of others? I'm the damn lucky one."

Shiny-eyed, Armi tugged at his bottom lip before covering his mouth in a heated kiss he'd remember forever. "You are the one. You give me strength. Self-worth. You accepted me and didn't try and change me. The only one who's ever stood up for me. I think I fell in love with you that first day you came to the office and got in Jacob Whitmore's face to defend me."

Hayden nibbled on his neck and cupped Armi's ass. "That was fun. And I'll do it over and over if anyone ever messes with you again, but I don't think I'll need to."

"Why? He's never going to change." Armi's scrunched up face was so adorable, Hayden couldn't help kissing the tip of his nose.

"Yeah, but you have. Don't you know how strong you are?" He squeezed Armi's ass. "Let's go take a shower and go to bed. I'm not finished with you yet."

They picked up their discarded clothing, and hand in hand walked up the stairs.

CHAPTER TWENTY-FOUR

It had been the most perfect weekend he could remember. For the first time, Armi walked through the city as part of a family. Saturday, they'd strolled through Central Park and the zoo, stopping for pretzels from the cart, and then they'd taken a car downtown to the 9/11 Memorial. Later, for fun, they'd ridden the Staten Island Ferry to get a close-up of the Statue of Liberty, walked across the Brooklyn Bridge, and had pizza. At times, he and Hayden had walked hand in hand—another milestone for him—or he'd talk to Jim about the Kings and what he hoped to accomplish, and Nikki had wanted to know all about how he'd started raising roses.

After dropping Nikki and Jim at Hayden's apartment to rest up before dinner, they headed back to the town house so they could shower and get ready. Like the previous evening, he wanted to call in a favor and get them a seat at a coveted restaurant. "We can go to one of the best in the city—Carbone. I want to make the weekend special."

Hayden, who'd showered first, lay on the bed but sat up quickly. "You don't have to do this."

"Do what?" He stripped off his sweaty clothes.

"Take my parents to all these expensive restaurants. They're just happy to be here with us. I bet they'd be happy if we just ordered in sushi. They have no good places upstate close by."

Armi shrugged. "I want to make a good impression." He walked to the bathroom and turned on the shower, letting the water rain down on him. A few seconds later, Hayden opened the door and joined him. He put his arms around Armi and held him tight.

"I don't mean to make you feel bad, but you don't need to spend all that money to make them like you. They love you because you're a good person with a kind heart." Hayden's kiss was warm and soft, and Armi clung to him. "And I love you because you're all that, plus you turn me on like no one else."

"I've had such a great time with them, I just wanted to make sure they knew the weekend was special."

"They do. They don't need fancy dinners to know you care. And all I need is you."

Armi kissed him. "Sushi it is."

Sunday was a stay-at-home family day, and Armi loved every minute of it.

He and Jim did the crossword puzzle, while Hayden sat next to him, playing with the hair that curled at the base of his neck. Contentment spread through him whenever Hayden's fingers brushed his skin, and every once in a while, they'd catch each other's eye and smile. But—and no offense to Hayden, who knew this—the best part of the day was spending time with Nikki in the greenhouse and yard. Armi knew Hayden was interested in his roses, but Nikki shared his passion, and she'd been thrilled to help him with his latest grafting project. It had taken the better part of two hours, but in the end, he was satisfied with the result.

He stripped off his gardening gloves. "If it takes, I'm going to call it the Nikki rose."

Big green eyes, so like Hayden's, grew wide, and beamed bright. "That would be amazing. Will you send me pictures if and when it takes? I'd love to see how it grows." They walked outside to the garden, and she bent to smell the different flowers. "My blooms never get this big or smell sweet like these."

"I'm going to send you home with a list of things I use and some samples of special fertilizers and treatments for black spot, fungus, and other diseases that specifically affect roses."

"Thank you so much." Nikki wandered some more, stopping at each bush, then with determination in her step, strode over to him. "I'm very happy you and Hayden are together. I think you're wonderful, Armi. And I see how you and Hayden look at each other, and know that you care about him."

"Uh, y-yes. I d-do. A lot."

"Hayden's always felt he must do everything on his own and be the strong one. We just want him to be happy."

Never having dated or met anyone's parents, Armi wasn't sure how to answer her, but decided to speak from his heart. "Nikki, I can honestly say that meeting Hayden changed my life. And I'm going to always try to make him as happy as he makes me, but I'm not sure that's possible."

Apparently, that was a good answer, because she hugged him. "I think it is. Let's go inside, and you can show me the rest of the house. It's beautiful." She hooked her arm through his, but he held back.

"Can I get your opinion on something?"

"Of course."

It had been weighing on his mind for several days, and Armi figured Nikki was the perfect person to tell him if he was doing the right thing.

"I, uh, was thinking of asking Hayden to move in with me. I'm here all alone in the house, and I know he's got his apartment, but we're together all the time now..." He chewed his bottom lip.

"It hasn't been that long, has it?" Her brow furrowed. "Only a few weeks or so?"

Face flaming because there was no way in hell he'd ever tell her he and Hayden had hooked up that first night, he ducked his head. "Well, uh...not really. It's been longer than that." He wanted to be truthful. "I've liked Hayden from the first time I met him, and the feeling has only gotten stronger."

She took his hand in hers and squeezed it. "I understand. It was the same when Jim and I met. But maybe...take it a little slower? Give it a bit more time?" She paused, and Armi sensed she was choosing her words with deliberation. She didn't know Hayden had revealed his past to him. "I'm sure there are things you both need to learn about each other."

Armi appreciated her wanting to protect Hayden, and though they'd only just met, Armi felt a special closeness with her. "I understand. We're not kids, and both of us come with baggage."

"Everyone does, but the trick is to find that one special person you want by your side for a lifetime of adventures. They can help you carry the load." She hugged him again. "Let's go inside. I bet those two are hungry. I know I am."

The sun came out, and the roses nodded in the light breeze, as if in agreement with what Nikki said. In the family room, Hayden and his father were talking about the latest innovations in computers. His heart squeezed tight, envying their shared laughter and the easy friendship and love. Something he'd always wished for with his own father but never had. And never would.

Hayden met his eyes, and as if sensing Armi's thoughts, spoke a few words to his father and crossed the room to join him. "Everything all right?"

No way would Armi ruin their good time with depressing thoughts about his relationship with his parents. "Absolutely. Your mom and I were in the garden. I'm going to send her some rosebushes, but she doesn't know it yet."

"She'll love them." Hayden slipped an arm around his waist. "And after they leave, you can tell me what's bothering you."

It was harder saying good-bye to Hayden's parents later that afternoon than waving off his mother for her yearly six-month trip to Europe for the fashion shows. He gave Jim some of his father's collectible memorabilia—signed jerseys from Hall of Famers and a Joe Montana personalized football.

"These are very valuable." Jim regarded everything as if they were fragile works of art. "Are you sure you want to give them away?"

"I think you'll appreciate them more than I ever could. And don't forget you're going to come to the season opener with us."

"Thanks, Armi. This is incredible. I'll treasure them."

Nikki held the bag of garden goodies he'd given her, and he whispered in her ear, "I hope you have room in your garden for some more rosebushes. I'm having half a dozen sent to your home tomorrow."

"Armi." She squealed with delight and flung her arms around his neck. "That's the sweetest thing anyone's ever done for me."

"Hey," Jim protested good-naturedly, and they all laughed when Nikki blew him a kiss.

"I heard you like to enter your roses in some local contests, so you'll have to let me know if they win."

"If?" Nikki scoffed. "You mean when." She kissed him again. "Thank you."

He'd arranged for them to travel home by car, and he watched them both hug Hayden tight before climbing into the back seat. The limo drove away, and Hayden put an arm over his shoulder.

"I think you're now the favorite son."

Armi laughed. "Don't be ridiculous." He leaned into Hayden's chest. "You're so lucky to have parents who love you."

Hayden kissed his neck. "Let's go inside. It's a workday tomorrow, and I have things to go over tonight."

They stopped by the kitchen to pick up some beers, then settled on the couch in the family room. "You're going to go to your apartment now?"

"Yeah, why?"

Armi sighed and drank some more of his beer. "Just that we had a great weekend, didn't we?"

Hayden smiled. "The best. I can't thank you enough for everything you did for my parents." His foot traveled up Armi's shin. "They love you."

"I think they're wonderful."

"Did being together all weekend upset you? You were a little quiet earlier. Is it because of your father?"

"It shouldn't bother me, right?" Armi picked at the label of the beer bottle. "I mean, I'm almost forty, and he's gone. He and I never had that closeness you have with your parents. And my mother...yes, she loves me, and we're fine together."

Hayden frowned. "I thought you were close. The two of you had a nice lunch together."

"She and I have a good relationship. Now. Growing up...she wasn't around much. Besides, I have no desire to dump all my problems on her. She's helped me with some of the issues with the team, but I can't run everything past my mommy, and I don't want to."

"You're hot when you get riled up," Hayden teased, then grew serious. "I'm sorry you never had support when you were young. But these past few weeks I've come to realize something about you."

Armi hung his head. "Yeah? What's that?"

"Look at me," Hayden commanded, and Armi was surprised to see Hayden's fierce expression. "Our first night you said you'd never done anything like that—picked up a guy and had sex."

"I-I hadn't."

"But you were amazing."

Armi's face burned. "It was special."

"But it's more than that. All your life you've listened to people tell you who you are, and you believed them."

He winced. "Yeah. That's pretty obvious."

Hayden's piercing green gaze met his. "But now that we've spent all this time together, I've seen the rapid change in you, and it made me think maybe you've always had the desire to work on the team. You've just never had the opportunity. Because your father was such an overwhelming presence, you let his negativity get under your skin and mess with your head."

"I never thought I'd enjoy it, but...I kind of do. It's just going to take time for everyone else to see that I'm not going to give up. Russell, especially."

"That fucker," Hayden growled, and Armi grinned, loving his possessiveness. "How do you plan on dealing with him after your talk?"

"I'm not sure. He won't be back for several more weeks, so I have some time to think about it."

"I think you need a plan as soon as possible. I would've fired him."

Armi wanted to heed Hayden's opinion, but he also knew that Russell possessed a deep wealth of helpful knowledge that would be almost impossible to find elsewhere.

"I know, but..."

"But you need him. I get it. I don't have to like it, but I understand. Just...be careful. I didn't trust him before, and I sure as hell don't now." Hayden finished his beer. "I'd better get my stuff together and go." He got to his feet, stretched, and headed for the stairs.

"Wait," Armi called out.

Hayden turned around. "What's the matter?"

"I want to ask you something. Sit for a sec?"

Hayden returned to his recently vacated spot. "Something wrong?"

"No. I hope you think it's right."

Puzzled, Hayden pushed his hair out of his face. "Okay. What's up?"

Armi licked his suddenly dry lips. "I was thinking...we had a great time this past week. Spending every night together, and this whole weekend."

Eyes soft, Hayden smiled. "Yeah, it was amazing. Every minute."

"What would you say about making it full-time?" Armi shifted closer. "Move in with me?"

CHAPTER TWENTY-FIVE

Hayden blinked. "You want me to move in here and live with you?"

Armi's smile shone with hope. "Yeah."

"I-I don't know...I mean, I'm crazy about you, and we've spent the whole week together..." He puffed out a long sigh. "I can't afford to live here and keep my apartment. I just bought it this year."

"There's no mortgage. Just the taxes and monthly expenses."

As if that made it better. Hayden shook his head. "There's no way I could contribute to both places." He saw Armi's mouth open to speak and held up his hand. "No, wait. Please don't say I wouldn't have to, because that's not right."

Armi's eyes dimmed. "I just want to be with you all the time," he whispered. "The thought of being here alone in this big house is depressing."

He held out a hand, and Armi took it. "I don't have an answer right now, but we'll figure something out. I don't like being without you either." He leaned in and nudged Armi's cheek with his nose. "I've gotten used to having you next to me in bed. Naked." He took Armi's lobe between his teeth and tugged.

Armi turned adorably red, and the pace of his breathing quickened. "I can't think when you do that."

"*Mmm.* Who said anything about thinking?" He licked the shell of Armi's ear. "Come home with me tonight. That's the way we started this weekend. Before my parents popped in on us."

Armi brightened. "Are you sure? When I suggested it Friday night, you didn't seem that keen on it."

Hayden threaded his fingers through Armi's dark waves and took his mouth in a deep kiss, licking and sucking his tongue. "I'm keen on you. And this weekend has shown me one thing." Hayden rested his forehead on Armi's.

"What?" Armi murmured.

"I don't want to sleep without you anymore."

The following morning, he showered and dressed while Armi lay sleeping. Hayden still found it hard to believe they were together. In love. The words in his head made him feel warm and gooey, and he smiled into his coffee. Who was he? For years he'd rejected getting involved with anyone, only to fall in love with his boss. The one rule he'd set for himself he'd broken, but it wasn't his fault.

To know Armi was to love him. How no one had seen that was a mystery, but Hayden was damn lucky Armi had overlooked all his shortcomings. He knew they'd face obstacles—their different upbringings being the first and greatest to overcome.

"You look like you're wrestling with the devil." Armi's quiet voice roused him from his deep thoughts. Armi stood, eyes still blurry with sleep, hair in messy waves, naked from the waist up. Adorable and gorgeous.

"Did I wake you? I tried to be quiet." He set his coffee on the island and crossed the small space to give Armi a kiss. It was impossible to connect with him for only a brief moment, and Hayden groaned as Armi rubbed up against him. "You can't do that. I have to go in a minute."

"Next time wake me. And is something wrong? You have the most serious look on your face."

He picked up his mug, and seeing it was empty, put it in the dishwasher. "I was just thinking about how it will look when people find out about us. They'll think I'm after you for the money. It's such a cliché."

"Why do you care?" Armi crossed his arms. "People are always going to have opinions—mostly wrong—about people's intentions. We know how we feel."

Hayden grabbed Armi. "I told you before—I'd want you even if you had nothing. Like that night at The Vibe. From the first time I saw you, I wanted you. Before I knew you had everything."

Armi's lips touched his. "I didn't have everything. I didn't have anything because I didn't have you." His eyes glimmered. "The only company sharing my bed was loneliness and insecurity, and even though they weren't welcome guests, I had no idea how to get rid of them. Until you."

"I promise you'll never be lonely again." Hayden kissed him. "And saying that, I have to leave. The door locks behind you, so don't worry." He bit his lip. "I—if you want, I can get you a key."

Armi's eyes lit up. "I'd like that. I'll have one made for you for my place too."

He smiled. "I'll see you at the office."

The sun's rays beamed down hot and humid, and Hayden was grateful for the cool blast of the air-conditioning inside the office. As usual, he was the only one in at seven thirty, and he preferred it that way. It gave him a chance to go over the day's calendar and sort through all the notes Armi would need for his meetings. The weekly delivery of roses arrived, and he set them up, leaving the beautiful pink Queen Elizabeth bouquet for Armi's office. His phone buzzed with a call from Janice.

"You little devil," she chuckled. "Why didn't you tell me about you and Armand Winters?"

Damn. How the hell had she found out?

"What are you talking about?"

He should've known better than to try and play dumb with a smart as hell woman like Janice. "Don't be coy. I saw you at dinner with an older couple. Daniel told me Armand had called for a table. Were they your parents?"

"Yes. They came for a visit."

"So? What happened to your rule—no messing with the boss?"

His lips twitched up in a grin. "I guess rules are made to be broken." The smile faded. "It's not a joke, though. I-I'm really crazy about him," he confessed. "I never intended for any of it to happen, but I've never felt this way about anyone. He's the best person I've ever met."

"Don't sell yourself short, sweetheart. You're pretty terrific yourself, and you deserve a break. I hope you're happy."

"I think I finally am. I'll stop by soon, and we'll talk."

The delivery for the breakfast meeting arrived at eight, and he was directing the service people to the placement of the food and coffee stations when he spied Russell hobbling into the office.

"Fuck," he muttered to himself. "What the hell is he doing here?" He made sure to keep a damper on his emotions and hurried across the space. "Mr. Anders. I didn't know you were coming in today. How are you feeling?"

"Like crap, but if I stayed home any longer, I'd lose my mind."

"Let me get you a chair, please." Hayden pulled one over from a nearby desk and helped him lower himself into the seat. "Can I get you a coffee or something to eat? I was just having them set up for the breakfast."

"Coffee and a bagel with cream cheese would be good."

"Right away." Hayden took his time, getting his head together in preparation for the verbal sparring. "Here you are, sir." Anders took the plate and set it on the desk without taking a bite, but sipped the coffee.

"Armand took you on the scouting trip."

"Yes, sir. I was able to take extensive notes that I sent to all the board members and Coach Jackson. I think both Tom and Mr. Winters were really happy with how the two players performed in their respective games."

"*Hmm.*" Anders took a bite of his bagel, chewed, and swallowed. "What about you?"

Hayden blinked. "Excuse me, sir? What do you mean?"

Anders's lips thinned, his eyes turning crafty. "Was Armand satisfied with your performance?"

Thankful for his nerves of steel, Hayden ignored the twist in his belly and stared down Anders. "I'm afraid I don't know what you're talking about."

"Don't play dumb with me. I know."

Hayden squared his shoulders, and despite his heart thumping wildly, he kept his cool. "I'm not sure what you think you know, but I don't have time to stand around and play guessing games, so please excuse me."

He returned to his desk. That conversation had so many hidden meanings. Did Anders know about him and Armi? Or was it something else...like his past? A man as rich and powerful as Russell Anders, someone used to getting whatever he wanted, wouldn't be above bribery to have records unsealed. Thank God he'd told Armi the truth, but that didn't mean he wanted the entire organization to know about his past.

"Dammit," he swore.

"Is something wrong, Hayden?"

Armi's mother stood in front of his desk, an inquisitive look on her face.

"Oh. Mrs. Winters, I'm sorry. No one called me to say you were on your way. Mr. Winters isn't in yet."

"I know." She smiled at him. "I'm here to talk to you."

His mouth dried. "Me? What about?"

"Come inside Armand's office, please, and close the door behind you."

Dread dogged his steps as he followed her and did as she requested.

"Sit, please," she directed him and took the seat opposite him. "Are you and my son lovers?"

He blinked, and this time his poker face failed him. Warmth crept up his neck. "What...why would you ask me that?"

She set her Hermes purse on the conference table. "Because Friday night, my dear friend Marion Pearl was having dinner at Daniel's, and she saw Armand." She fixed him with a stare. "She said he was with an older couple and a very good-looking blond man. Marion told me you were very affectionate with each other."

With every passing word, Hayden's heart sank deeper and deeper until he was certain it rested in his churning stomach. Jesus, was everyone at dinner in that damn restaurant? Eight million fucking people in this city, and they were all watching him.

"Uh–"

"Please don't lie to me. That's not a good start to our friendship."

And suddenly Hayden had reached a tipping point. Why the hell was he nervous and unsure? He and Armi weren't teenagers sneaking off to do something illicit. They were grown men in love. He raised his chin.

"Yes. That was me. My parents came in for the weekend as a surprise, and Armi arranged to take them out to dinner."

"I see," she answered softly, and to his shock, her eyes filled with tears. She reached into her purse to grab a tissue. "I would've loved to meet them. And I just want to know if Armi has any intention of telling me about the two of you. All I want is for him to be happy."

It was a fine line for him to tread—Hayden wasn't sure if Armi was ready to speak to his mother about them—but he didn't want to get on her bad side.

"Mrs. Winters, please don't be upset. It was spur-of-the-moment. I wasn't expecting my parents to visit. Next time they come, we can arrange something, if you'd like."

She dabbed at her eyes. "What I'd like is to know more about this relationship. This is very fast, isn't it?"

Squirming under her unflinching gaze, Hayden decided to be nothing less than truthful. "We've worked very closely together and learned a lot about each other. We might come from different backgrounds, but it doesn't really matter." He met her gaze directly. "I couldn't help falling in love with him. Armi is wonderful—he's kind, sweet, and smart as hell. I have to remind him not to let people take advantage of his good nature and to stand up for what he wants." Hayden found himself smiling. "And I'm the lucky one because he fell in love with me too."

She studied him. "I think you're telling the truth—at least I hope so. Armand has been extremely lonely, and he needs people on his side."

"I think he'd love a closer relationship with you," Hayden found himself saying, wondering when he'd become so daring, but he wanted Armi to be happy, and if it made Eloise Winters annoyed with him, so be it. Maybe he'd learned that love means putting someone else's happiness over your own. "I know you're very busy, but he needs his mother. He'd love to have your support. I don't know what I would do if I didn't have my parents in my life." His lips twitched. "They're very involved and give me their opinions, whether I ask or not. I might complain about them, but I wouldn't give any of it up."

"You're more than a pretty face." Her blue eyes twinkled.

The knot in his chest eased, and he laughed. "Thank you. And Armi is more than who you think. And who his father thought."

"I'll admit I wasn't the best mother when I was younger. I'm trying to rectify it." Her lips tightened. "I regret the estrangement between Armand and his father, but there was little I could do to bring them together. Randolph was a hard man and had little patience for people who didn't fit his world."

"Which was athletic, extroverted, and one of the good-old-boys type," Hayden mused. "And of course, not gay."

Shaking her head, she sighed. "He had a warped sense of what made a man. Sensitivity and kindness were considered weaknesses."

"I feel sorry for him. His team might've won the Super Bowl, but as a father, he was the loser, for not seeing what a great son he had."

"I think I like you, Hayden Porter."

"Hayden, are you–" The office door opened, and Armi walked in, his jaw dropping with surprise. "Whoa. Mom? What's going on?" His uncertain gaze shot to Hayden, who reassured him with an easy smile.

"Your mother and I were having a chat. I'll leave you both and get to work." He held out his hand. "Very nice to get the chance to speak with you, Mrs. Winters."

"Don't be silly." She held out her arms. "Call me Eloise."

"Uh...can someone tell me what I missed?" Blue eyes comically wide with shock, Armi's eyes ping-ponged between him and his mother.

Hayden passed by him and gave his shoulder a squeeze. "I'll let your mother explain."

He left them and closed the door behind him. At his desk, he went through the calendar and arranged Armi's notes for each meeting, then checked his emails for anything that needed an immediate reply. Of course, he also kept an ear open, but all he heard was the low murmur of voices, until his attention was caught by the sight of an angry-faced Russell Anders.

"You walked away from me before we had a chance to finish our conversation."

"I don't know about that." Hayden returned to his typing. "I was finished."

Anders set his crutches down and braced his arms against the surface of the desk, sticking his face near to Hayden's. "But I wasn't. Tell me something." His voice dropped to a husky growl. "Do they still call you Hungry Hayden?"

His fingers fumbled on the keyboard, and his stomach plummeted. "I don't know what you're talking about."

"*My hole is hungry,*" Anders sang off-key. "*Hungry Hayden wants to know if you'll fill it.*"

Fuck.

Somehow, by some means, Anders had seen the video he'd made. Hayden bit the inside of his cheek and remained silent.

"Tell me, Hayden, does Armand know his tight-ass, buttoned-up assistant used to spread his legs and show himself to anyone with some bucks to spend? He'll be so disappointed."

"I have a job to do. Please excuse me." Hayden rose to his feet to go to the printer.

"Don't be too sure about that," Anders called out. "Once I let everyone know—"

Armi's door opened, and he walked out. "Know what, Russell?"

Hayden's heart sank. All these years he'd kept his secret, and now it was about to blow apart. He didn't care about the job. But would Armi still stay with him after everyone–especially his mother–found out about his past? It was one thing when it was the two of them and he didn't get into specifics, but Russell would make sure everyone would find out. How could he put Armi in the position to make the choice between the Kings and him? Pain seared through Hayden at the thought of losing Armi. But if he was going down, he wouldn't go alone. The mask was off, the costume he'd worn torn away to reveal his reality. He was ready to fight for what and who he wanted.

"Your boy here was in a cheap porno. Selling his naked ass and dick."

Armi crossed his arms. "And?"

Hayden could've cheered.

"*And?*" Anders sputtered. "What the hell do you mean, *and*? Is this who you want working here? A porn star?"

"Thanks for giving me the accolades, but I was never a star," Hayden jumped in. "And it was hardly a career. A mistake I made twenty years ago."

"The Internet is forever, Hungry." Anders's eyes gleamed. "Did you know that was his nickname, Armand? He made one movie, *Hayden's Hungry Hole*, where he got it on with someone in front of the camera."

Face flaming, Hayden glowered at a smirking Anders. "I told Armi everything already. He knows."

That seemed to take Anders aback. "You told him? Everything?"

"Yes. The cam work and the movie. There's nothing else. How did you find out? Those records were supposed to be sealed."

Anders laughed out loud. "And you're supposed to be smart. You know money talks."

"Apparently so do old fools, like you, Russell." Eloise walked out of Armi's office. "Too much."

Hayden cringed. Knowing Armi's mother had heard everything, he couldn't face her and kept his eyes trained to the floor, but not before seeing a group of employees standing by their desks, unabashedly listening to the conversation. Armi slipped a hand in his and laced their fingers together. "I'm not going anywhere, in case you were wondering," he murmured.

Feeling sick to his stomach, Hayden lifted a shoulder. "I couldn't blame you if you did."

"You taught me to stand up for myself and fight for what I believe in. Well, I believe in you and me. Us."

He didn't deserve a man like Armi, but if somehow he came out of this unscathed, he'd do everything to make sure Armi knew how much he was loved.

"Eloise, I'm glad you're here to see who your son is mixed up with."

"Is this true, Hayden?"

Shame coursed through him, and he nodded while keeping his attention at his feet. How could he ever look Eloise Winters in the eye again? She might've accepted him being in a relationship with Armi, but now, finding out he'd done porn would be a death knell. He could feel his heart break into pieces.

"Answer me this, Russell."

"Anything, Ellie. I can only imagine how disgusted you are with all this ugliness. Armand is your only child, and you must be as outraged as I am. I know Randolph would've been horrified."

"What I'm outraged about is that you're airing Hayden's personal life and pain in a public forum, intending to embarrass him. But let me ask you." Something in the tone of her voice had Hayden raise his head. Armi squeezed his hand. "How did you discover Hayden's unfortunate mistake?"

"Is that what you're choosing to call it? Ellie, he—"

"Answer my question, Russell. You know, I still have a vested interest in the team. Randolph might've been brilliant in running a franchise, but he was stupid when it came to keeping his papers up-to-date, and he never removed me from his will either."

"I knew Hayden was sniffing around Armand and that Armand would fall for whatever Hayden told him. Hayden's an opportunist, probably out for the money. So I hired a private investigator who found what I needed."

Eloise's smile was thin. "And you watched the movie, didn't you?" Her blue eyes blazed. "I used to see you looking at Armand when he was younger, and it made my stomach crawl. He was a teenager, but that didn't matter to you. So I did a little investigating of my own and discovered you've always had a young male lover on the side, haven't you? You'd sit with Randolph and hear him say terrible things about his own son and gay people and say nothing."

"What?" Lucy's shocked voice rang out. "Russell, no. Tell her that's not true. You don't like men. You said you loved me."

"Be quiet, Lucy." Russell reached for a chair and slumped into the seat. "I couldn't tell Randolph. He wouldn't have understood."

Hayden's head spun as the accusations flew in the air. All he knew was that everyone at some point had failed Armi. Not anymore.

"You made your choices in life." Face flushed and shaking with anger, Armi pointed a finger at Russell. "In your desperate need to run the Kings, you're willing to destroy Hayden by trashing him in front of people he works with. What does that say about your character? What kind of person does that?"

Hayden put a hand on Armi's shoulder to soothe him. "It's okay. Don't get all worked up about him. He's nothing. You, on the other hand, are everything."

"Your intention was always to grab full control of the team, wasn't it?" Eloise flanked his other side. "I'll bet you sabotaged his efforts at every turn to make him look bad. But it's all moot because Armand is strong and capable of making his own decisions." To Hayden's surprise, she placed a hand on his shoulder. "You never had a chance in hell, Russell. With Armand, or your scheme to discredit Hayden, or taking over the Kings."

Armi stepped forward. "You're still on disability. I advise you to leave and think about whether you want to return or retire. Just know it won't be the same if you do decide to return. Things are going to change."

With no one rushing to help him, it took Russell several attempts to stand, but he finally limped out of the office. Upon hearing Eloise's accusations, Lucy had left, and Hayden felt sorry for her as another pawn in Russell's life. The staff stood awkwardly until Armi spoke.

"Everyone, please go back to work. We have plenty to do around here, I think?" They dispersed, but Hayden knew he'd be the topic of conversation for days to come.

Still reeling from the embarrassment of his personal life being put on blast, Hayden remained behind his desk. It was only the three of them, and Hayden braced himself, waiting for Eloise to speak. She might've been holding on to her true feelings for the sake of a public front.

"Hayden?" Heart hammering, he met her gaze. "No one goes through life unscathed, without missteps and mistakes. Some are small, and some have lasting impact. It's how we choose to recover from them. I think you've suffered enough. I know you care for Armand, and that's what matters to me."

Armi hugged her. "Thanks, Mom."

Alternating between nausea and wanting to pass out, Hayden wiped at his burning eyes. "Thank you. From the first I told Armi we'd keep it professional, that the two of us together was a bad idea, but I couldn't stop thinking about him. Maybe I was wrong."

Armi pulled him to standing and slipped an arm around his waist. "Maybe, huh? I think we've learned that some bad ideas can turn out to be the very best."

CHAPTER TWENTY-SIX

The breakfast meeting was tense, but Armi was determined to proceed normally. Hayden had begged off and he'd agreed, knowing how traumatized he'd been after the confrontation with Russell.

"So I've gone over the salaries, and our take from advertising and adding the two players from the NAIA won't strain our budget or exceed the NFL cap. If we offer the two standard contracts, include offset stipulations but also incentives, we have a good chance of signing them."

Silence reigned for a moment.

"That sounds good, Armand." Troy Geiger shot a quick glance at a scowling Whitmore, who sat mute. "Jacob and I will review the contracts and forward them to you."

"Thanks."

Coach Jackson held up a hand. "Can I just say we all owe a thank-you to Armand? If it wasn't for him insisting on us expanding our scouting beyond the high-profile college players and free agents, we might've missed these two potential stars. My coaches are already looking forward to the start of the season and going through the lists of these D3 and NAIA schools to see if we can scope out some rising juniors. I'm liking the new path you're putting us on."

Troy nodded. "I agree. It might've taken you some time and a few stumbles along the way, but I think you're getting a good handle on how to run this team."

A warm glow filled him. Armi wasn't used to so much praise heaped on him. Or any at all. Maybe it was poking the bear, but Armi wanted to know. "Jacob, you've been pretty silent. What do you have to say?"

"Where is Russell in all this?"

Armi's brows drew together. "Meaning what?"

Whitmore frowned. "He's the GM. We should wait until he's back full-time before making these major decisions."

God, he hated confrontations. His heart pounded, but he tried to remain calm and folded his hands. "Why?"

"What the hell do you mean, why?"

"There's no need to raise your voice," he responded quietly. "I asked you a simple question. Why should I wait for Russell?"

"Because," he snapped, "he's the one in charge. Russell has always been involved in all the major decisions regarding the team. Next to your father, he was the leader. He should've been—"

"The new owner?" Armi filled in. "Don't deny it. That's what you think, isn't it?"

"What if it is?" Jacob challenged. "You don't know shit about running a football team."

"Maybe it's time we stop doing things the old way and listen to new voices. New ways of thinking." Armi tried to remain civil simply because he'd been taught to be respectful. Even to people who might not deserve it.

"You mean your way?" Jacob demanded and stood. "I'm not taking orders from some kid who doesn't know the difference between defense and offense."

"I believe in listening to all voices. That's how a true team operates. If you can't guarantee that you'll agree with that, then maybe it's time for you to step aside."

"I don't have to listen to this bullshit from some flower-carrying fairy. Come on, Troy." He walked to the door and flung it open. Troy remained seated, and Jacob waited. "Troy? What the hell are you waiting for?"

"I'm waiting for you to stop following Russell like a puppy and think for yourself. Yeah, Armand's made some mistakes, but he's trying, and if we don't help, isn't that only hurting the team and our bottom line?"

Armi held his breath as Jacob went apoplectic. "Are you out of your fucking mind? Bad enough we've got an owner who sleeps with men, didn't you hear what happened this morning?"

"No. Should I have?" Troy glanced around the table.

Coach shook his head. "Not a clue."

Armi's face burned. "There's no need to bring that up here. This is a business meeting about the Kings. Not a referendum on my personal life."

"Your personal life reflects on the team."

"No. It does not," Armi snapped. "Go into any stadium and ask a fan who the owner of the team is. I'll bet most don't know, and even more importantly, a hundred percent won't care about his or her personal life unless they've committed some unforgivable crime."

"He's got a point, Jacob," Troy agreed.

Jacob snorted. "His boyfriend was a porn star. You all okay with that image for the team?"

Troy's and Coach's brows rose.

"What does his boyfriend have to do with the team?" Frowning, Coach looked to him for an explanation.

Armi met his eyes. "He works here. It's Hayden. My PA." Their brows disappeared under their hairlines, and he rushed to explain. "It happened when he was seventeen—a kid. The record was supposed to be sealed and the one video destroyed, but Russell dug it up and tried to humiliate Hayden and me. But we're not going to allow something that happened decades ago to hinder us, personally or professionally."

"It's not that big of a deal, Jacob," Troy stated. "I'm not interested in what someone did when they were seventeen. Maybe you never got into any trouble when you were young or did stupid things you regret, but all I have to say is I'm glad there was no Internet back then. And considering some of the messes our players get into now..." He shrugged. "Porn is pretty far down on the list."

"Amen," Coach muttered.

"You're all assholes. Wait until advertisers pull their spots, the endorsements dry up, or players don't want to sign with you because of this gay garbage."

"What do you mean, with you? Aren't you still part of the team?" Armi asked.

"No. I'm done. The Kings' days are numbered. I'm not willing to circle the drain with them and watch a lifetime of hard work vanish. I'm retiring."

He slammed out of the room, leaving the three of them staring at each other.

Armi cleared his throat. "Well...that was...interesting. I guess I'll be looking for a new legal counsel for the team. If you have any suggestions, let me know, and I'll put out a call to some headhunters. I would think Jacob has up-and-coming people on the team to step into his shoes."

"Don't let him burst your bubble, kid," Troy said with more kindness than Armi had ever heard. "I know it's been a rough road with your father, and none of us really helped you or showed much faith in your ability to take over the team. I personally wanna apologize for that. I was wrong, and I'm sorry. But I gotta say, you've come a long way these past couple of months, so whatever you're doing, keep it up."

Hoping his face didn't reveal his wicked thoughts, he nodded. "I plan to. Trust me."

"Keep it up? You've got to be kidding me," Hayden gasped. "And you kept a straight face? You're a better man than me." Howling with laughter, Hayden fell on his bed. With no need to hide their relationship any longer, he and Hayden had left the office together and decided to have dinner at Armi's house. He didn't care where they stayed except for checking on his roses. They'd showered and were relaxing in bed before ordering dinner.

"I've been waiting for this moment all day." Armi pounced on him, and they rolled together until they lay side by side, legs tangled. Joy and light radiated from Hayden's face, and Armi loved seeing Hayden free and filled with peace. "I know it was rough for you, but I'm glad everything's out in the open."

Hayden's eyes glimmered. "It was, and it's a crushing weight off me. As humiliating as it was to have everyone in the office hear about my past, it's nice not to be waiting, wondering if that was the day someone would find out."

"I hate that you've lived like that for so long." Armi touched his face and guided their lips together. "I only want you to know love from now on." He pressed kisses to Hayden's neck, then traced with his tongue the ink patterns on Hayden's arms. "I want to give you that love."

"You do. And I love reciprocating." Hayden's fingers skimmed his face as he continued to kiss and lick his body. Armi grasped his heavy cock and lapped at the slit, swirling his tongue over the wide crown. Their eyes met and Armi engulfed the full rigid length in his mouth.

"Ohh, yeah." Hayden sighed. "*Mmm.* You're so perfect."

He pushed Hayden's legs apart to kneel between them and took him deep to the back of his throat. The thick shaft filled and stretched his jaw, and he gasped for air but continued to rise and fall on it, the pleasure washing away the pain. His fingers dug into Hayden's muscular thighs as he licked and sucked hard, his tongue sweeping against the pulsing vein of Hayden's dick.

"Baby, oh fuck." Hayden twisted the sheet in his fists, hips snapping as he keened and thrust deep. His entire body stiffened and he came, shooting down

Armi's throat, and Armi eagerly drank it all. "Give me a minute to recover." Hayden cracked an eye open.

"Don't worry." Armi gripped his aching cock. "I can do it."

A grunt burst from Hayden, and Armi found his legs over Hayden's shoulders and Hayden's mouth on his ass, biting and kissing the cheeks. "But I can do this." He nudged his slick, wet tongue past the rim, working it in fully, and Armi cried out, his body springing to life as every nerve ending leaped into flames.

"A*hh*, God, it's too much." But he lifted his ass higher, forcing Hayden's tongue farther inside. It was so good. So damn good.

Hayden slipped his thumbs in to pull the tight opening wider. "You love this, don't you? Love having your ass eaten. I love tasting you." Hayden's breath ghosted past Armi's skin. "So delicious."

No one had ever given him this kind of pleasure, and Armi thought he'd explode from the emotions flooding through him. It was so...primal. So wanton and filthy and yet incredibility hot and sexy. Armi gripped his cock and ran his hand up and down its throbbing length. But Hayden didn't let up, and Armi was buffeted from all sides, his skin stretched to the limit.

"I'm gonna...gonna..." He writhed beneath Hayden's wicked mouth.

"Let go, baby. I love you." With his tongue buried up Armi's ass, Hayden pressed a finger on the smooth skin behind his balls, and Armi saw stars.

"Oh, fuck." He came, spraying across his chest and stomach. "Hayden."

"I'm right here," Hayden murmured, lips moving slowly against his sweat-drenched skin. "I'm not going anywhere."

They lay cuddled together, Armi waiting for his heart to settle. "After that first time, I never thought I'd see you again. But to have you love me the way I am? I'm the luckiest man in the world."

"Next to me, you mean." Hayden's fingers played in his hair.

"*Mmm.*" Armi wasn't going to argue. Not when he lay limp and boneless, a puddle of contentment. "I didn't get a chance to tell you the most interesting thing that happened out of that whole meeting."

"Yeah? What?"

"Jacob quit."

Hayden's eyes flew open. "You're kidding."

"Nope. And Troy apologized for not being more supportive and letting my father–"

"Be a dick? A piece of shit?" Hayden grimaced. His thumb traced Armi's cheek, and Armi leaned into his touch. He couldn't imagine a time simply being close to Hayden wouldn't turn his bones to water.

"I've learned a lot about myself since my father died."

Hayden pulled him near. "Oh?"

"I thought I was doing this to prove to him that I could. That I wasn't the failure, the loser he always said."

Hayden held him tighter. "You're not. You never were."

Armi continued as if he hadn't heard Hayden. "But then I realized, somewhere along the line, it changed. And I was no longer doing it for him. I was doing it for me. I wanted to take responsibility and prove to myself, more than anyone else, that I could succeed."

"I still hate that your whole life he kicked your confidence to the curb and made you feel less than.

You do know you're doing an incredible job with the team, don't you? People respect you because you lead with kindness. And contrary to what your father said, that doesn't mean weakness."

"I'm happy, though. Because of you, I feel more. More alive, more capable. Freer to be who I always wanted but never imagined possible. That first night we met, I was so far out of my comfort zone, I might as well have been on the moon."

Hayden drew circles on Armi's shoulder with his fingertips. "I know. You were such a surprise—a wonderful, gorgeous surprise. I could see you weren't a hookup kind of guy, but you opened up to me, like one of your roses." Hayden leaned in to kiss him. "And I couldn't resist getting pricked by your thorns."

Even though they'd already had the conversation, Armi tried again. "I have an idea. About living together. Because I don't want to sleep alone."

"I don't like it either–"

"So how about a compromise?"

Hayden wrinkled his nose. "How would that go?"

"Weekends here and weekdays at your place. I'd need to check the roses and spend time with them, but I think we could work it out. And in the winter, after the season is over and before the trade deadline hits, we can go to my house in the Hamptons or, if we want someplace warm, take a long vacation. I have someone I trust to come in and care for the roses when they're not in bloom."

"I don't know…I don't want to feel like I'm living off you. And won't people in the organization resent you showing favoritism toward me?"

"We wouldn't be the first office romance. And I still need you as my PA. That's not going to change."

"True, true." Hayden heaved a dramatic sigh. "Who else could you get to keep you in line and out of trouble?" His eyes twinkled. "And clean up your messes?"

"All while being the most fabulous lover? No one." Armi kissed him. Excitement brewed in his chest, thinking of the two of them starting a life together. Here or wherever they decided.

"I can't disagree with that." Hayden's eyes sparkled like polished emeralds. "But it's easy to make love to you. All you have to do is touch me, and I'm hard."

"You mean like this?" Armi threw his leg over Hayden's hip.

"I've created a monster."

"*Rawr*," Armi teased, licking up and down Hayden's throat. "Still think this is a bad idea?"

"Impossible. Loving you is the best idea I've ever had."

EPILOGUE

Super Bowl Sunday

"Hold the line. *Hold the line.*" In the owner's box, surrounded by family, friends, and coworkers, Hayden screamed as the Kings were facing pressure at their forty-yard line. They were sixty seconds away from winning the Super Bowl, but in football time a minute was a long way away.

"Ow." Armi stuck a finger in his ear and wiggled it. "I think you broke the sound barrier."

"I can't believe I'm so excited about a football game, but it's the Super Bowl and we're about to win it." He jumped out of his seat.

"Shh." His father hugged him and covered his mouth. "Don't jinx it." He threw his arm around Armi next. "I never thought I'd be able to afford even a ticket to a Super Bowl game, but to see it from the owner's box is beyond my wildest fantasy. Thank you."

"It means even more to have everyone here who matters most to me." Armi's eyes glittered bright with true happiness. "I never understood the how and why people get so invested in a game, but now I do." He pumped his fist. "Go Kings!"

The crowd roared as the quarterback was sacked and the Portland Stingers lost another ten yards, making it fourth and twelve.

Trevor and Marianne high-fived Hayden. "We're so looking forward to vacation next week with you two. Ten days in Bali. Total paradise."

Hayden couldn't wait, especially since he and Armi were taking the full month. "It's gonna be amazing. The pictures I've seen of the resort are incredible. I've never been so far away from home." His gaze found Armi, who was surrounded by the board and Hayden's father, all of them intent on what was unfolding on the field. "But as long as Armi's there..." Realizing how sentimental that sounded, he ducked his head.

"Don't be embarrassed." Marianne kissed his cheek. "Have I told you how much we love you and Armi together?"

"Not at all, Marianne, just every time you see them," Trevor joked, laughing harder when she glared at him.

"You be quiet. Don't pretend you haven't said the same to me. We've never seen Armi so filled with self-confidence and self-love, but most importantly, he's happy for the first time in all the years we've known him. Thank you."

"I'm the one who should be thanking you for being his friends and recognizing what I did—that he's a special man and deserves the best."

"I've got the best." Warm lips tickled his ear. "You."

"This is so exciting. Go Kings!" his mother cheered, raising her margarita to toast Eloise, and he laughed. The two had become close friends. They talked all the time, and their families had spent the holidays together—Thanksgiving at his parents' house upstate and Christmas in the city at the town house. Hayden couldn't help but love the sight of them wearing matching Kings jerseys, planning a girls' weekend at a spa out west.

"Twenty seconds left," Troy called out.

"I'm so nervous. Is this really happening?" Armi held a bottle of Dom Pérignon in preparation for the big win.

"It's happening." Hayden pointed. "Look. They're going for a Hail Mary, and I'll bet a whole bag of Flamin' Hot Cheetos that our defense will be all over the receiver's ass."

Hayden watched Armi and his father, along with Troy, Dex Reiner—their newly hired GM—and Felix Amaro, the legal counsel, shout and point to the field as the quarterback did exactly as he'd predicted, but the King's star linebacker caught the ball in the end zone for an interception.

Everyone erupted in shouts, and Hayden's ears rang. The crowd went wild, and the floor beneath them shook.

"They did it! Oh my God, they're Super Bowl champs." Armi flung his arms around Hayden. "We won! We won!" he screamed.

"We sure did. And they're winners because of you." They hugged, and Hayden watched as Armi was swept up by everyone in congratulations and accolades. His flushed face was bright with happiness, and Hayden recorded it all on his phone, wanting to keep this moment for Armi, forever.

With a decidedly evil grin, Troy handed him a bottle of champagne. "You know what they do to the coach with Gatorade. I think we need to do it to Armi."

"I like the way you think."

Troy had stepped up and become the confidant Armi needed to maintain the running of the Kings after Russell and Jacob left. He'd acted as an interim GM and was instrumental in giving Armi advice in hiring their new GM and legal counsel. The team's inner circle was now run as a truly collaborative effort.

Hayden positioned himself behind Armi, who was accepting congratulations from other club owners who'd crowded into their box. He dumped the contents of the bottle over Armi's head, yelling, "Super Bowl champs!"

Armi jumped and spun to face him, pretending outrage. "I can't believe you did that."

"Blame it on Troy. It was all his idea."

"I have a better one." With a wicked glint in his eyes, Armi grabbed him, and to clapping and shouts, spoke so only Hayden could hear.

"As long as I have you, I'm a winner. Kiss me."

"Now that's the best idea you've ever had."

I hope you enjoyed reading Armi and Hayden's story as much as I enjoyed writing it. Football is one of the few sports I watch and enjoy, even if I am a long-suffering NY fan. (I'm lookin' at you Giants. We don't even bother to talk about the Jets....).

Bad Idea is the beginning of a new series, *The Brooklyn Kings*, and will continue on with the next book, *End Game*. Quarterback Devlin Summers and Tight End Brody Martin have been together since college but keep their relationship a secret to play pro football. Their story is so sweet and sexy and filled with love and hope.

If you'd like to read the first chapter of *End Game*, you can find it here:

https://bookhip.com/VMDSWJK

FELICE STEVENS writes romance because what is better than people falling in love? Her favorite part of a romance novel is that first kiss...sigh. She loves creating stories of hopes and dreams and happily ever afters. Her stories are character-driven, rich with the sights, sounds, and flavors of New York City, and filled with men who are sometimes deeply flawed but always real.

Felice writes gay romance because she believes that everyone deserves a happily ever after. Having traveled all over the world, she can safely say that the universal language that unites people is love.

Felice has written in a variety of sub-genres, including contemporary and paranormal, and she has a mystery series as well. You can find all her books listed on her website.

Felice is a two-time Lambda Literary Award nominee and a Lambda Award winner in Gay Romance for her book *The Ghost and Charlie Muir*.

BOOKBUB
https://www.bookbub.com/profile/felice-stevens

NEWSLETTER
https://tinyurl.com/y85e69ab

READER GROUP
https://www.facebook.com/groups/FelicesBreakfastClub/

FACEBOOK AUTHOR PAGE
https://www.facebook.com/felicestevensauthor/

INSTAGRAM
https://www.instagram.com/felicestevens

GOODREADS
https://www.goodreads.com/author/show/8432880.
Felice_Stevens

WEBSITE
felicestevens.com

PAYHIP STORE
https://payhip.com/FeliceStevensAuthor